You Made Me Love You

MATRIMONY! BOOK THREE

BY JO-ANN POWER
WRITING AS CERISE DELAND

DRAGONBLADE PUBLISHING, INC.

ARE YOU SIGNED UP FOR DRAGONBLADE'S BLOG?

You'll get the latest news and information on exclusive giveaways, exclusive excerpts, coming releases, sales, free books, cover reveals and more.

Check out our complete list of authors, too!

No spam, no junk. That's a promise!

Sign Up Here

www.dragonbladepublishing.com

Dearest Reader;

Thank you for your support of a small press. At Dragonblade Publishing, we strive to bring you the highest quality Historical Romance from some of the best authors in the business. Without your support, there is no 'us', so we sincerely hope you adore these stories and find some new favorite authors along the way.

Happy Reading!

CEO, Dragonblade Publishing

Additional Dragonblade Books by Author Cerise Deland

Matrimony! Series
If I Loved You (Book 1)
Because of You (Book 2)
You Made Me Love You (Book 3)

Naughty Ladies Series
Lady, Be Wanton (Book 1)
Lady, Behave (Book 2)
Lady, No More (Book 3)
Lady, You're Mine (Book 4, Novella)

The Lyon's Den Series
The Lyon's Share
The Lyon's Perfect Mate

Fleetside Chronicle
Serving London and environs

NUMBER 31—Volume LXXXI. Monday, December 12, 1814
Price~Fourpence

WANTED: Matrimony!

Frustrated in your search for domestic tranquility? Search no more!

Search no more!

Place your advert with the *Fleetside Chronicle*!

News sheet now totally devoted to marital bliss.

Find happiness in a trice!

Affordable!

Exclusive. Confidential.

The strictest honour observed!

June 3, 1814

A Wife Desired by a Gentleman arriving from the Indies.

A Gentleman who arrives from the East Indies wishes to settle permanently in England. He has long been away and seeks to establish his household quickly upon his arrival home. His family are respectable and his prospects great. He is thirty-one years of age and has some favor. He has no requirement of the lady as to fortune. However, he wishes his wife to be in possession of excellent manners and a good education. She must be attentive to the demands of a prominent social life. In addition, she must be of suitable age for him, of respectable nature and with a sweet disposition. The Gentleman expects no connubial relations to be necessary. This will be a union of likes, committed to each other in word and deed.

Letters to said Gentleman should be posted to G. Hammond, Publisher, 140 Fleet Street, London, before April 30, 1815, to allow for receipt and subsequent responses by Gentleman in Calcutta. The Gentleman will communicate with any appealing applicants in early January 1816, as he prepares to leave Calcutta March 1816 and journeys back to Britain. From among a final two applicants, he will make his choice and communicate such to those ladies via East India Company mail and/or the publisher of this newspaper.

April 1, 1815

Suitable Situation Wanted with Respectable Gentleman.

A Widow of fine disposition wishes to place herself in a companionable union with a true gentleman. She wants a situation that will benefit her while she, in turn, will bestow her attributes on her new household. She is twenty-three years of age and has taught English at a private girls' school in York. She is resourceful, a good cook, and an excellent baker. She is eager to find happiness but will be very particular in her choices.

Miss M. R.—

Responses to G. Hammond, Publisher, 140 Fleet Street, London.

April 15, 1815

A Widow seeking a Companionable Husband.

A Lady wishes to establish a rewarding marital relationship with a Gentleman of Substance, Ethics, and Earnest Intentions. She has an excellent education, a refined social life, and speaks eloquently. Her previous marriage was a loving one—and while she understands connubial affections are never forced nor arranged, she wishes a companionable relationship with a gentleman husband. She seeks a friend, first and foremost, a boon companion in times of stress, a joy in times of peace. She is thirty years old, and of good health and cheer. She has no objections to a true marriage of more than mind, but cautions that her opinions on female equality in thought, word, and deed are very advanced. She will fight to keep them.

Mrs. T. W.

Responses to G. Hammond, Publisher, 140 Fleet Street, London. She will respond personally to every prospective gentleman whose missives delight and intrigue her. She has no deadline for marriage, as finding the most excellent partner is her only goal.

Chapter One

October 1, 1816
London

KENDRYCK HOLLENS LIKED his journeys short and few. Yet, for most of his life, his trips had been numerous—and tedious. Most not by horse, but by sail, camel, or elephant. Many had been dangerous to life, limb, and sanity. Each trip conspired to prick his good nature. This he had kept to himself, as one did when the choices presented were not one's own, but assignments imposed by some pompous factotum or overzealous military commander with a grander idea of himself than reality could prove. However, this morning's trip from Southwark to Viscountess Peregrine's house was not only blessedly brief but in a comfortable carriage.

Eager to get on with his plan, Kendryck had little patience to wait for the coachman to climb from his perch and do his duty. He pushed open the thing himself and bided his time before he hopped to the step and the cobbles.

He examined the elegant Palladian house before him. His arrival in town had been announced, curse it, by the city rags, and he had no wish to engage with anyone who might have noted that the new Baron Strade of Rhoose and Gary had hired a fine private hack at the George. He would decree when he would meet anyone in town. He was not yet ready to set that time.

So with a nod to all that might be outside his control, he paused to button this frock coat and assure himself his top hat was affixed properly. His Bengal tailor had done the best he could, which was, by nabob standards, the best money could buy so many continents away from High Society. The fabrics gave with his flex and flowed with his form. The fit across his shoulders and down his back was precise. The cut of his trousers, the same. He had demanded of High Tailor Vin that the flow of the wool be as easy as that of his silk pajamas. The man had done an excellent job. So fine, in fact, that Kendryck did not think so much about the form of his clothes as he did the effect of them on the native British he would meet this morning.

He flicked his gaze upon the step of the townhouse before him and surreptitiously surveyed the matching symmetry of its neighbors. Ivory, pristine, stately. Exactly what he expected. Precisely the kinds of friends he needed. He stiffened his spine in resolve.

Behind him, the jarvey flicked the reins of his coach and went off to circle around. The man was to return, as Kendryck had ordered, within twenty minutes. To remain inside longer would be rude of Kendryck. He called before regular calling hours, inviting himself by note to Lady Peregrine only two hours previous. But that breach of protocol could not be helped. He had to hope that the lady upon whom he called would receive him, and do so with open arms. She was one of the few women in his life he admired, and perhaps the only one he had ever trusted. Which, of course, made the subject of this interview hard to bear. But he had to do it. He owed himself the clarity his visit would bring.

He stepped toward the door. Dropped the knocker. Waited for a forbearing butler to pull it open. Like this visit this morning to a lady of the *haute ton*, he would accept all invitations to appear at any time, anywhere, and do what he must to raise his only goal upholding every social rule. A model of propriety, he would devote himself to the development of the life he'd created for himself and discard all those elements others had put upon him since he was a tender sixteen years old.

A grizzled old dumpling in stiff cambric and pressed black serge stared up at him. "Good morning, my lord." The edge of inquiry in the butler's rasping voice denoted his examination of the stranger at his doorstep. The little fellow extended a gracious hand, then stepped backward and allowed Kendryck the privacy of the spotless, blue-veined marble foyer.

"Good morning." Kendryck removed his hat and gloves, then handed them over with a smile. Kindness always smoothed the road toward one's acceptance. "I do apologize for upending your morning's routine. I hope to make it up to you in some small way."

The dumpling could barely suppress his shock at the apology from a gentleman. His jowls jiggled as his surprise turned to delight. "No need, sir. No need. My lady invited you to come as soon as possible. Do come with me."

Up the broad stairs they went, a procession that took Kendryck back to the last time he'd had the honor of visiting with the lady of the house. The sun shone down on them from the glass rotunda above and cast the whole foyer in shades of gold. The fragrances of beeswax and lemons rose up to him, so crisp and smooth, uncomplicated. The scents of England were faint, fewer than the myriad mixes of ambergris, musk, and a thousand others that perfumed the hair, teeth, and clothes of native Hindus and Muslims. Every inch of this house, just as those of many nawabs, spoke of daily attention to the tiniest crevice. Even those British who looked down upon him from their gilded frames upon the walls had the mien of efficiency—and superiority.

Kendryck winced in recognition of the hauteur. Too much of that and in the snap of fingers, entire groups of people prospered or died. *None of that here, Kendryck. Lady Peregrine is not one you've dealt with in the Company.*

He forced his mind to relish the other differences between this home and those he'd visited far from here. He'd been in many a lavish abode in his journeys. The Nizam of Hyderabad's bejeweled stone palace. The nawabs of Bengal, who lined the walls of their homes with sheets of gold. The colorful red and black chintz tent of one of the defeated Mughal sultans of the northern hills. He was shocked, however, that he felt so refreshed to sail up the cool, creamy stairs, past dead ladies who had achieved their status here by bearing their husbands heirs and smiled for their portraitist. Not as one Muslim sultan's wife who had disliked what her painter produced and threatened to skin and eat him.

The little butler paused before the closed double doors and eyed Kendryck warily. "I tell you confidentially, my lord. My lady has not been well, and she has not received anyone for weeks. You requested twenty minutes."

Kendryck had earned his reputation with those in the Company by being honest in his dealings and precise in his statements. His fame with Hindus and Muslims was based on finesse. "I assure you, my business will be done quickly. My coach returns at precisely the ordered time."

"Very good, sir." At which the little man turned the filigreed handles upon the doors.

Kendryck was presented with the serenity of blush walls and the contrasting drama of deep magenta damask appointments. Color had so seeped into his consciousness these past fifteen years that his impressions of the resulting aura always had him matching the atmosphere to the personality of its owner. Here was the bloom of Lady Peregrine's *joie de vivre* combined with the spark of her spontaneity.

"Ma'am." The butler stood rigid on the threshold. "Baron Strade of Rhoose and Gary."

Kendryck noted three people before him, but focused only on his hostess. She sailed forward, hands out toward him, a joyous welcome wreathing her long, finely sculpted face. In all the years since he'd last seen her, he had fondly remembered how she had fought for him to return to Eton rather than go to the jungles of

Bengal. Of course, she had changed. Thinner, she moved with the caution and stoop of age. Stark white was her hair, but bright was her attitude. Yet the snap in her hazel eyes and lines about her smiling mouth still told of the pleasure she took in other people.

"My darling Kendryck," she enthused as she put her hands in his. "I am so glad you have come so quickly to see me."

He bent down to give her a kiss on each cheek, the only woman he had ever wished to honor. "I planned to but was pleased to receive your note yesterday."

She accepted his homage with equal fervor. "I am so delighted to see you here, grown from the respectful boy to robust man. Allow me a moment to examine how tall and broad and dashing you have become. Fifteen years have served you well in a country which so few survive."

"Dear lady, you put me to the blush." Those who had seen him grow robust to inches over six feet tall were those he had dealt with these past fifteen years. All were prominent Indians or Lord Wellesley's and Company men. This lady did him the honor of recalling the year when last she'd seen him in her drawing room. "I am meanwhile starstruck, a callow youth behind in his duties to state how beautiful you are."

She tipped her head. He had taken her aback, he could see. "Kendryck. My dear sir, you are most kind. Chivalrous, too. Ever were you thus. I saw it then. And you were how old when you last stood here?"

"Sixteen, ma'am."

She reached up, sighing as she surrendered to whim and sank her fingers into the curls of the hair that persistently fell over his brow.

Had anyone else done that, he would have flinched. From her, it was an endearment. His eyes fell closed, but only briefly. "Forgive me, ma'am. No woman has done that since my mother…"

"I daresay you need a loving wife who will do you a similar honor, Kendryck." She grinned—and he laughed. She was flirting with him! "Even as a boy did your black hair fall as it does now over your forehead. Oh, forgive me my desire to coddle you, sir." She snatched her hand away, and held both palms up in praise of his appearance. "But I am astounded at your bold good looks, Kendryck. You are quite a sight. Ever so many feet taller, my boy! And broader, too. Is this what comes of a life in the Indian sun?"

A life in sun that caresses or burns. In heat that delights or kills. In the company of men who have had their ethics ingrained so well that they thrive, or scorch their brains so thoroughly that they die to all morals.

"Thank you, my lady." He rushed on, changing the subject to lighter fare. "You are too kind. Ever were you good to me." *The only one who stood for me.*

The laughter died from her eyes, and she grew taut with a memory that sobered her. "You were sixteen and put upon. Your mother was not here, and you needed an advocate."

He did blush deeply then. She had argued with his grandfather not to send him to what she termed "the cesspool of India." She had failed, and Kendryck sailed away, never to return. Until now, when he could fling away every ugly thing about the British in India, save the colors of his mind—and his resolve to tell the world of his convictions.

"Farewell, yesterday! Come, come." Rallying and waving a dismissive hand, she claimed his arm and stepped aside to do the honors of introductions of the two others in the room. A shorter woman, young, possessed a solid manner about her that denoted her as a matron. She was pretty, with a round face, full pink lips, and a halo of rich sable-brown hair. "Allow me to introduce my niece, Mrs. Hammond. You may recognize her name from correspondence, as she is the publisher of the *Fleet-of-Heart Chronicle.*"

"I do indeed recall your name, Mrs. Hammond." He had been surprised when he received her packet of responses and noted that "G. Hammond" was a woman. To his knowledge, no other females owned a London newspaper. Then, too, no other owners of papers offered the services of making matches for those adventurous enough to advertise for a complete stranger to wed. Kendryck had often questioned his own decision to do so. Still, he was grateful for the lady's help. "Thank you for coming this morning and on such short notice, ma'am. I appreciate all you have done for me."

"It has been a pleasure to serve you, my lord. Would that this might have been a more joyous and less disturbing process."

"I assure you, Kendryck," Lady Peregrine intervened, "Germaine has had much success and very few problems with her matrimonial services."

"I thought as much myself, my lady." He turned his gaze to the gentleman in their midst.

"Allow me to present to you, Kendryck, my nephew, Mr. Jack Shaw. Lord Strade, sir. Mr. Shaw is a Runner with Bow Street, and one of longstanding and notable achievements. Mrs. Hammond and Mr. Shaw are cousins, my sister's child is Germaine, and my brother's is Mr. Shaw. Mrs. Hammond and I found it appropriate to hire Jack's services last week to help us find the lady you seek."

"I am most pleased to meet both of you." He was happy to meet with Mrs. Hammond in the presence of her aunt. Lady Peregrine, with whom he had corresponded for all the years of his exile to Bengal, had been the one to recommend the services of the *Chronicle*. Never would he have thought to advertise to seek a wife, but Lady Peregrine had assured him that her niece's process of finding a proper mate was not only secure but also confidential. *Would that it had also been without incident.*

Kendryck thought it was wise of Lady Peregrine and Mrs. Hammond to have invited the Runner, Shaw. Kendryck understood that Runners were often hired by private citizens to solve crimes. Kendryck's situation was not so much an offense as it was a mystery. One he had few resources or time to untangle, but which he felt duty bound to unravel.

"Please." Lady Peregrine offered the settee opposite hers.

"Let us get to the matter. Your note, Kendryck, said you called for only a few minutes."

The three resumed their seats.

"Indeed. I do not wish to be a burden." Kendryck took the overstuffed chesterfield. "I am grateful you have responded to my inquiry so quickly. I had no wish to startle or inconvenience you."

"Good matches," said Mrs. Hammond with a crisp tone that any man in the Company would applaud, "are our business. Any that go awry are ones we wish to correct if we can or, in this case, discover reasons for their failure. Allow me to explain."

"Please do," he said.

"All correspondence I receive," the young woman added, "I lock in my safe each night. I review the applications in the mail each morning and afternoon and sort them according to prospective matched applicant, if I can discern a match at that time. Then I lock them away. No one sees them. Only me."

Lady Peregrine silently offered him tea.

He accepted, placing the china on the table before him. "Did you have many young ladies who applied to my advertisement?"

"We did." Mrs. Hammond smiled, easy in her skin, proud of her service. "I would say there were more than thirty I thought worthy. As per your initial instructions to me, you wished me to decide which among them all was the most appropriate match for you."

"You sent to me two from which to choose." He had read both women's initial letters and a few subsequent ones. The first applicant wrote poignantly in her appeal to his senses. The second woman appealed to him more. Not only did she take the time and effort to correspond with him in four letters, but he liked her prose, her humor, and her eloquent description of her past.

"I deemed both suited to you," Mrs. Hammond said with some pride and much despair in her soft hazel eyes.

He nodded. "The first, Miss Roundbridge, wrote a few times and was eager to get on with things. In fact, she rather pushed herself to make her own deadline—and declared she would arrive in Wales at the end of September. That letter she wrote to me I received six days before I was to sail home from Calcutta."

"When did you leave, sir?" Mrs. Hammond asked.

"March first. I knew the mail would go two days hence on our Indiaman *Royal Anne,* and I wished to ask both ladies to come to London instead of Wales. I wanted to make my selection and theirs easier. I had initially asked each lady to do me the honor to come to my home at Strade Rambles in Wales and bring a lady friend to accompany each, as a chaperone. I offered to reimburse them their expenses."

"That is a long way to go, sir." Mrs. Hammond frowned.

"I know, and I was not pleased to ask it, but I changed my mind and had to come to London first. You see, I had received word of many problems at home. Foremost among them were financial issues. With the death of my older brother and my sister more than a year before, my household was in chaos. My estate manager could not control the finances of my stepmother, half-brother, and sister. But I ran into problems. I began to write my letters to both ladies, but I was called away from my post to tend to an urgent matter in the hills. Figuring I had enough time before the next mail ship, the *Royal Anne,* would set sail, I went off to my duties. But I was wrong in postponing that. Problems there took two weeks to solve. I regret it all.

"When I returned from my business in the hills, it was the night before another ship, the *Quick Robert,* was to set out. I wrote my letters quickly and had my man run it to the dock. Alas, he met with an accident along the road. A swarm of monkeys attacked his carriage, and he never arrived to deliver the letters before the mail packet was to go on the tide the next morning."

"And therein lies one problem, my lord." Mrs. Hammond pressed her lips together. "We now know that, according to Miss Roundbridge's parents, she did not receive your letter. Nor did the second applicant, Mrs. Wallingford."

He sighed. "That is as I surmised. It is unusual that the Company mail does not go through. But, of course, when my own ship restocked in Good Hope at the south of Africa three months later, I heard the news that our *Quick Robert* was lost in Algoa Bay three weeks before."

"Therefore, Miss Roundbridge," said Mrs. Hammond, "assumed you were still committed to her application, and she proceeded to your home in south Wales posthaste."

"And Mrs. Wallingford?"

Jack Shaw, the Runner, said, "We have, as yet, no word of her plans. It is Miss Roundbridge we are very concerned about. Her parents tell us that she began her journey via mail coach to South Wales in the middle of September. But other than their statement, we have no proof of that."

Kendryck frowned. "What do you mean?"

Shaw continued. "I have spoken with the drivers of coaches during that month from West London to Milford Haven. Only two young ladies of Miss Roundbridge's description took journeys west. Neither went farther than Bristol. She has not been heard of since she left London. They say that is not like her."

"I am dismayed," Kendryck said with a heavy heart. "No one has heard from her? Not even any friends?"

"Not a word," said Mrs. Hammond. "She has vanished."

"Her parents approve of my investigating," said Shaw.

Mrs. Hammond went on. "When they wrote to me inquiring as to what I might know about their daughter's whereabouts, I asked Jack to make his inquiries of the mail coaches. I knew, Lord Strade, that you arrived home from India soon, but I felt it behooved me to learn as much as I could as soon as possible. Parents," she said with a sad glint in her eyes, "always wish to know how their children are."

Not all. Kendryck inhaled, ignoring the urge to shift in his chair. All families were not like his. "I agree. I am most glad you took up the investigation. And having done so, I am prepared to reimburse you for your previous outlay, and sir"—he regarded Shaw—"I wish to retain you to continue your search. Miss Roundbridge would not have ventured so far alone were it not for the proposed meeting with me. I should not have asked it of any ladies. I failed them. Years in India have imbued me with genteel manners for my native friends, and now I hope to reclaim for myself those manners of this country."

"You must not blame yourself, Kendryck."

This from Lady Peregrine was kind, but it failed to absolve him of responsibility. "I do, ma'am. Such a journey is not one ladies make by themselves. Not even in India."

The two ladies checked each other's expressions and nodded in agreement.

Shaw sat back. At his leisure, he examined Kendryck as he should, given the man's job was deducing the nature of those who experienced unusual events in their lives.

But Kendryck had nothing to do with the woman's disappearance. He was not in the country when she went missing. She had vanished on her own. So Shaw could look all he wished. Kendryck had nothing to hide. The only thing the Runner could not see was Kendryck's determination to break from his past and make a sound marriage to aid him in his new life.

Thus he asked the only other information he needed. "I arrived in Dover only yesterday. This morning I left my rooms at the George in Southwark and plan to leave by ship for Cardiff day after tomorrow. Have you any knowledge of the current wishes of the other candidate to marry me?"

Shaw nodded. "Mrs. Wallingford may know what she reads in the newspapers of a missing lady, though she may not connect this matter with you, sir."

"As to whether she journeys to Wales, sir," said Mrs. Hammond, "we do not know."

Chapter Two

November 2, 1815
The Strade Rambles
Glamorgan, South Wales

"Of all the men you might have chosen to marry, Tynley Wallingford, did you have to choose one who lived in an eagle's nest ten million miles from London?"

With a wrinkle of her nose, she regarded the atrocious mix of castle, keep, and dreary Palladian stone mansion atop the cliff before her. The weather up there had to be many times as bad as this down here on this barren, chiseled coast.

She wrapped her arms around herself, snuggled into the giant collar of her thick wool coat, and tried to find some comfort among the spare squabs of the carriage.

Her hired coach from the little village of Rambles had stopped again. The snowflakes were as big as her fist and slippery as grease. She knew because she'd had such a hard time standing on the white layer of it as she waited for the coachman and his second to push the carriage from a rotten hole in the road.

Now, to make matters worse, was her view of the home of Kendryck Hollens. His formal name of Lord Strode of Roost and Goose only tested her good nature. His real title escaped her. She'd reminded herself to trim her humor and learn the proper form before she appeared before him. But to her, he was everything from Strange of Stoke and Poke to Stoke the Fire. Not a good way to begin.

"But then," she asked the frigid air of Bristol Bay that stung her face, "becoming your bride has allowed me to see worse, like that poor horse dying in the road?"

"Eh? W'at?" Her hired driver stopped his work and squinted up at her. He was as hoary as the landscape. Did all Welshmen blend in? "W'at say, Mrs....?"

She excused him his lapse of memory of her name. She lifted a hand. "Just jabbering to myself, sir. I'm fine. Warm." He'd kept asking her if she were warm. "Do not mind me."

"Aye. Aye." He bent his back into it. Which was not to say much, because his poor spine was already bowed over the rickety old coach that had ambled into that hole in the road. "Be done in a bit."

We both hope.

"Goin' up there," she heard her driver's assistant mutter to his master. "She ain't muzzy. Don't look good for her."

Her driver grumbled at his man. Sounded like he'd told him to shut his mug.

So, no, I am not muzzy. Why would I need to be to go there?

Lady Peregrine—whom she called by a courtesy title of Aunt Juno—had told her much about the man she was to meet. To marry, too, if she liked him.

"You will adore him, my darling," the lady had assured her more than a month ago, patting Tynley's hand and offering her more tea and biscuits. "Kendryck is a dear. Always has been. What's more, I am certain he will be he arresting. The men in his family usually are very good looking. I daresay if I were young, I'd be tempted to bind myself to him. Inheriting his family title and lands, Kendryck is a catch. Don't you think, Germaine?"

The young publisher of the *Chronicle* gave Tynley a polite nod. "He seems very appealing from his letters."

From the date she'd written her advert for the *Chronicle*,

Tynley had promised herself to be careful about choosing a man, sight unseen. Her Aunt Juno, who had that epithet as an honor to the friendship she bore Tynley's parents, had a tendency to be overly enthusiastic about many things. She had an old title, older money, and a distinguished reputation that allowed it. But the lady's glowing descriptions of Kendryck Hollens also held a discordant note, and Tynley hoped she could ferret out what that implied. She always preferred to know the fullness of any person's nature. When she had trodden the boards, she did well when she knew each fictitious character's qualities. In real life, knowing another's motives and failings served her better.

But that could take years. She sighed. *Decades.*

Aunt Juno had responded with a grin full of mischief. Her answer focused on the importance of having good-looking children.

Babies were not Tynley's primary concern here. She had had a beautiful child sired by the most wonderful of men. And though her husband had been an accomplished actor in Drury Lane, in looks, he was no Adonis.

She sniffed back the fond memories that could summon tears. Not welcome on a cold and blustery day. No indeed.

Besides, her intended did declare in his own advertisement that he did not require conjugal relations of his bride.

What sort of man did not care about hopping into bed? Or heirs? Especially if one was the sixteenth Baron of Strike and Pike. Or whatever he was.

"All done, ma'am!" The coachman gestured her toward him and his carriage. "Hurry, do. We're up to the Ram, we are. Tommy," he called to his groom, "let's get along."

"Do people call it different names?" She paused with her hand on her hip and indicated the Gothic expanse of gray rock and white stone that dotted the brow of the hill.

"That monster?" He scratched his head beneath his cap and gave her a little wince of apology. "They call it what'er they like. Funny bits go on there, aye. 'Tis an odd place. Always so. Strade's

Strange. Ram. Rambles. Roose the Goose. All good! Everyone knows where you mean."

She accepted that and plunked herself in the carriage for her last bumpy ride. At first she sat back and watched the craggy landscape fall to forests, then treetops fall to billowing clouds. As the road curved around and rose higher, she marveled at what the view might be from the widow walks outside the turrets. Surely, the sight of sky blending with the sea would bring the feeling of floating above all the earth.

The horses took a sharp bend in the road that presented her suddenly with the broad front portico of the mansion. Six bays wide, three to each side of the door, the windows were dark panes topped by trefoils. The door, reflecting a new coat of paint in the sun, was an eye-popping forest green. The three-story-tall manse was of old stone. An ancient curtain wall of an old castle with arrow slits crumbled to one side. Jutting up from inside stood a tall medieval keep. The whole effect was of an old troll hunched upon the brow of the hill, scowling down upon those on the road.

She drew backward, into the collar of her good winter pelisse, but told herself to shake off the shivers that consumed her. She gazed again at the structure. A mix of old, new, ugly, and decayed, it was far from welcoming. Nor did it have potential to be. Indeed, she could not honestly say if she admired the mix of architecture or hoped someone might knock it all down. In truth, the building was many times larger than what one could term a humble abode.

The coachman pulled under the portico and brought his horse to a halt. "Go ta the door, Tommy. Tell 'em we're here. They've not been expecting us."

He spun around to give Tynley a quick flick of his head toward the manor. "Butler's hard of hearing. Never comes unless you bang down the door."

"Too much bangin' in this house," said the second groom as he jumped down.

The coachman told him to be quiet, then explained to her, "Creatures in the rafters."

"House is that old," said the groom.

"Bats," yelled Tommy over his shoulder. "Lots of them!"

"Harmless." The coachman held her eye to let his word sink in. He laughed as he helped her alight.

She could not suppress her shiver at the idea of black creatures that lodged in one's hair. Her mother had had the bad experience of it once and never failed to make a grand moment of the retelling. That very story was the one Tynley knew so well that she had used the example of good drama. It was one that propelled her toward the stage.

Would that I had been as talented as Mama with her shrieks and blathering. I'd still be acting, not climbing the steps to this monstrously large house.

She dropped the elaborate brass knocker on the old carved door.

"Do it again," said her coachman after he came to stand beside her and plunked down her reticule.

She did. And then again.

Her fingers were going numb in the frigid air. Her nose froze, too.

She knocked again.

Behind the door, a cacophony erupted. A dog barked and a cat screamed. A young woman ran around yelling, "Jericho, give it to me! Now! Now!"

Tynley tapped her toes and questioned the depth of her desire to enter this old, odd house.

The huge wooden door yawned wide. Dog, cat, and yelling female had disappeared.

Only one person appeared behind it. "Good afternoon, madam." The balding fellow who poked his head toward her looked as if a gust off the shore might send him airborne.

"I am Mrs. Wallingford. I am here to see your master."

The butler pondered it for a second, then let a light shine in his blue eyes. "Mrs. Wallingford? Good, good. Do come in. We did not expect you today."

"I came quickly." *I need to know if this outrageous arranged marriage might work. If not, I will return to my little cottage in Clerkenwell and dream up another alternative for my future.* "Please announce me. I am tired, cold, and rather hungry."

"Yes, ma'am. Of course you are. Your hat and coat, ma'am."

As she removed her gloves and handed them over along with her other attire, he bellowed for a footman. The man might be deaf, but he yelled like a fishwife. He'd have done well in the old Totham Theatre, where the acoustics were nonexistent. She'd remember to stand far from him lest he blow out her eardrums.

A younger man appeared, and the butler gave him directions, then focused on her once more. "Right this way, ma'am."

He led her down a long hall and up stairs of gray marble, banded by mahogany rails and bannisters. The walls, unlike in so many grand homes, bore no portraits of great ancestors. She approved the lack of pretense that one's predecessors deserved to look down and intimidate one and all for decades ever after.

Cold and drafty as the ground floor, the first floor held little charm. She followed her man right and to the first door.

He knocked lightly, to which a bark of "Enter" was given.

At once, she was in the center of the most glorious library she'd ever seen. The shelves rose three tiers high. The cavern smelled of old leather, bad ink, and fine parchment—and perched upon a truly huge, elaborate Elizabethan ladder was a truly huge and handsome man.

He gazed down at her, mouth open. She considered him in a like manner.

"I say," he said with a push of glasses up his fine, straight nose. "Are you…?

"Mrs. Wallingford. I am she, sir. Are you Lord Strade of"—it took her a moment to put it all to rights—"Rhoof and Gary?"

His square jaw firmed. His eyes smiled. "Not that I claim it often. But yes, I am he of Rhoose and Gary."

"Ah. Good." She folded her hands before her, ready to be fed and warmed and made to feel at home. "A fine way to begin."

"If we each agree."

She held her ground and craned her neck. He was right. She, too, needed time, but she would not give any quarter until he had treated her to some compensations like the weary traveler she was. "I have journeyed here in dire weather, sir, betting on the odds that you do agree!"

"Are you so bound to matrimony yourself?"

If he thought to wheedle his way out of this easily, he was mistaken. So quickly upon first meeting, too! "I am here with an open mind, though in truth I will not be happy if you have changed your mind before we've met."

"I did. I wrote to Lady Peregrine and to Mrs. Hammond."

She sniffed. "When?"

"Yesterday," he said, and had the decency to appear disturbed by it himself.

"So your letter to dismiss me and I have passed in the night. Odd. Dear sir, I have not come all this way to be told once more that the mail has failed to do your bidding." *Your other applicant, as I understand from my Aunt Juno, has failed to appear.*

With the speed of one incensed, he climbed down from his ladder and stepped toward her. *My, oh my.* He was a tall one, wasn't he? Not a feather, either, but broad of shoulders and lean of hips. Long legs, too. With curly hair as dark as midnight and morning beard. And with bright eyes of blue flame, he gazed down at her as if he could see right through her serviceable wool gown.

Let him. "I assure you, my lord, you cannot intimidate me by glaring at me. I've experienced scrutiny in many more ways than you could imagine. What you wish to learn of me, I will gladly tell. And without so much as a question. I expect the same from you. After all, to advertise for a spouse, sight unseen, requires more brass than brains. So. Shall I sit and do we talk? Or is there some test of yours I have not passed that means I must remove to the nearest inn for the night before I return to London?"

His comely, dark lashes fell over his gaze for a moment. Then he returned to the living. "I have bad manners."

She lifted one brow. Some statements required no agreement.

He snorted. "Please. Forgive me. Etiquette is one element I must relearn."

India was not the end of the earth. She was no chuckle-head.

He tried to smile. But he extended a hand toward one of his library chairs.

"Thank you." She took the seat. It was so much more comfortable than the blasted coach. She sighed and breathed more easily.

"Carter?" He called for his butler to step forward, but kept his eyes on Tynley. "I think we are in need of a bracing tea. Sandwiches. Perhaps a hot pasty or two, if Mrs. Swan has any left from luncheon. Also a few glasses for brandy or… What do you prefer, Mrs. Wallingford? Brandy or whisky?"

"Whisky. Scotch. Neat. Three fingers' worth."

Strade grinned his approval. "We will have it shortly, won't we, Carter?"

"Yes, yes, sir." The butler turned away to hobble toward the kitchens and Mrs. Swan's beneficence.

No sooner had he disappeared than in loped a short-haired collie and his pal, a squat, pudgy bit of caramel.

At which point, the bigger dog decided to come look Tynley straight in the eyes, while his friend, the short Corgi, did a little dance of welcome. She scratched both animals' long, silky ears. "Hello, friends. Do you prefer brandy or whisky? I bet *you* have not forgotten your manners."

"No, they have not. That rangy fellow was my sister's hound, and is the best gentleman in the family, much to the dismay of the smaller gent."

"And his name?" She beamed at the large critter with the long, slobbery tongue.

"Jericho."

"A noble name, sir," she told the dog. "And your friend is whom?"

"Richard the Third," Strade provided.

"Hmm. A motley duo."

"Indeed. Charlotte decided that the collie was so large that no one would ever attempt to overcome him with horns or shouts."

"Like the city in the Bible, I presume?"

"Precisely."

"And this fat little chap? He is named for royalty because…?"

"He's very fat and gassy." Strade made a pained expression.

"Like a certain prince regent?" she asked.

Strade nodded in the affirmative. "Jericho can win hearts but never a crown, Charlotte said. She trained them both to protect her and anyone else she loved. Would that they could have saved her."

"Forgive me, do I detect that your sister is…no longer alive?"

He pursed his lips. "Correct."

"My condolences."

"Thank you." He took a chair opposite her and folded his hands in front of him. Long fingers with neatly trimmed nails were stock still in his lap. The attitude told the tale of one who contemplated the world at his own pace. His azure stare flashed, full of distaste for their current topic. "Charlotte died long before I could return home to comfort her in her passing. I loved her. Jericho did as well, and I see by his acceptance of you that he is able to transfer his allegiance to you. Up until now, he did that only to me, but now he favors you, and influences old Dick, here, to do the same."

She tipped her head, hopeful but ready to be tossed to the courtyard in a trice. "Do my new friends convince you that their acceptance might be a sign you and I can cease our swordplay?"

He chuckled silently. "I wonder. Have you training in the art of the duel?"

"I am quite good and have played the cavalier often." Though he probably would laugh if he knew when and where and in what costume. "I will warn you, I play only with a guard on the tip."

"Not bent on running through an opponent?" He liked this repartee, inviting more of it with the look of pleasure on his bold, starkly handsome face.

"Never. Swords fiddle about the matter. I much prefer daggers."

"Straight to the point, eh?" He spread his hands out wide.

"I dislike games."

He rested his elbows on the arms of the chair. "Then we are jousting to no good end, Mrs. Wallingford."

"Ah, sir, you seemed to invite the match. I would rather talk plainly, if you think you might as well?"

"I would prefer it."

"We are agreed, then."

He nodded and crossed one long, lean leg over the other. In black trousers, frothy cambric cravat, and scarlet wool waistcoat, he was the picture of the lord and master of his domain. In fact, he was so at ease, he did not bother to put on his frock coat. "Do please tell me why you are here. I did not expect you. When last you wrote, you indicated two weeks before you'd leave."

"From Cheltenham? Yes, I was with a friend. She recently had a baby, and I was helping her with her new responsibilities. Her husband was wounded in the wars. Very badly so, I am afraid. He has lost the use of his left arm. But he suffers from memory loss. He drifts in and out of consciousness, and Annabelle and I fear for him."

"That is a shame. Hard to live with someone whose faculties are gone. Can he find work? Regain his former position, at least?"

"He may not be capable. You see, before he enlisted three years ago, he was an actor. A good one. Or rather, he would have been quite renowned, but he chose to go off to war. We doubt now he would be able to memorize lines."

She was beset by visions of the man ranting and raving at Annabelle, reliving the charge of the line. He frightened Annabelle with his reenactments of the cries and shouts of his friends.

So like the actions of her own husband, returned from war.

Tynley put a hand to her mouth. "Forgive me. I… She fears him."

"I knew a gentleman in India who had fallen from an elephant's howdah and hit his head. He had similar symptoms. Difficult to live with, that is. Did you wish to stay with your friend? To help her?"

"I offered, but she did not want me to change my plans to suit her need. My friend is very independent."

"Like you."

She met his gaze, which seemed to glitter with humor. "Like me."

"It takes great courage to agree to marry a man sight unseen."

"Or a woman."

"Why would you?"

She inhaled. "My whole life story in a few sentences, then?"

He offered her a small smile. "If you can, yes, tell me."

"I like marriage. I am a widow. I was well matched to a man I adored. We had a child. A boy. He…he died last year of fever."

"And your husband?"

"A week before."

Strade pulled his heavy, dark brows together. "I am sorry."

"Thank you. My husband was…a sweet, caring man. I have few options for my life now. I do not wish to be anyone's governess, nor anyone's housekeeper or companion. I am too old and too opinionated to be anyone's mistress. I know more about life than to be willing or able to subject myself to a man's pleasure. I won't teach. I won't sew. I won't work in anyone's shop. Surely some man, I thought, would welcome my humor. I have enough nerve to have ambition."

His large eyes narrowed to bright blue flame. "How much?"

This man could intimidate many a woman. He could be charming. He could be appealing. His looks were devastating to a woman's hope to remain indifferent. His past in India was exotic, perhaps even daunting. She could admire his charm and be lured by his staggering good looks, but what fascinated her was how he survived in the hotbed of chaos and disease that was India. What did he want in a wife? Strength? She had it. Courage? That, too, she possessed.

She tipped her head. "How much ambition do you need?"

Chapter Three

Kendryck sat back. She challenged him—and he more than approved it; he *relished* it. "Rather a lot."

"You will tell me why."

Not a request but a demand. He smiled. "I can. However, the revelation may run you off."

Through this odd churn of conversation, she continued to scratch one dog's ears and the other's silken muzzle. Did she take her serenity from the nearness of creatures who loved so well? Of course she did. *Like Charlotte.* She locked her emerald eyes on his. "Why is that?"

Time to be brutally honest. Push her away. Avoid desiring her, complicating his life. "I plan to become a sensation, Mrs. Wallingford. In London. In the literary world. In politics."

"I've heard lines like that in plays, sir. Few in real life. Those are unique goals."

"Some would say unattainable."

She did not flinch or gasp, but lifted her exquisite chin and held her ground. "Not I."

Who was she? Like no woman he had ever met, bold and proud. "Why is that, Mrs. Wallingford?"

"I understand drama, the power of the word. The impact of a look, a stance, an attitude. As a former actress, I know the workings of theater and a few of the dynamics of the London *ton.*

I am not deterred by the magnitude of your ambitions, sir. I have a different question about the value of their pursuit."

"Ask it," he invited, because he was caught now, within mere minutes, ensnared in her intricate web of intelligence and beauty.

"I wonder at the toll they will take upon your character."

He did not know whether to laugh or snort. Tynley Wallingford had him in her grasp. "You fear I will change?"

"Success leaves its mark, as does failure. When the end comes, will I still like you?"

"You like me now?" Impractical, insane as it was, he hoped to God she did.

"Some aspects, yes." She inhaled, and her visage held breathtaking delight, as if she knew she had him. "But the day is young."

He barked with laughter. She must not hold such fascination for him. *Which aspects thrill you?* he wanted to ask, but dared not. He'd be flirting with her. "Well then. I say that if your ethics are sound, yes, Mrs. Wallingford, you will like me better. Or I hope you will. Are you in possession of high standards?"

"For myself, yes. I've told you what they are. As to how I can claim them, I have lived a paragon's life."

Even for a woman who has been an actress? "And you are not afraid of censure, Mrs. Wallingford?"

"Censure? Will it be that bad? What will you do, sir? Start a revolution?"

For a long, hot moment, he stared into her eyes and wished to reach down into her soul. "I may."

"Intriguing."

That was her reaction? Did she not wish to exclaim, examine, protest? He had to counter, and learned forward. "I would rather die than not tell this to the world."

Carter appeared on the threshold. Kendryck was spared the need to give all his plans away to her. The lady who sat with him was a model inquisitor. He'd told no one his plans. He'd even warned himself that disclosure would diminish his devotion. Why and how she should be so compelling that she could draw such secrets from him was a mystery. And not as galling as he had once thought.

Why? Why? He ran a hand through his hair. *She is so different from…*

"Sir?" Old Carter stood at the door, his heavy tray rattling the china upon it. "May I serve?"

"Do, please."

The man ambled in, filling the time and space between Kendryck and this beguiling woman who had the courage of a lioness. Through his revelations, she did not wince, she did not blush, and nor did she run. Good, then. She was no sylph. No siren. Yet she was an astonishingly beautiful redhead with lips that lured and breasts that invited. She could lure him out. Yes, he'd not had a woman in so long, but he was no callow boy. No fool for a pretty face and a comely figure.

Curse it. He was enraptured that she also had intellect. But no, he was not going to commit to her on the basis of teatime repartee.

This meeting was a simple matter. He was well and truly met, rhetorically. And this encounter was nothing more than a well-matched parlor game of… What? Discover your mate?

He remained silent as Carter served them both. Meanwhile, he pondered what this woman thought of him. This widow—wise, lively, and beyond lovely—who sat, ready to partake of tiny sandwiches and tarts, seemingly unruffled by their odd encounter.

With a sharp inhale, he'd bent to pick up his teacup when, at the door, another figure appeared. And another.

Jericho growled low and long, true to form whenever Kendryck's half-brother appeared. Little Dick the Third said naught, but his round little eyes never left Kendryck's two young siblings.

Mrs. Wallingford imbibed every detail before her. The two who hesitated at the door. Kendryck's frown.

Well, do let us get all the oddities displayed at once. The better for this jewel of a woman to collect all evidence she needs to impel her to leave.

"Come in, come in, do," he bade his half-brother and sister. The boy, age twenty-one, and his half-sister, age seventeen, were the mirror image of each other. With the same slim figures and strawberry-blond hair, the same wide, indulgent mouths and startling brown eyes, they were beautifully handsome devils. "Allow me to introduce you, Mrs. Wallingford, to Barbara and Gerard, my sister and brother."

"How do you do, ma'am?" Each murmured a charming hello and made a polite little bow of humility.

"Very well, thank you," his visitor responded to them. A smile was in her tone—and why not? Aside from the failure of the two dogs to welcome either newcomer with any approval, she knew them not. *Yet.*

May she not be there long enough to be treated to their worst.

That was a ridiculous hope. His young siblings were who they were. Spoiled, abrasive, and quick as snakes.

"We've not had tea," said Gerard like the impertinent boy he always was. "Might we sit with you?"

Mrs. Wallingford turned her emerald-green gaze to Kendryck.

"Yes," he told the boy. He would tolerate them for a few minutes. "Do join us."

"Thank you, sir." Barbara hurried to the chair opposite the lady. "You were brave to come in the storm, ma'am." She dug to learn how and why this lady was here.

"Is it still snowing?" his visitor asked, as if this were just one conversation among many she'd had with this young woman.

"Badly. My maid says it is to be a foot or more by dinnertime. I say, Mrs. Wallingford, are you pouring for us?"

"No, I am not." She tipped her head, the light in her eyes implicating the girl's forwardness to ask.

Kendryck suppressed a snort. *He* was not going to play servant. "Do pour for your brother and yourself, Barbara."

The girl went to her task with a pleasant smile and the grace of a girl who had been sent to the finest finishing school in England. Kendryck knew because he had approved payment of the bills for the past two years.

"Will you remain with us for Christmastide, ma'am?" Barbara asked as she finished her duties and passed tea and a full plate to Gerald. All of this Barbara performed as if she were a princess of the realm.

Mrs. Wallingford sipped her tea. "I have not yet discussed that with his lordship. Are you both home for an extended stay from school?"

Kendryck licked his lips. She knew how to turn the tables! Bravo for her.

Barbara smiled, unruffled. "I have finished my years at school. I came home in August when Gerard's and my mother was ill. She has a weak heart, and her maid could not lift her."

"Good of you to do that, Barbara." Mrs. Wallingford was more than kind. "It is always important to help family to good health."

"Mama improves, and we are so pleased. She wants to begin the preparations for my London Season. Strade has promised me a London debut." She curled her shoulders in delight. "I am most eager."

This attempt by Barbara to show how highly she regarded herself was exactly what Kendryck expected of the girl.

"Oh! I hurried as soon as I could!"

Kendryck sighed. The appearance of his stepmother sooner rather than later was also predictable. She would not bear any mystery in the house. He stood. "Please come sit with us, Madeline."

The woman sailed forward, stately as ever, and smiled at Mrs. Wallingford. "We are so happy to have visitors."

Kendryck did the introductions and paused while his stepmother took her time arranging herself on the settee opposite him and Mrs. Wallingford.

Neither dog moved a muscle. The world could come and sit in this parlor, and they would remain by the side of their lovely visitor.

Kendryck moved to cut short the questions that would drag out this unhealthy teatime. "Mrs. Wallingford visits us from London. I did not expect her arrival so soon, and we debate her length of stay. You might each be so kind as to carry the conversation for a bit, as our guest has traveled far and wide in a very cold and uncomfortable mail coach. She needs her tea, her sandwiches, and a good rest."

"Well, my, my," offered his stepmother. "I quite agree. You must refresh yourself, Mrs. Wallingford. We have few visitors, but we do enjoy them."

Kendryck refrained from rolling his eyes. His father had been a cad who brought home his doxies to put in the spare bedrooms. He'd brought home few others, only other men who wished to have at the same women. Madeline had tried to rise above her husband and develop ties with those in Cardiff Society, but she had failed. No one wished to associate with her, his father, or his grandfather.

That older man had been not so much a hermit as a critical old libertine. Those in Rambles, Rhoose, and Gary hated him. Those in Cardiff ignored him. When he died five years ago in June—so Kendryck's best friend, Walter Drummond, wrote to tell him—two people had bothered to attend his burial. The two were men to whom he owed money. For that burial, as well as that of his father, his older brother Owen, and his young sister Charlotte, Kendryck had been in India. Away from the heartache and scandals.

"Tra-la-la. There you are. There you are!" A diminutive lady waltzed into the parlor.

Why not add the last member of family to the gathering? His grandmother often escaped her maid.

"Grandmama!" He shot up and walked over to the little lady who stood upon the threshold half-clad in her translucent white muslin morning gown and red velvet dancing slippers. A white lace cap sat at an odd angle over her left ear. He removed his waistcoat and swung it around her shoulders in a move to make her more presentable. "Do come in."

"Thank you, darling boy." His grandmother was a tiny specter of her former self. She'd once been the talk of London, a viscount's daughter with raven hair and sea-blue eyes, a diamond. Now, she shuffled toward Kendryck, her trembling arm out for him to lead her to a chair. She smiled, but knew not at whom, for aside from the fact she remembered fewer people by name each day, she had, as she usually did, left her spectacles somewhere she'd promptly forgotten. "I heard the commotion. Servants always titter when someone new has come to play with us. Who is it, Kendryck, dear?"

Yes, *him*, she knew. Heaven knew why. He'd been away for fifteen years. But he took it as his honor and bestowed on this lady in his house, who honored him even in her aged fog, the graciousness she richly deserved, and of which she had enjoyed so little.

"We have a lady come from London to visit us, Grandmama." He helped her to toddle over to take a chair nearest Mrs. Wallingford. "She stays for the evening, perhaps longer, since the snow does not abate."

He checked the lady's expression at his words and was pleased to see she played along with him. His grandmother proclaimed by her sorry state of dress, if not yet by her verbiage, that she needed no arguments this afternoon, nor any other day.

Mrs. Wallingford was all delight as she caught his grandmother's hand and helped her to settle in the chair. "I am very pleased to meet you, my lady."

He nodded, grateful. She even got her address correct for his grandmama, for the older woman was still Lady Strade.

"Good of you, my child." His grandmama patted Mrs. Wallingford's hand. "Saw your coach from the window. Hired or mail, eh? Why did you come like that? Kendryck should've sent for you. Bad of you, sir, not to bring her to us in comfort. Drink up. Do." She flitted her fingers over their visitor's cup and saucer. "No pneumonia for you. As for me, I'd like tea. Whisky, too." She sat back. Her gaze landed on her daughter-in-law, and she wrinkled up her nose. "Don't tell me I cannot have any. Maddy is a witch, you know. Maddy is a baddy. Maddy is a baddy."

Kendryck rose to take his grandmother upstairs. They did not need a commotion today.

In the doorway appeared his grandmother's maid. *Just in time.*

"Lucy!" Kendryck waved her toward them. "My grandmother was just settling in for tea."

The maid darted toward her charge. "My lady, I have your tea ready in your rooms. The very best biscuits, too. Jam and honey also. May I assist you up?"

The lure of biscuits was too great for the lady, and with a pat of his hand and promise to see him at dinner, off she went.

He did not resume his seat. He'd had quite enough of his family's inquisition of Mrs. Wallingford. He would take her away. "Do forgive me, all of you, but I will usher Mrs. Wallingford away to her rest. She only just arrived and has had no chance to refresh herself. Do come, madam. I will escort you up the stairs to your rooms."

"Thank you," she said, and dispensed with her tea at once. To the rest she said, "I am so happy to meet all of you."

He took her elbow, and she came closer, her simple citron *eau de vie* nearly sending him to his knees with want. *Why, why?* he asked himself, and put the cause to his lack of the comfort of a woman for so very long.

Mrs. Wallingford was so different from the charming Muslim girl who had been his loving wife. This one was tall, standing nearly high as his chin. This one was highly colored, all red hair, pale skin, freckles on her nose, pouting pink lips, and plump cheeks. Not dark-haired or black-eyed or hennaed.

This one wrapped her arm through his instantly at his offer. She was not shy or coy or prohibited from touching him by parents or religion. This one came readily and walked beside him. Refreshed at her immediate reaction, he smiled at her as she let him lead her away to the foyer.

At the foot of the stairs, she took a huge breath, a hand to her chest.

"Trying, I know it is, to meet them all," he told her, sorry for the scene she'd been subjected to. "Thank you for bearing with them. They don't have many visitors, and you were a new confection to pick over."

She stared up at him, her appreciative, jewel-like gaze drawing him like nectar. "I was not put upon. I like people, as a rule. But I appreciate your rescue."

And I, your generosity.

Up the stairs they went to the next floor. "Our guest suite is down this hall. I am sure Carter has ordered a footman to put your belongings in here. Perhaps by now, he has even assigned you a maid. Do ring if you need anything."

They approached the door to her rooms, and he stopped there. "I will let you rest. Dinner is at six. We keep country hours. No need to dress formally."

"I hope you and I will talk again," she said with that low, sensuous contralto that flowed into him mellow as good wine.

His body grew warm, intoxicated by her. "After dinner. We can get to know each other better."

"Just you and I, I hope?"

"Anything you wish."

She beamed at him and threw back her head to laugh. "I want it now."

I want you now. My lips to your cheek when you laugh. To the arch of your throat there, bared now to me.

"But time brings prudence." He ordered his hardening body to behave. "Tonight we shall resume," he vowed, and wondered to whom he promised such delights.

Chapter Four

THE NEXT MORNING, Tynley rose by six and rang for her assigned maid. She wished to find his lordship in the breakfast room alone. Contrary to his invitation yesterday, he had not invited her to join him after dinner last night. In fact, he'd been quite a grump during the meal. His family and she had carried the conversation and made it a congenial hour and a half. But Tynley had felt the brunt of Strade's rejection. In the spare two hours she had spent in his presence, she had grown to like him. *Too much.*

She took the stairs with all the new hopes that mornings promised. She had ordered her maid, Seren, a pretty, apple-cheeked girl of fourteen, to do her hair in a loose chignon. Then she had quickly donned her forest-green gown, the newest and finest of her day dresses.

The warren of the back of the house was a puzzle, and it took her a few minutes to find the right room. Seren had told her the path but the house had more halls and nooks and crannies than it appeared it had from the Palladian frontage. She was not put off. Adventure was part of her nature. Had she not run away from her cheerful, charming parents to Drury Lane at the age of sixteen to try her chances on the stage?

She stood before the circular breakfast table and nodded to Carter, who was supervising a footman's work laying out the silver of a sideboard.

"Ma'am, good morning to you." Carter, gracious fellow, was wide-eyed at her appearance. "We are not quite ready."

"I see that. I do not mean to be a bother, Carter."

"Do sit as you will, ma'am. I will bring the tea and coffee. Service will be shortly."

"And Lord Strade? Has he broken his fast yet?"

"Yes, ma'am. He was up before dawn."

"I see." She let the butler see her disappointment. *Why not?* He seemed a right sort, and nothing allowed for friendship like displaying the truth of one's emotions.

Carter drew his bushy white brows together. "His lordship keeps long hours."

"Does he?" For Carter to divulge such an intimate detail of his new master's schedule to a guest was a rarity. That suggested he considered her not only innocuous but an ally. She responded with the only conclusion she could glean from this and what Strade had told her of his intentions. "Driven to succeed, I would gather."

"He is, ma'am." He gave a deferential nod and headed for the far door to the kitchen. But there he paused and turned to face her. "He burns too many candles. Reads too long. Writes profusely. After breakfast, he usually takes Jericho and goes for a walk in the woods."

This information had her smiling at the man. "The day seems sunny. I saw from my window the snow has stopped."

"Mrs. Swan—she's our cook—has good bones. They tell us that the storm has passed on."

How fine of Mrs. Swan to be our bellwether. "After breakfast, I may go for a walk myself."

He grinned. "That would refresh you. After being crushed in a coach like a walnut, it would do you well to stretch your legs."

"I agree. Might I ask you to show me the right path to take?" *You've already revealed so much. Why not more?*

"Yes, ma'am. We'll fortify you with good, hot food, and you can dress. You do have heavy woolens for this clime, I hope?"

"I do, sir."

He could not contain his pleasure. "We'll have Dick the Third go with you."

She could not contain her snigger at the dog's name.

"I know," Carter said with the look of one who was pained with laughter. "We could just call him Dick, but that would be so indecent."

"Richard won't do?"

"Too long. Too formal for a creature who is the funniest chap I've seen in the house."

"I welcome his company."

"As you should, ma'am."

WITHIN THE HOUR, Tynley was dressed in her chocolate-brown woolen coat, scarf high around her throat, and her best leghorn hat, lined in fine teal merino. She'd also slipped into her reliable brown boots and good wool socks. Off she went down the side of the hill that Carter had come to the edge of the woods to point out to her.

Dick was happy to come with her, running around her like a child let out to play. He ran ahead, returning every few paces to bark, as if to say, "Why do you dawdle?"

"I'm coming! How do you go so fast on those short little legs?"

The path that Carter had pointed toward was a well-worn clearing down the hillside. Beyond, it appeared to go all the way to the beach. Well protected by the trees from the wind off the shore, she poked along the rough, rocky way. Today, the sun had warmed the ground more and the snow had thinned upon the earth. Thus, the greatest danger to her was the slick snow that was melting.

But she came to a fork in the path that had her stopping to

decide which way to go. Both required her to contemplate how to maneuver what was a significant drop. One measured more than a foot. The other would require her to stretch out to grab a tree limb. She liked neither choice.

At once, Jericho came prancing through the dense green-black foliage. He barked in a playful rhythm, then paused, hunching on all fours as if he were challenging her to follow him.

"I'd love to, boy," she told him, "but I am rather stumped."

"Come along, then," said the tall, broad fellow who emerged from a tight copse of evergreens with a hand out and a smile of welcome. "I'll help you down."

She gazed down at him, and her breath left her. He was devastatingly beautiful. Men, of course, were not supposed to be. But this one was beyond the pale of handsome. She'd seen it yesterday in the light of day. Last night, amid the golden glow of candles. And now, in the sunlight that sent rays across the black of his hair and kissed his chiseled brow and cheeks and lips with the shadows and lines a sculptor would capture, if he could.

She had schooled herself yesterday to give him little reason to think her forward. She was no virgin, no girl fresh from a schoolroom, but a widow, used to a man's caresses and instant desires. Married to a gentleman she had loved, she had given in to Graham's needs, just as he had showered her with his attentions when she required his. She had fallen in love with her husband slowly, over a year or more. She had admired Graham for his humor and his acting skill long before she had wanted him as her lover, as her mate. They had not married until she was eighteen.

"We wait, Tynley, so that you can know yourself better." Graham was six years older than she, a man who had enjoyed women since he was fifteen. "I'll not ruin you. You'll marry me and be my own, my one and only forever. I promise you that."

To lust for a man was a yearning she knew. Far too well. The rush of heat in her blood. The swelling of her breasts. The need to clamp her thighs when the desire for a man's touch filled her loins. That she should want this one, whom she'd known so briefly, surprised her. Here in the forest, where wild creatures rustled the brush, and birds darted about ruffling the leaves, wind rushed though the barren limbs and crunched and cracked and roused her raw desire to a ridiculous madness.

Strade had walked closer as she went down memory lane. "The fresh air has pinked your cheeks."

Little did he know the true cause. And if he did, what would he do?

He waggled his fingers at her. "Will you continue?"

She thrust out her hand. "I will."

⇶⟫✕⟪⇷

HE COULD NOT help himself. He had to feel her in his arms. And so he grasped her, two hands to her small waist, and brought her down, flush against him. *Wrong,* said his mind at the rigid response of his manhood. *Right,* said the hot blood coursing in his veins.

But reason niggled at him, and he steadied her on her feet. "Fine?"

She nodded quickly, like an embarrassed child.

He moved backward.

Yet she clung to his hands.

He shot her a quizzical look.

She managed an apologetic wince.

She could not want him. Not so soon. Why would she?

"I'm glad you came out," he said, fighting for words to fill the silence. What was he? A boy? "The weather is better than yesterday."

"This path becomes treacherous. Carter did not say."

But he knew I'd come across you. "He knew you'd do well. Carter has an instinct for people. I learned that early, as a boy."

The two dogs frolicked together, yipping and chasing each other in circles.

"He assigned Dick to come with me," she said as she dropped one of his hands and turned to take a few steps.

He still had her other hand, and he was not giving it up. "Always a good idea to have one of them with you in this woods. Drops like that one back there are the usual." They picked their way along the rocky path. "No need to rush along. We can walk like this. No one is about to see us. You are safe."

She glanced up at him, and the look on her face told him she did not agree.

Well then. Neither do I.

"Do you like to walk?" he ventured, because he could think of nothing else to discuss but the here and now.

"I do."

"Would you prefer to walk alone?"

"No!" She halted, and the expression on her face told him she was partly insulted and partly dismayed. "Why would you think that?"

He considered the clouds scudding along the treetops. "You are upset with me because I did not welcome you to join me after dinner."

"I am." She turned to him those luminous green eyes that had stared at him all night long.

"I am sorry."

"Were you ill?"

"Ill. Ahh. No. Not ill." He gave a laugh. *I had to think. Digest why I found you so appealing. The hours brought no answers.* But what could he say now? "I thought it best to allow you your rest. You had had a difficult journey."

"I had hopes we could talk freely. I was disappointed that we could not continue a frank discussion. I need to know you, sir. If I am to commit to marry you, if I am to aid you in your quest to conquer the world, I must first learn who you are."

"You are right. I do apologize."

"You must not put me off because you can't…"

She had stopped, and since he had her hand and would not let her drift away, he stopped too. He swung around in front of her. "Because I can't reveal what I truly feel? Because it would be improper?"

"Yes." She held up her chin in defiance. "You have already told me much. Your silence speaks as strongly as your words. Your gaze as eloquently as your avoidance. Your stance, your grace. I can see, even if you cannot speak to me of yourself."

He smiled. *So much for concealing one's thoughts.* "I should ask for a summary of all your conclusions."

She sniffed. "Why would I lay bare my thoughts and make a fool of myself?"

"Of all that you are, Mrs. Wallingford, a fool is far from reality."

"Tynley is my name. You will use it. And yes, I do agree, Kendryck. I am no fool. Which is why you are on your best behavior, and I… Well, so am I."

They strolled a bit, and he was grateful for the respite to reorient himself to the practicalities of their situation.

At last, he asked, "What shall I tell you about me?"

"Everything." She spun away, but he pulled her back…and this time, she came full against him once more. Her hand to his chest, she quieted. "What you like for breakfast. How long you stay in the library working only under candlelight, which cannot be good for your eyes. Why your grandmother does not like your stepmother."

"Eggs. Hard-boiled. Usually until midnight or until my eyes burn. And Grandmama never liked my father's second wife. Something happened between them to poison her against Madeline. I daresay now, Grandmama does not remember it. And Madeline will never tell."

His heart pounded. What was this that she stirred in him? The need to know all of her as well. Her past, her ambitions, her failures. He might understand his own desire for her if he could part the veil of their newness to each other.

"I wish to learn about you, as well," he said with more serenity than he felt. "We will do nothing rash until we know each other better."

She lifted her face to the sky and shook her head. "Uncanny."

He laid his hand atop hers, afire to claim more of her than that. "What is?"

She gave him a sad, sweet smile. "That is what my husband said to me when first I told him I liked him more than as a friend."

"And how long did it take for you both to know each other?"

"A year. More."

Kendryck could not wait that long to know…to taste…to savor her. She was too luscious—and though he might declare celibacy, it was a new vow for him. He'd fed his desires in Bengal. Was that hedonism not what drove him to display the idiocies of British rule to the world? He'd had so many Bengali women, one he had destroyed. He'd hurt no Englishwoman. And never could he harm this one. "We should not take so long."

"We won't." She locked her languid gaze on his. "A week."

"That's all?" he said as his heart rebelled.

"It must be so. I am a widow, but not without some reputation to maintain."

"Then we must fill this week with all the knowledge of the other that each demands."

"You agree to that?" she asked, a winsome look to her that told him she already knew he would comply.

"I do. We will walk here each morning. You will dine with me—"

"For breakfast. And tea."

He nodded. "In the afternoons, you will come to me in my study to read my notes."

"On what?"

"My novel."

"Is that so?" She grinned. "About what?"

"India."

Her dark red brows knotted. "I know so little."

"You will be astonished. I was."

"I can comment. And help. Your rhythm. Your pacing. Your sense of drama."

That surprised him. "Your experience with the stage may help."

"It will. I am rather good. I was often the one to hold rehearsals, and I would make copies of scripts for all to use."

"Actors forgot their lines?"

"And made them up." She grimaced. "You'd be surprised. 'To be or not to be' could become 'I am and I am not.'"

He chuckled. "Terrible to bastardize good English."

"Are you a good writer?" Her words were a challenge.

"You will tell me."

"Quite bluntly, too. You may wish me gone by week's end."

He slid his other hand around her waist and pulled her tight against him. God, she was heaven to hold. "I do doubt it."

"So do I, sir." She tossed him a carefree look and stepped out of his reach, then pointed toward the alluring seclusion of the forest. "For now, we will walk and you will tell me all about your novel. And India. And how you are so bound up in it that you wish to shake the world."

Chapter Five

THEY TOOK UP a routine. Breakfast at seven together alone. At eleven, they walked into the forest with Jericho and Dick. Review of his notes for his novel would be at two. Tea was at four, alone in his study next to his bedroom suite on the upper floor. And at night, after supper, they parted, and each went off to his or her respective bedroom alone. They bade each other good night, and their farewell became fonder each evening.

Each day she had learned more about him, and he about her.

The first day, it was his preference for breakfast. With his eggs, he liked toast, butter. Tea and coffee. His news sheet. And frivolous stories she told him about the theater and how she was better as an assistant to the manager than as an actress.

"Why did you leave home?" he asked their second morning together over breakfast.

"My parents had a dim view of those on stage. My father is a baronet, but a poor one with little land to support him. He owns a book shop off Piccadilly. That's where I learned to love the written word. I was supposed to be the shop girl, but I would read in between patrons. I told them when I was twelve I wanted to be an actress. They thought it charming. When I turned sixteen and refused to marry the hatter's son, I told them again. They were appalled. He and my mother did not want me to become notorious."

"But when you married, did they accept you then?"

"No. My parents and I are estranged. We do not write or visit. Have not since I wed twelve years ago. They do not care what I do," she said, staring down at her teacup.

Kendryck took her hand up and kissed her knuckles. She melted at his sweetness. "But you do."

"Yes, I do. I have a good reputation, and I know it. I am proud of it."

The next day as they strolled in the woods, he returned to the subject. "If you and I marry, I may develop a reputation that many will term notorious. People do not like a man who wishes to show the world the truth of their folly. Not Society. Not politicians. Not those who will have their lives altered by changes in how business is conducted. How will you bear that?"

"I have witnessed how many people wear fame. Often, over time, the clothes do not fit. I'd welcome being known for a good reason. I would wager your reason is a noble one."

He took that with a nod of appreciation.

The next day, she let pages of his notes fall to her lap as they sat in his study. "I catch a glimmer of why and how you went to India. I foresee the details of that will take me reams of paper to understand. But explain to me, please, why and when you decided to return home."

"My grandfather sent me to India when I was a shy boy of sixteen," he began. "The man was a crusty old bugger, brutal and mean. Forgive me, but it is true. My grandmama and Lady Peregrine, your Aunt Juno, tried to dissuade him. He would not relent. My grandmama is the finest person among us. She was kind, and bore with her husband and my father's whims and failures. I hate that her mind is gone, poor thing."

He sucked in a harsh breath.

"For thirteen years, I served in the government in Bengal, doling out their records, dealing with the nawabs and sheiks. They were my friends. They had given me treasures as gifts— jewels, gold, items I did not earn. Items I was told I could not return, lest I insult my hosts and the Company's friends and allies. Yet I was disgusted by the corruption and waste, by the greed of the East India Company. I had had enough, and I wanted to come home to tell the world. I began to plan for that—and told no one what I wanted. Then, more than two years ago, my older brother died all of a sudden, and I inherited the barony. I was happy to come home to claim it all. I often thought being master is an honor and a duty, a sentiment my grandfather and brother thought a romantic notion. But they were gone, weren't they? They had taken their views with them, too.

"A month after my brother Owen died, when my sister Charlotte wrote to me and told me she was ill, I hastened to prepare for my replacement and subsequent resignation. She wrote the next month to say that she was worse, and the family surgeon told her she had a cancer of the breast. After that, I hurried to prepare my resignation. That took many months, as a replacement for me was difficult to find. Once I did, I began to prepare to sail away. I did my best to disentangle myself from my responsibilities and book passage home. It all took so much time."

The tears that collected on his ebony lashes drew her to him.

She rose and bent to kiss his cheek.

He pierced her with his gaze. "This is not wise."

"To comfort you? Yes, it is."

"I want your comfort, your happiness," he said, his voice rough with desire.

"I believe you." Longing to crawl into his lap, she warned herself against the impulse and drifted backward. "Teatime…"

"Cannot come soon enough," he whispered, and in a gush of delight, she laughed and spun away.

KENDRYCK LEFT THE double doors open to the main salon that evening after supper. He did not expect Tynley to appear.

Evening discussions were not part of their schedule. But he had taken to opening all the doors of his home, save his bedroom, to ensure an air of rectitude.

Their strolls in the forest were another matter entirely. Unsupervised, unchaperoned, the two of them could do as they pleased in the solitude of firs and oaks and the birds of the sky. He had controlled himself. Tynley—except for yesterday's kiss in his study—had, too. He would not lead her on. That would not be fair.

His conduct meeting Tynley alone could be construed by some in Society as verging on the unacceptable. He knew it. But he condoned it because he had to get to know her. He admired her. He desired her. But he could not become carried away by lust. Judging by many couples he'd seen, including his father and Madeline, he knew lust often died a hideous death. Respect offered more rewards. He had seen a few examples of marriages based on that, including his own. He wanted it for himself. Once more.

But Kendryck also observed decorum to preserve Tynley's reputation, because he'd lost rights to his own good name years ago in India. True, he had worked diligently to restore his stature after the death of Marinda and their child. In the last three years of his term, a few notable English ladies in Calcutta had opened their doors to him. That was some measure either of their forgiveness or their forgetfulness. But his guilt had led him to remain celibate, and he had succeeded in curbing his appetites. The loss of two people one loved had done that.

He would not hurt Tynley. She was innocent of his past and had journeyed so far to him in good faith. They had to take some time to decide if they might do well together, and this desire he felt for her would not become a trap for either of them. He would be rational. Logical. Else he reneged on his own promise to himself never to allow lust to carry him away. He would not give in to his passions and become the replica of the grandfather, father, and brother he had detested.

After picking up his reading glasses from the library table, he opened the old folio of maps he had purchased from the Sultan of Naz before he sailed. The maps, hand drawn, were more than seventy years old and had been commissioned by the previous sultan from a renowned Bengali cartographer. Kendryck had purchased the rare drawings, wishing to pinpoint the locations of a few villages that had been obliterated by British raids fifty years ago.

"Strade?" His stepmother appeared at the threshold and glanced about. "You are working this late?"

"I am, Madeline. I often do after dinner." But she knew that. They had even discussed it on occasion. He indicated the oversized pages draped over the large, circular table in the center of the library and gave her a quizzical look.

She craned her neck this way and that, ascertaining if anyone might lurk behind the numerous wooden bookcases. She advanced a step inside. "Yes, well. You are alone. I wish to speak with you."

He removed his glasses and stepped away from the table. "Would you care to sit?"

"Thank you. I would." She marched over to the four chairs situated before the white stone fireplace.

He was not surprised she had come. He had expected a visit from her the first evening after Mrs. Wallingford arrived. But no. His stepmother had put aside her curiosity in favor of gathering information over time. Prudent of her. Especially now that she had that special posture about her, which connoted she'd done her research and intended to prevail. She had come to make her preferences known. He would do the same. *Armed for battle, we march forth, madam.*

"Come, then, let us sit," he said to her, then took his pre-ferred wing chair and put his glasses on the chess table.

"I am concerned about Mrs. Wallingford."

"In what way?" He knew Madeline feared Tynley was about to usurp her powers as lady of the house. Madeline had already felt the pinch of his return home, the curtailing of her numerous expenses here and in Cardiff, plus her extravagant plans for Barbara's come-out. But she always took her time surveying the battlefield on which she fought against him. He would draw her out, let her assert her power, spread out her desires like soldiers to the line…until she felt his own hegemony once more.

"She is a lovely person. Thoughtful. Kind."

She knows little of you and how to deal with you.

"A widow, too. Poor thing. And so she has the ability to do much which a young girl may not."

Here we go. "Such as…"

Madeline trained her dark brown eyes on him. "To be alone with you constantly."

"The doors are open always," he said. "You may join us at any time."

"Barbara has contemplated it."

And eavesdropped, I don't doubt. He folded his hands in his lap. "And overheard something she questioned?"

She put a finger to the auburn curl at her ear. "You two are very jovial."

Someone is watching us. "Humor is not permitted?"

"Heated glances that are enticements."

"Barbara has also hidden herself from view to spy upon me and report back to you."

The woman huffed. "This is not good. You know we have so much to overcome with those two bastards of your father's whoring in the village. We dare not have more to add to their fire."

Kendryck set his teeth. His father and his grandfather had more bastards than the village of Rambles could ever hold. "Madam, the fire you speak of was burning long before Mrs. Wallingford arrived here. The straw that first burned was the rumor that my father took two servant girls into the same bed with him and impregnated them. Hence, the two young ladies who live in the village with that taint and their mothers' maiden names as markers."

"Stop that!"

"The next was that Father brought home the youngest daughter of a viscountess, whom he seduced in her own home and whose father forced him to marry her."

"Stop! That is not what we speak of."

"No?" *Of course it is. The result is Gerard. But my father did not stop there, did he? He went to Cardiff on a regular basis and found amusement wherever he chose. Or brought his amusements home. A duel and a dead man are the next stories. So many!*

"There is nothing for the past, Madeline. But the future, I will deal with. I wish instead to discuss why Gerard is suddenly home from university." His brother would not speak of it, and neither would Madeline.

Her lower lip quivered.

Kendryck knew it a ruse. "He arrived home the day after I came from London. I deserve to know why he is here and not at university."

She straightened her spine. "Gerard is innocent."

"Is he? I have asked him, and he tells me he attends to his own absolution. I get no details. I am entitled, as I pay to put him in brandy and pin money."

She was on her feet now. "I should have known you would not speak calmly with me about this."

"It is you, madam, who raise your voice, not I."

"I merely wish to preserve whatever dignity this family has left."

He nodded. "A fine ambition. I do applaud it."

"I want it to benefit Barbara and her debut."

"As do I."

"Do you?" Her eyes narrowed. "Then create no scandal. Barbara deserves to marry well!"

Don't we all?

She stamped her foot. "Better than live out her days in this morbid pile beyond the pale of nowhere!"

"I would suggest that you look to your own behavior, Madeline. See to it you continue to treat Mrs. Wallingford with all the respect you would any lady you would meet in London."

"I have done nothing wrong. Nothing to harm our guest."

"Do tell Barbara to stop spying on us. Mrs. Wallingford and I do nothing more than get acquainted."

"Will you marry?"

"We have not decided yet."

That reality flummoxed her. "But...where... How did you meet?"

"By advertisement."

"What?"

Enough of this. He got to his feet. "Mrs. Wallingford and I have decided she remains for a few more days, at the least. For now, we are friends. I will tell you when she and I decide what the week's end brings."

"This is most extraordinary."

"I agree. Now, if there is anything else?"

Her large eyes turned bleak. "No. Not now."

"Well, then. Goodnight."

He watched his stepmother hurry away and knew what her visit forced him to do. Friendship was built not only on shared interests and values, but a belief that each could trust the other.

Tynley could not unless she knew the worst of him. He prayed that when he told her, he would not drive her away.

Chapter Six

ON THEIR FOURTH morning, Tynley tingled with expectation as she rushed down the stairs at seven. Her excitement rose despite her new worry.

Last night, when she had returned to her room after dinner, she found one of her gowns—her favorite blue-green silk that Kendryck told her he especially liked—was ripped at the hem. The dress had lain on the wardrobe floor, crumpled. She had not left it like that, but had it hanging upon one of the sturdy hangars. Seren, the maid assigned to her, had seemed dedicated and shy. Tynley did not suspect her of any wrong, yet she asked her about the gown's presence on the floor. The girl was surprised. She even declared she had not seen anyone enter Tynley's rooms. Tynley had not asked her about the torn hem. Seren had not done that, she felt certain. But the tear bothered her. In fact, it appeared to be worse—a slice from a pair of scissors.

The shiver that had wended through Tynley upon that discovery was one she decided to dismiss. She did not have evidence to accuse anyone of the deed. Plus, she could mend the tear. She was good with needle and thread, and had often mended costumes for the stage. She would open her mending box and find a band long enough to decorate the hem and hide the tear. She would count it as one of those odd things that happened now and then.

She had decided to devote herself to enjoying her new enchantment with a man she'd come to understand quickly. Her delight was girlish, and she chastised herself for allowing the thrill of romance to wing through her at the advanced age of thirty. But she liked Kendryck. His cleverness, his humor. Most of all, she appreciated his cautious approach to selecting a marriage partner. She had done the same.

This exuberance that she discovered in Kendryck's presence filled her with a joy she had not felt since the years of her marriage with Graham Wallingford. Before her husband had joined the army to fight Napoleon, they had enjoyed a wonderful friendship and love affair. After he returned from war battered and bewildered, they had struggled on. Graham was not himself; his memory was spotty. He could not retain dialogue and could not return to the stage. Moreover, he understood his weaknesses, and his anger could be explosive.

She had found work as a manager's assistant for two different London theaters, and filled in their irregular income by doing fine needlework for a Half Moon Street modiste. When Graham became ill with fever and their son caught the same illness, the weeks that followed were harsh. Both of them dying within weeks of each other had sent her into long mourning that sapped her physically and emotionally. She doubted she could ever laugh again.

Then one day she'd received an invitation from her Aunt Juno to come to tea. The older lady encouraged her to join her for walks each day in Hyde Park. Their promenades were the beginning of Tynley's recovery. After three months of that, her natural ebullience—always her asset and her flaw—was revived.

Aunt Juno had spoken to her of Germaine Hammond's success in her new venture of matching couples. That, however, was after many occasions with her aunt over tea when Tynley had revealed her loneliness and her desire to meet acceptable men. After that, her aunt had invited her to numerous dinner parties where Tynley met many eligible fellows. No one appealed. She placed an ad in the *Chronicle*. The chances of finding a man who appealed to her seemed so very small. A gamble. A challenge. Yet somehow, the probability seemed greater that she would discover as much or more of a man's character in his prose than she had about those in Aunt Juno's salon.

She had advertised in the *Chronicle* and later responded to Kendryck's advertisement for a wife with good reasons of her own. She believed that she could be happy again. She wished to do that with a good man.

To her delight, she had found him.

And so she wended her way along the endless corridors down to the breakfast room. Kendryck was there. Always there before her. Seated, his large, elegant fingers holding the latest news sheet, he looked up at her, and she knew by the lazy appraisal of his blue eyes that he welcomed her.

Each morning she had moved to a chair closer to Kendryck around the circular table. Though ever nearer, he never touched her. He did caress her with his eyes and lure her with the enticing expressions of his wide, masculine mouth.

Carter, smart man, disappeared. The butler had learned that retreat was a discreet move.

This fourth morning, they ate leisurely. Finished, Tynley rose and was ready to bid him adieu. "Until eleven."

"Not today." Kendryck shook his head. "Before we take our usual walk this morning, I want to show you a portion of the house. It's old. Part of the original castle. I will meet you on the front steps."

The tension in his words disturbed her. Unable to tend to her mending as she had planned, she rushed upstairs to walk the long gallery. There, she implored herself to memorize the names and dates of previous family members whose portraits hung upon the blood-red walls.

At ten minutes to eleven, she rushed to her room, donned her brown coat and teal leghorn hat, and ran down the stairs. She was just at the landing to the second floor when Barbara appeared below, a book in her hands.

"Good morning, Mrs. Wallingford." She turned her dark blue eyes upon Tynley with a pleasant smile as she climbed the stairs toward her. "How good to see you. I miss you at breakfast each day. You arise very early, Carter tells us."

"I do. It has always been my nature."

"Welcome each dawn, do you?" she said with a flick of her wavy blonde-red hair so similar to Gerard's. As she stopped before Tynley, she critically eyed her worn hat and coat. "I wish I were as inclined. But I favor naps. I say, have you been taking walks each day? The weather here can be beastly. Gales off the Atlantic come in. We've had shipwrecks, it can be so horrid. Did you know?"

"No." Tynley shook her head. What was this inquiry really about?

"The fifth Baron Strade was so fortunate to discover gold doubloons from a galleon wreck on our shore. The story is he ordered no one else to go near and gathered them up off the sands himself. Meanwhile, Spanish sailors died upon the rocks. He allowed no one to go to them to aid them. Yes, he left them to die while he picked up the coins. Such a noble fellow, Strade. He used the coin to build this house." She swept her hand wide to indicate the manse. "A monster, isn't it?"

"A maze." Tynley could be nothing but honest.

"Ha! Indeed." Barbara put a hand to Tynley's wrist. As reassurance, it was a sham. "Like his descendants. Complicated and dark."

The girl was warning her away. *Why?* "I don't see that."

"If you stay long, you will. Shall you? Stay long?"

"A few more days. At least."

"Judging if you like our Kendryck, I know. A good idea to take one's time to decide if one will marry. Lucky you. Would that a woman had all the time she wished to decide if she could lash herself to one particular man, eh?"

Is that really what bothers this girl this morning? "No matter what anyone tells you, Miss Hollens, you should take all the time you wish for that. Infatuation is for the moment. Marriage is forever."

The girl lost her hauteur, appearing grateful for the advice. "I will remember that."

"Do. Now, if you will excuse me?"

"Off to your walk."

"I am. Good day."

TYNLEY SHOOK OFF the chill of that encounter. She was going to enjoy her time with Kendryck, and whatever he wished to show her, she was ready to see it. She hurried, the promise of something new giving her feet wings.

She pushed open the heavy front door and scanned the terrain before her. The front steps were broad, leading down to the Doric columns of the portico that was wide enough to accommodate two carriages side by side. The skies were gray today, laden with the threat of more snow. She shivered, anticipating little delight in whatever Kendryck would show her.

He approached from the tangled wilderness of the dense forest. His shock of black hair beneath his top hat blew in a gust of wind. His cheeks were rosy. But no nonchalance stood in his expression. Instead, his visage drawn in tight lines, he sent her a forced smile that held the sadness of an apology.

Jericho and Dick ran pell-mell from the dark of the forest. Their long pink tongues hanging out, they came to her, yipped, and danced around her. Tynley could have sworn they had smiles on their faces.

She was glad some creatures did. "What's wrong?" she asked Kendryck.

"I wish to tell you more about me."

"Marvelous. I will do the same," she said, on a bright note.

"Not all will be good to hear."

"Ah, but sir, I can tell you things about me that are not likely to get me into heaven."

That did not move him, and so she decided to allow him his brown study. The sooner he'd tell her all, it would be over and done.

He wound her arm through his and patted her hand as he led her around the frontage of the Palladian house on a slate path to the back. Fog rolled in with a blast of cold air. They passed a portion of the structure that was Tudor period, built in half beams and half plaster. Next to that, stone walls rose twenty or more feet high up into the mist.

"How old is this?" she asked him, marveling at the huge blocks of limestone. She knew the characteristics of medieval architecture, having often admired the construction of the Tower of London.

"Some say 1110 or 1240. We have original drawings in the library. I should hire an expert from Cambridge to come examine them. They are written in Old French, and I cannot make sense of them."

"That is wonderful. I agree. You should do that. It is heart-warming to know whence you came."

That elicited curiosity from him. "Do you know a lot about your family?"

"My mother comes from York. Her family were landed gentry, holding small plots. My father is a Londoner. I was comfortable, proud of them, until I told them I wished to be an actress. They were angry; ashamed, too. Afraid of what others would say if they learned I had done that. But I could not care. I wanted it. Perhaps I was too adamant. Perhaps they thought me unable to make sound decisions. But I left home anyway, escaping one night after they had gone to bed."

"You have not communicated with them since you left home?"

"No. My father's family are very devout. To them, a woman

should be docile and never boastful. As an actress, I threatened to be all of that and more."

They walked on for a few long, silent minutes.

"My family speculate on our relationship," he said, breaking their peace with regret in his voice.

"Barbara met me on the stairs as I came out. She knows we breakfast together and walk in the woods each day." She sighed. "We knew they would learn and might object. Despite our keeping the doors open and allowing anyone to join us."

The family had, too. Come and gone, at first it seemed by need to converse with him or her about this or that. Later, they had tried to surprise the two of them and catch them in some inappropriate clutch. Neither had happened.

"My stepmother, Madeline, is not so much one to pry as one who wishes everyone to keep the rules. She came to see me last night."

"She complained?" That surprised Tynley. "I did not detect she was disturbed."

"She is. Very. I assured her we are quite respectable."

"Quite," she agreed with a smile and a nod to the need to remain so.

His expression clouded. "She can be wily, changeable. Unpredictable. I wish you to be aware of that. When a young mother, she was very harsh. Rules were the way she commanded and punished. She believed in the strap as the means to beat a child into compliance."

"Dear heavens," Tynley said, alarmed that anyone would do that to a youngster. "Barbara and Gerard were raised that way?"

"My father approved. So, yes. Madeline used it liberally. You could hear their cries throughout the house."

Tynley shuddered. "Did she hit you and your brother and sister?"

"Owen, my older brother, was off to Eton when our father married Madeline. Less than a year later, he was at Cambridge when Gerard was born. As for Charlotte and me, she was six and

I was eleven. Though I was at school, and home only during holidays, Charlotte was here through it all, and she and Madeline never got on. Charlotte grew lonely and rebellious. Madeline demanded obedience in all things and enforced it with her whip. I never knew she used it on Charlotte, though, until one Christmas, when I was home, Madeline took aversion to Charlotte bringing in rock samples from the forest paths."

A forlorn look washed over him, and he paused in his reverie.

"There are a few tunnels, too, under this part of the old castle. They run, according to the medieval drawings I told you about, down into the hills here. Down to the coast. Hard to find. Treacherous to navigate. Steep and slick. Charlotte explored them all the time, on her own, with a lantern in hand. She was adventurous and bold, too much so. Our father caught her when she was six and warned her not to go, but she never stopped. It was her fun, and she snuck out anyway.

"Each time she went and brought back samples, she was caught because of the mess she tracked in. Madeline sought to stop her by beating her with her thick leather strap. That morning near Christmas, I found Madeline at it and caught the strap in my hand. I told Father, too. He did nothing, of course.

"He never did. He wished nothing to do with rearing children, only begetting them. Always begetting them. Madeline was quite a beauty in her day. But Father had other ladies as well. Rumor had it that he had quite a few children on the wrong side of the blanket. Two of those live in Rambles. They hate us for that, even though their mothers declare the stories to be false."

"I would."

"Any woman does," he said, looking at her with pain lining his eyes and mouth.

Suddenly, Kendryck strode away and turned right toward a large opening, once a gate with portcullis, now yawning wide and empty. Tynley joined him and saw a vast medieval castle courtyard open before her. Overgrown with weeds and littered with debris and stumps and stunted trees, the expanse spoke of decay and neglect. The walls of the old keep rose high, the building intact. But Tynley perceived Kendryck saw none of it as he led her across the courtyard toward the ancient keep.

"We'll go in the keep one day, if you like. The stairs are stone, hollowed from wear and steep. The railings are old wood and rotting. So the climb is treacherous. But the view at the top is a panorama that is fit for a king. You will see all that once was Strade land from the hills and valley to the sea. My ancestors sold much of it off, piece by piece. They were not good stewards of their lands. I've seen the record books. They bear it out. My ancestors took the money of the sales and bought investments. All of them paid handsomely and continue to do so. It is how we live."

He led her toward the half-timbered Tudor house, perfectly intact. His attitude gave her a sense of foreboding. "What I want to show you today is inside here."

What had begun as an adventure alone with him dissolved in the mists. From the corner of her eye, she detected that he frowned. He fought within himself about some issue.

She struggled to find a way to resurrect their camaraderie.

The dogs charged off, running toward the gate and barking sharply as if to warn them of danger approaching. She and Kendryck paused to watch, but the two quickly shied away as if threatened.

"We have a skulk of foxes in that patch of the forest. Jericho caught a kit last spring, and the vixen failed to save her pup from him. The two dogs always bark like that when they approach. Do not worry. Jericho had his fill of them, and Dick follows him. They just make sure we know the foxes are around." Dismissing the animals, he pointed toward the old house. "I've brought you here for good reason. I want to ensure you know who I am, Tynley. This business of marriage requires more than a simple agreement."

"I do agree." She was not afraid, but at his serious tone, she was concerned.

He took from his greatcoat's inner pocket an old, corroded iron key and turned it in the rusty lock of the door to the half-timbered house.

Inside, leaving the heavy door ajar, he led her across the foyer toward another smaller door. For this he produced another, smaller iron key and pushed the portal wide. He kicked across the floor a wooden wedge and lodged open the door.

The dogs trotted in, sniffed around, and left for the bailey.

Tynley stared at what stood before her.

Old shelves lined the walls. Tables lined up, one in back of the other. The room might once have been a larder or closet, but it was clean, as if newly swept this morning. No cobwebs hung from the solid crossbeams. No animals scurried to hide in any corners. Cloths draped countless items of different shapes and sizes. A few hangings appeared to be sheets, others old rugs or draperies. They covered boxes, chests, and bowls. Against one wall, the items cloaked appeared to be tall, folded screens.

One by one, Kendryck yanked at the cloths.

She gaped at the number of chests before her. Most were leather and iron-strapped curved wood, all of different sizes. She counted nine. Most were two feet wide and as deep. One was long as Tynley was tall and fit for a pirate of the Spanish Main. Closed, the top was covered in hammered gold leaf. A latch of pin and hook locked it shut.

Next to it, on another table, sat stacks three feet high of elegant silver plates. Next to that was a huge bowl of polished silver. Inside lay dozens of finely wrought goblets. Two shelves below held stacks of smaller plates and serving dishes, all of the same glittering silverware.

Tynley shot a glance at Kendryck, who stood as mesmerized as she, and took a moment to turn to her and blink.

"Go on," he said with a nod toward the other tables. "Examine them all."

She could not take them all in. There was too much. It was too grand. Too blinding.

A child's chair. Fit in gold leaf, studded with ivory and jade stones in an intricate pattern that was repeated, exactly, up the legs, along the wide arms, and to the back and seat of the chair.

Against the walls stood folding panels, screens, all of inlaid quartz, ivory, and stone depicting scenes she could not in the light decipher.

"Open that chest against the wall," he told her. "It has no lock."

She lifted the lid. Inside stood carved ivory, wooden, or molded porcelain animals, monkeys and rats, dogs and cats, some as small as her thumb, others big enough to swallow her hand. Their expressions were human and their bodies contorted in the throes of joy or agony or death. Their eyes were emeralds or sapphires, their bodies studded with black or white pearls, some with citrines. All shimmered in the few rays of sunlight streaming through the old medieval glass windows.

"See the red velvet pouch inside that chest?" he told her. "Take it out. Draw the strings."

She did, and inside, a thousand tiny stars winked up at her. She put her finger in to stir them. Diamonds, hundreds of them, tiny, dancing beams. "All this is yours?"

"Mine."

She replaced the pouch and closed the lid of the chest. "Tell me how you acquired it."

He nodded. "We will sit in the courtyard. I cannot bear to be here for too long. It eats at my nerves, and I become the man I promised myself I would bury in the dust of my past."

He covered the displays in haste, then led her outside to a stone bench near the wall of the keep. They sat together as the sun tried to part the clouds.

"I must be honest. I am not a good man. No, no, don't object. Listen to me, please. I come from a family steeped in licentious behavior. The Hollens family descend from notorious Norman knights who cared for themselves and naught for others. It is a wonder any of this was built," he said, and extended his arm to denote the bailey and the castle, "let alone that any of it survives. My grandfather, my father, and my older brother were all rogues of the worst sort. They gambled, drank, ignored their land and tenants and took women as they pleased. They bragged about it, too, and sprinkled the earth with their by-blows. Never gave their progeny a penny. Their own pleasure was their only thought. The head of the family has for centuries always been dubbed the Unholy Hollens."

"You are not like that," she said. It was what she knew in her soul.

He stared at her, rejecting her sentiments. "I am. I am."

She examined him. He was forthright, sincere. She knew a gentleman when she saw one. "How?"

"I sailed to India at sixteen. A skinny, frightened youth, sent away by my grandfather, who did not wish to support me. I was, after all, the second boy. You see, there was already another one, Gerard. My father was a laggard, there were mouths to feed, and my grandfather had to cut his expenses. I was the expense he cut."

Kendryck shot to his feet, strode around in a circle, removed his hat, and beat it against his knee. "He bought me a clerk's position with the East India Company. I sailed for Calcutta and the Company's offices in Bengal. I had a legible pen and a good ear. I took notes and did mathematics others had no skill for. I caught the eye of senior East India clerks in Calcutta who needed an attentive assistant. With regularity, I had promotions.

"Oh, they weren't all given to me because I worked hard. No. Men died. So very many men died. Of the eight who sailed out with me, six were dead within two years. The heat exhausted them. Fevers burned them up. Or insects bit them to a raving madness. And then there were always the monkeys who nipped at you and took a finger. Or worse, the occasional tiger who crept into your tent when you went north to the hills and had been foolish enough to forget your rifle."

She had heard some of these tales before, but had not felt the sting of them until now. "But that does not make you an immoral man."

"It made me lucky." He threw his hat away, and it sailed like a black dragon over the courtyard into the fog. "What came next made me greedy, covetous, needy of everything I wished for."

Still she was not moved. What he claimed was too extreme to fit his person. Like the suit of bad clothes she had discussed with him. The crimes did not fit his person.

"I received a promotion and went inland. I was appointed secretary to an Englishman who was the ambassador to the nadir of Hyderabad. All in the embassy lived very close to the Muslim court and, like the chief resident, I not only dressed the same way but ate the same as my Indian servants. I also took an Indian girl as my mistress. She came from a fine family, a secondary branch of a maharaja's line. I took her as my wife. It was not a Christian ceremony. But no matter. We had a child. A girl. They lived with me in my little house, and my association with my wife was beneficial to me."

"Did you bring them home with you?" If he had a mistress or a woman whom he considered his native wife, Tynley would not stay. Nor would she marry him.

"No. A year after my change to Hyderabad, I was sent back to Calcutta. There, the Company leaders disapproved of those who embraced Indian culture, especially taking Indian wives and mistresses. I prepared to bring her to Calcutta with me anyway, but her family refused. They came one night and abducted her and my daughter. They refused me even to see them. The father left me a note that he was shamed by me and my colleagues. Meanwhile, my Company officers told me the same thing. I would not receive promotions any longer. That did not hurt me as much as the loss of my wife and daughter. But then, months later, worse news came. I was told by a servant of mine that both of them died of a fever."

"That's terrible! Did you believe your servant?"

"I did. But their abductions and deaths proved to me that I

had to expose the prejudice and corruption I knew existed in the Company." He looked across the bailey toward the door to his treasures. "I brought all that home not to use it or sell it, but to prove the corruption. To show the world what we have taken from people who knew not what we stole from them. And all of that? It is but a drop of water in a sea of stolen wealth and a glorious culture shamed and ruined."

"It is all…unfathomable." Tynley took his arm.

He did not move. "After I learned my wife and child were dead, I was quite insane. For over a year, I did what I had to. But I drank. I lived…very low. And one day, ill as I had never been before, ragged and thin as paper, I saw what I had become. A duplicate of the three men in my family whom I had reviled. And I hated myself.

"'Twas then I decided to come home. I am not one to negotiate with any man. I want my way. But I do write well. So I planned to use my skill. I would write something, somehow, to enrage others here, to show all the horror of the English in a foreign land. I told myself I had to correct what was wrong. To tell all I know of the problems in India. I began to collect records of abuses by those in the Company. Who they demoted for becoming too Hindu or too Muslim. Who had changed religions. Who wore pajamas and turbans. I have a vast library of those crimes, and I will write them down so that all the world learns about them."

She was proud of him, but afraid for him too. "That is a noble goal—"

"Which I am committed to. But you are not. You walk into this innocent. I fear for you with the revelation of all of this. I will rile the East India Company, ship builders, merchants, Parliament, and a million others! I will not be accepted, but denounced. I am ready. I am able to withstand the scandal and their hatred. But this is not your fight, Tynley. It could destroy you. It means that you should go," he said with sad conviction in his blue eyes. "Return to London. There you can find a man who will give you a peaceful life with children and a long life. So many men would be better men than I."

Her mind had one answer. She could not be hasty to agree. But her heart had another. "No. I do not wish to go, Kendryck."

"You must." He said it like a decree.

She stared at him. Here was a man who had been thrust out of his family. They had been unjust, and they had also been cruel. They had sent him as a tender boy far from home to a land he knew not. In that terror, he miraculously survived. He used his skills, his talents, and his dedication to carve for himself a reputation. One that was more than the part of his loving relationship with his mistress and child. After their loss by dreadful means, he had made a plan to return home and correct the problems and injustices he saw.

She would help him. It was noble and just. She could keep her head and rise above any criticism he endured. He was a baron, with power and money. Not like her, a mediocre actress and a failed playwright, a woman who wished for fame and acknowledgment.

"Kendryck, look at me. I want to help you."

He regarded her. "Dear lady, you are a beautiful woman. With intellect and solid character. I more than like you—I care for you. Together, we would find more. But this could drain all the joy from you."

"Or, like you, it could give me purpose."

"Do you need one so badly?"

"We each do. What is life without a goal…and someone to share it with?"

He rounded on her, his black hair tousled over his brow, his azure eyes burning. "That is my problem here. I wish you to stay. Stay for breakfast and tea and walks in the woods. Stay to be my succor and my strength."

"Then don't make me go."

"But this emotion between us is too fast, too strong. I am a man of great passions. Love, hate, ambition. Desire. I know the results of impulse—and I fear them."

She shook her head. "Impulses can often be followed for good reasons. You and I have been honest with each other. Even to this." She opened her hand to the castle and the old house with its treasures. "Kendryck, I can be your partner in this. I am up to the task. I am no coward."

"I believe you, but—"

"Kendryck, no one will come to take me away." This was England. Such things did not happen.

"You may take yourself away!"

"Kendryck, you fear shadows of the past. And if I feared the future you describe, I would be gone now."

"I am tempted." He touched her cheek, an angel's endearment. "So tempted to rush you, promise you that in my arms and in my bed you will find all that heaven allows. But I do not wish to seduce you."

She grew wistful. "And what if I am already seduced?"

He set his jaw. "Lust is not for you, my darling. Love is what you should have."

"I agree."

"I told you yesterday I want your comfort and your happiness."

She sighed, smiling beneath his soft caress of her cheek, and let her head fall back. Her hat slipped its ribbons, and her hair slipped its pins. She hugged him tightly to her, all that she wanted. "I want yours, too."

"Oh, don't be rash."

"I am too old for that—and too young not to seize what I want. And I want to be brave. With you. That's what you need in a partner. Oh, Kendryck, the world awaits your fine correction. I want to help you achieve it." She shook back her hair and gazed up at him with all her desire unveiled for him to see. "I want this challenge, and I want you—"

"Oh, you are a maddening woman." He pulled her close. "I want your stubbornness and your resolve. I want all of you, this spot here…" He bent to press his hard, warm mouth to a point on her throat.

She reeled in the euphoria of his regard, but needed to assure him of more. "Listen to me, Kendryck. I wanted my husband so dearly. And I've never been tempted by any other man. Until you. Dashing, noble, stalwart you."

"Don't say that." He was a tormented devil as he smiled down upon her. "We have days to go. Three before we agreed to decide."

To prove she could wait, she teased him. "You are horrid to count them."

"Trust me, sweet lady." He took her arm and considered the sky with wide eyes. "I count each minute."

"Stop counting," she whispered. Finished with his arguments and his delay, she wound her arms around his neck. "Just kiss me."

"You are a ripe temptation. What can I do but keep you?"

"You can call banns. That will give us a month to decide. After that, if you do not want me, I will go."

"You may not want me," he said.

"I have already decided."

"You are fast—and stubborn." He was won over to her cause and smiling about it.

She grinned. She liked to win. "A good match for a man who considers himself too impulsive."

He snorted and clutched her close. "If I agree, will you kiss me?"

She fluttered her lashes. "I'll think about it."

He scoffed. "How long?"

"That depends on whether—"

His kiss was quick and hot and decadent. His lips were everything a married woman craved in a lover. Firm and insistent, sweet and searching, his kiss set her body ablaze. No coy boy took her. No longtime spouse. But one full of the passion that hot dreams were made of.

Her eyes remained closed as she floated in the euphoria he created. When she opened them, one look at him and she knew neither of them was going to change their minds. She would marry him and want possession like that forevermore. He would marry her...and she would keep him all to herself, her life's ambition.

Chapter Seven

"I'd like announce our engagement to the family at dinner tonight," Kendryck told her as he walked her to her chamber door.

"The sooner the better," she agreed. No one was in the halls, and she pulled him close. "We should also tell them that we'll have banns read. They'll think that's wise. They will want to know we are prudent."

He arched dark brows. "They'll want to hope we are celibate."

She loved when he was pointed. It kept her on her toes. "They would not be so critical."

"They can be. For Gerard's sake."

"That's…awful."

"The desire for only one male heir is a long, hideous tradition in this family. My continued good health breaks with that hope."

"We will give them other things to think about. A wedding."

"A breakfast reception. A party. Days apart from you and me as we go on our honeymoon."

She grew flirtatious with him and petted his cravat. "We want them informed. Included. Happy."

He stroked her cheeks. "I want us happy."

"We will be. And soon." She wished to kiss his lips, possess him. She outlined his lower lip with a fingertip. Where was her intention to remain sweet, untouched, and his friend? Gone! Fled with his charming manner and potent good looks. She overruled her flirtatious urges. "The timing of the banns will be good, since we can marry just before Advent."

He chuckled and caught her hand. "If you keep fondling me, madam, I may have to get a special license so we marry tomorrow!"

She wrinkled her nose at him. She did like playing with him. "On the contrary, sir—we are going to act like the mature adults we are and not hop into beds or anything else too fast."

He covered her hands. "Much as I hate to agree, I will. But what, if any, preferences do you have for the ceremony?"

"Not here," she blurted, and wondered why she did not feel comfortable being married in his home.

He frowned. "Yes. The Rambles does not convey itself to festivities, does it? No, do not answer that. Your quick response to my question said it all. I've never liked the house..."

She cupped his cheek and sought more from him about the manse.

"It is such a mélange of styles. Relics of so many through the centuries who did not care for it well. Fragments of yesterday that stand as testimony to everything the family has done to destroy others. No, my darling, I do not wish to be married here either."

It would not bode well. She shivered at the thought. "Where shall we go? Do you have a church here in the village that you attended?"

"Not I. Not my grandfather, either. I think they may have run him out as the heathen he was. No, I have another suggestion. Would you agree to our wedding taking place in a twelfth-century church along the main road near Cardiff? The vicar is a childhood friend of mine, and I know he'd like the honor of marrying me. He often wrote to me that he thought I never would."

She smoothed the line of his frock coat down his chest. She appreciated the feel of his strong ribs beneath the supple fabric.

"Yes, we must do that. To be wed by a friend seems the perfect choice."

"Do you have any friends who might take the journey to witness us wed?" he asked, as she traced the line of the lapel on his waistcoat.

"I do have one friend whom I'd like to invite. She currently stars in a play in Drury Lane. I will write and ask, though I doubt she can attend."

"What about Lady Peregrine?" he asked with a mischievous light in his eyes as she fiddled with a button on his waistcoat.

"Aunt Juno?" She nodded. "Now that is a very good idea. I will send her an invitation. She might well be eager to see us close the deal begun by her niece, the publisher."

"Near the church is a fine carriage inn," he added. "I will notify the innkeeper that we have a few guests for him for the wedding."

"We can have the wedding breakfast there," she suggested.

"I think my friend and his wife would host that at their vicarage."

"That would be so good of them."

Kendryck grinned and caught her hands. "I want you to stop fiddling with me, and yet I would love it if you went on! So we must be proper."

She pressed her breasts to his chest. "I like fiddling with you."

"You are a tease, madam. Come now, or I will have you here."

Her eyes popped wide. "What an intriguing idea!"

"Stop, please." He chuckled. "Turn your mind to the wedding, my lady. Now…I like this plan more and more. To prepare, we shall go to Cardiff in a few days. We will visit my friend, Vicar William Drummond, and ask him to put us in his register for the first of December. While we are there, we will visit a milliner for a new hat for you and—"

She tsked at him. "My poor hat."

"Terrible colors. It will be gone, and none too soon, either.

We will also visit a modiste. We go to London in the spring, and you will need a wardrobe."

"We cannot go alone. Not to Cardiff."

He frowned. "You are right. We will take Madeline and Barbara. They will love the idea of visiting shops. And thus dies the idea of a journey together."

"We will have many of those in years to come," Tynley said as consolation. "What I really want to know, sir, is where we go for our honeymoon."

"Not here. Not Cardiff. A surprise, madam!" He lifted her hands and kissed her knuckles. "No more of your caresses. I am on to my study. See you at supper."

⟫⟫⟩⟨⟨⟪

THE CANDELABRA BURNED brightly as Kendryck rose from his chair to inform the family of the coming wedding. He had few hopes this would go well, but he would do his duty by them all. He told them quickly of his and Tynley's decision.

Madeline took his announcement with stoic ease, and congratulated both of them with a true smile.

Barbara sat, a mischievous look within her dark brown eyes, but, following her mother, she wished them well.

Gerard offered his hope for long life and happiness. "We knew it was coming. The way you two regard each other blinds us. No wonder you breakfast early alone together. You even escape to walk in the forest with only the dogs to view you."

Kendryck had raised a glass in honor of his bride-to-be, but with Gerard's impudent words, he froze. "However you feel about our actions, Gerard, I do ask you do the proper thing and raise your goblet in honor of the bride."

The young man pushed back his chair and sent to Tynley the most obscene flash of sexual desire.

Kendryck saw it. Who could miss it?

Tynley shot back in her chair, as if a sword passed through her chest.

Kendryck clutched his glass so hard he thought he might crush it.

Tynley stared into his eyes and gave a small shake of her head.

Later, Kendryck told himself. Anger never won with Gerard. But he would bend the boy, turn him to the right of things. He must. Gerard would never survive in the world as a hedonist. He needed some fine characteristic to commend him.

Dinner went on.

Tynley picked at hers.

His stepmother carried the conversation throughout the meal.

Barbara, never one to rally to anyone's cause but her own, ate well and conversed with everyone.

Kendryck waited until Madeline, Gerard, and Barbara had excused themselves, then took Tynley's arm. They strode slowly toward the bottom of the stairs. "I will speak to Gerard tomorrow morning, Tynley. He will not act so outrageously again."

Kendryck saw the anger in her eyes. "He was unprincipled."

"Not new of him. A wily boy, still. He has many challenges. I have not told you about them, but he must reform." Kendryck raised her face, caressing her chin. "He will. I will demand it."

"Thank you."

"Do not let him ruffle your feathers. I like your feathers, my darling, as they are."

She hugged him, but in her expression was trepidation.

He would improve her mood before she climbed the stairs to bed. "Can I kiss you goodnight?"

"No."

"But I accepted your proposal, Mrs. Wallingford."

"You did, and I am very happy about that, sir. But you have had your one kiss for today."

"Are you a stickler for order?"

"I am." She tried for levity with a toss of her head and a waggle of her fingers at him in goodnight. He could see it in her as she climbed the stairs, but at the landing, she turned and summoned a much-too-valiant smile for him.

The look of love upon her sublime features temporarily put at bay his anger at his half-brother—and raised instead a new fear at the new problems Gerard might create.

As soon as she left Kendryck's sight at the top of the second floor, she hoisted her skirts to run. She could not get to the sanctity of her rooms fast enough. She shut the door deliberately and caught it just before it slammed. She fumbled for the key and gave it a sharp turn.

Her eyes closed.

She breathed deeply. To be afraid of a boy, a silly, stupid one at that, was not like her. She had fended off many men in her early years in the theater. So many assumed a woman in the profession was an easy target.

But she had evaded all of them who would take her for a trollop. She might not have become a famous actress of the London stage, but she had not given in to the need to supplement her income by lying with men. Instead, she had turned herself into a proper assistant to managers who'd needed help with all sorts of problems of the production of a play. When she had married, she'd been a virgin. When she married Kendryck, she would be just as virtuous…and free of the likes of men like Gerard.

She made for her bedroom, noting the small fire Seren had left behind the grate of her sitting room. Tonight, she would not ring for the girl. She'd get out of her own clothes. She'd done it herself for years. And she did wish to be alone. If the girl were here, she'd be asking Tynley if she might bring her tea or something stronger to improve her mood. Tynley did not want that. Nothing would raise her spirits but her own strength of character. That, plus her reaffirmation of her belief that Kendryck would reprimand Gerard, would help. Certainly Kendryck was the one to do it. She had only the ability to reject the boy's immature behavior.

She struggled out of her gown and half corset, her shift, and stockings, donned her night rail, then crawled into bed.

She lay, staring at the plastered ceiling, focusing on Kendryck's and her agreement to marry. Perhaps a wedding was just what the those in his family needed to change their spirits. Had Madeline lived here since her marriage? Had Gerard and Barbara lived here since their birth? Gerard had gone to school and Barbara to finishing school. The girl had expectations that she would come out in June. If that was so, then all them going to London for the spring would be a refreshing respite from life in the Rambles.

Tynley could introduce Barbara and Gerard to those in the theater in London. Contrary to what many thought, not all working there were of questionable character. Many talented people worked there. Managers, producers, writers, stage designers, modistes, and tailors all contributed to the production of plays that entertained audiences year-round. They had stories to tell, lessons others could learn. Even young, bored women and salacious young bucks who thought the world revolved around them alone could find enjoyment there.

Tynley rolled over and sighed. Sliding her hand under her pillow, she froze. Her fingers sprang away from a slick, oily fabric.

She shot up from the mattress and threw off her pillow.

There, in graying shadows with only a few natural rays of moonlight streaming in to illuminate her bed, she stared at an oil cloth. Something was beneath it. Something that felt like carrots or young potatoes. Rotting, moist to the touch.

She pushed away from it and stood, her heart pounding.

Without thought, she backed out of her bedroom and turned

to unlock her sitting room door.

Down the hall on bare feet, she ran to Kendryck's door and, without permission, flung it wide.

"Tynley?" He wore matching navy silk shirt and pants, the length of which puddled at his feet. "What's—"

She went into his arms. Flat to his chest, she clasped him close.

"My darling, what's happened?" He gazed down at her and swept back her hair, his eyes narrowed with concern. "What's wrong?"

"Something…" She choked. "Something ugly in my bed."

His eyes narrowed in disbelief. "What? Do you know?"

She shook her head, her hair wild around her shoulders. She clutched him close. "I have no idea. It's…under my pillow. In a case. A cloth."

"Come over here. Sit down."

She took the chair he led her to.

He knelt before her, two hands to her cheeks. "Breathe slowly. Deeply."

She did, and stared at him. "I went to my room when we parted. I didn't call for Seren. Just managed myself. Then I got into bed, and under my pillow is this…thing."

He kissed her forehead, rose, and went to his sitting room. Within a minute, he returned with a glass and whisky.

She took it, gladly, and drank a goodly portion.

"Just a minute." He went to his dressing room, and she heard him knock.

He returned to her, but on his heels was the young man whom Kendryck had introduced one morning at breakfast as his valet. The boy was tall, slim, dark brown, a Hindu. Nishan was his name. He too wore a matching set of long shirt and loose pants. His were of emerald-green silk.

Kendryck described to Nishan what Tynley had found under her pillow. "Get it. Be careful with it. We do not know what it is. Bring it to us."

After the boy had hurried away and closed the doors behind him, Kendryck knelt before her once more. "You did not call for your maid? And you saw no one in your room? Nor was there any indication of anything out of place or missing or different there?"

To each, she told him no. "I was not purposely looking for anything odd."

Within a minute, Nishan rapped lightly on the door and entered. He stood, his nut-brown eyes locked on Kendryck, his expression sour. In his hands, he carried a dark pouch by pinched fingers to one top corner. "The cloth is oiled, *sahib*. A case. For tools, may be. I do not know. Strange, *sahib*."

"And inside? Did you look?"

"I did, *sahib*. It is a plant. Old." He curled his nose.

"It smells?"

Nishan nodded once. "Yes, very bad humor, *sahib*."

"Take it down and out. Place it far from the kitchen doors. Do not open it again. Get Carter from his bed and send him to me now. Then return upstairs to your room, and before you go to bed, wash your hands and face and nose. Change your pajamas. Send them to the wash tomorrow. We will go to inspect that thing in the morning."

The boy hurried away.

She began to weep. She didn't usually dissolve in tears in a crisis, but someone had done this maliciously. She had never been attacked like this, and she could not stop the silent flow.

To that, Kendryck stood and took her hand to lead her up. Then he sat down with her cuddled in his lap. "There now," he whispered, his lips in her hair. "Cry here." Kendryck drew her close. "I will have Carter send me one of the footmen, who will sleep outside your chamber door. Then I will have all the upstairs servants before me. We will learn if any have seen any of the others about."

He did not add that the servants might also indicate if they had seen any of the family about. But Tynley knew that Kendryck would probe that possibility.

"Do you trust your maid, Seren?" he asked her.

"I do." 'Twas then she told him about the tear in her hem. "I had forgotten all about it. Even then, I did not automatically think it might be she who had done it. But now it is clear, someone here does not like me."

"Shall we call Seren to come sleep with you in your rooms?"

"No." She pushed away from his chest. "I am not a child who needs… Oh, well, clearly I am a grown woman who needed you."

"I am very glad you did. I hope you will always come to me for strength and support."

"Especially when I find odd things in my bed?"

He smiled with benevolence. "Especially that."

She sank to his chest and curled near, her head on his shoulder. "I'm glad we marry soon."

"Me too." He stroked her hair. "Then I will be the odd thing in your bed."

She lifted her gaze to grin at him. "And what a fine odd thing you will be, too."

He kissed her lips quickly. It was a brand. A reassurance. A promise of safety. "Be still now. We will have done with this for tonight."

Chapter Eight

TYNLEY ARRIVED IN the breakfast room minutes before Kendryck. She sat, sipping her tea, happy to be up and doing something rather than attempting to sleep.

Kendryck sailed in, his greatcoat on, his cheeks ruddy. "Forgive me, my dear. I was in the yard inspecting that pouch." He discarded his coat and draped it over a dining chair, then ran a hand through his dark, ruffled hair. He approached her, lifted her chin, and looked her over. "Did you sleep at all?"

She shrugged. "Snatches here and there."

He kissed her cheek. "I hope you took some comfort from the presence of Conway outside your door."

She had met the young man earlier as she emerged from her suite to come downstairs. "He is impressive. Well spoken and pleasant."

"He is. A good lad. He also boxes in the village."

"Ah. That's how he remains so fit. Does he take matches?"

"He does. He wins, too, I am told." Kendryck regarded Carter and gave his usual sign that he could serve them.

The butler ambled away to the kitchen.

"What do you think is in that oilcloth?" She had to know, no matter how ugly.

"A decaying plant. Roots of something, most likely."

"And the odor? Does that tell you anything about its identity?"

"No. Just regular mold and fungus. I was concerned last night that it might contain the remains of an animal or the roots of a poisonous plant that grows here in South Wales. But no. It is neither."

She had set her teeth at his words, but felt relief sweep through her that the thing in the pouch was not more harmful. "A fright, nonetheless."

"It is." He covered her hand with his own warm one. "Conway guards your door each night from now on. During the day, I have charged your maid Seren with the duty. She will be relieved now and then throughout the day by the upstairs maid. Joan is her name, and Carter assures me she is a good girl. I have given strict orders no one else is to be in your rooms at any time for any reason."

"Thank you."

"I have also called Gerard to me in my study at nine."

Tynley had not thought of that young man's bad behavior since the fright of the thing in her bed. "I will be interested to learn his reaction."

"He will show good manners from now on, my dear. He must."

Carter appeared with serving dishes and placed them on the sideboard.

Kendryck shook out his serviette and smiled at her. "Now. On to happier matters. I thought we might journey to Cardiff day after tomorrow. We'll go for two or three days. We'll make arrangements for the banns and our wedding. Madeline and Barbara will come with us as chaperones, and, of course, they will simply have to introduce you to their favorite shopkeepers."

"Incentives are always welcome," she said with a smile.

But she could not wait to get away.

KENDRYCK AWAITED GERARD'S arrival with a determination to steer the boy in a new and useful path.

He'd had the boy on his carpet here the day after Kendryck arrived from London. Then he was surprised at Gerard's presence at home. Gerard had attended Cambridge for two years. That he would be home mid-term boded no good. Kendryck had asked the reason.

Gerard told him two of his friends had reported that he had beaten another boy so badly that the young man had to return home to heal.

He claimed innocence. "They blamed it on me. Frankford and Winton started the fracas. I joined in because Winton was flagging. Had to help him, didn't I? I can't help it if Cramdon fought harder and things just got worse."

"With you involved," Kendryck concluded. "Did your mother receive a report of this when you were sent down?"

"She did."

The day Kendryck arrived home and saw Gerard there, he had asked her privately why the lad was home, but she had said he was simply too high-spirited for the school. Madeline had said nothing to Kendryck about a letter. To press her never got him anywhere. She always held firm to defense of her children, no matter their failings.

But Kendryck knew how devious and irresponsible Gerard could be. When Gerard was no more than four, Kendryck had come upon him beating his baby sister Barbara—and he'd had a smile on his face. Kendryck had hauled the boy away and told Madeline, who seemed not to care. Years later, Kendryck's sister Charlotte had often written to him how Gerard's escapades got him into trouble, once for kicking a dog so badly that the animal died. The farmer who owned the collie had reported Gerard's actions to the village elders, and they had sent a complaint to the sheriff. Charlotte had reported that nothing came of that, as their grandfather appealed to the official, most likely with a goodly sum of money, and had the case hushed.

This morning, Gerard would answer for hurting so many. Kendryck would see the boy schooled or employed. Gerard would also learn a few manners.

"You told me to appear?" Gerard stood in his study. In aggrieved tone and stance, he challenged Kendryck's summons.

Sitting back in his chair, Kendryck examined his half-brother's haphazard attention to his attire. Kendryck had recently paid a large invoice from a Cardiff tailor for new woolens and fine cambric shirts for his brother. The bill had been incurred weeks before Kendryck arrived home, and so, unable to reject the purchases, he had paid it off. This morning, the boy had little excuse for his soiled waistcoat and untied cravat. Even less excuse for his slovenly appearance in front of the man whose good graces he should be courting.

Kendryck's first order of business today was the long-festering, unresolved matter of the injured boy at Cambridge. "Gerard, I told you that I expected you to make amends to the boy you attacked so that you might be invited back to school."

"You did."

"Have you begun that process?"

"I have thought on it."

Where had this boy learned to be so perverse? But Kendryck knew. Gerard had learned it from the other men in the Hollens family. "Thought on it. I see. How?"

"I drafted a letter to Cramdon's parents."

A letter. Paper for pain. Gerard would do more than that to make up for what he'd done. "Finish it today. Let me read it." *Then there will be more you must do.*

A false smile touched Gerard's lips. "I do not write quickly. I need more time."

"You have until four o'clock today. Bring it to me."

The boy smarted. "I cannot. I am not eloquent. But you could help me."

Kendryck folded his hands upon his desk. "I did not help you into this mess. You will help yourself out of it."

Gerard blinked. "I don't wish to return to school."

"Irrelevant to the apology."

He fixed his gaze above Kendryck's head. "I didn't like Cramdon. I won't apologize to him or anyone because I do not want to go back to university."

"Oh?" *Cannot look me in the eye, eh?* "Why not?"

"I'm no scholar."

"Really? And what exactly are you, Gerard?" *Bully, torturer, liar.*

"I have not yet discovered. I suggest you could send me to London. But don't open the house, of course."

Of course. Too big? Too staid? "Too costly."

"Right you are. You could rent rooms for me in the Albion, and I will find out what best suits me."

Anger ran through Kendryck's bloodstream, but he could not allow this boy an inch of pleasure at his loss of control. *The Albion. London.* Where Owen had rooms for years. Where his eldest brother learned how to carouse, gamble, and whore. "What precisely might you learn in London, Gerard?"

"Banking."

"Are you good with numbers?"

"I can learn."

"I see. Anything else strike you?"

"Trade."

Such a cocky little twit. "Of what?"

"Rum. Sugar. Black men."

Assignment to a West Indies trading group as clerk was a posting Kendryck would never make for his little half-brother. He would be visiting upon the native people of Africa and the New World colonists one more conniving rogue to rip them to shreds with his perfidy. No one in his family would do that ever again. From time immemorial, when Spaniards died upon the sands below the castle, the Hollens family had lived upon the loss and pain of others. His grandfather had invested in the circular trade of the West Indies merchants and earned thousands. His father had expanded the trade to the China ports and profited more.

Kendryck had plans to pull all his investments in those companies. He had identified a score of them in the past few weeks since he had been home. He would find more. Many more. The Hollens family fortunes would turn away from its past of investing in the misery of others when he liquidated the old stocks in the next few months. He would redirect all the money into viable commercial products and services that had nothing to do with destruction of native cultures or the enslavement of other human beings. Indeed, the rape of other civilizations for the prosperity of the Hollens family ended with Kendryck.

He regarded his callow little brother with such cool disdain that Gerard shifted on his feet. "No, Gerard. London is not for you. Nor is trade. And never will be."

Gerard set his jaw. "*You* were sent away to learn a trade."

"Correction, Gerard. I was sent away to die. Our grandfather did not like to support a lot of people in the grand style to which he alone thought he was deserving. Plus, he saw he had a new boy in the family. You were a scrawny, sickly baby, and I do swear, he most likely thought you would leave this earthly coil soon enough, leaving only our older brother Owen, who was disturbingly healthy. So strapping, in fact, was Owen that he survived syphilis repeatedly as he whored his way through London. From the Albion, too. He sired a child on one young woman whom he'd raped while he built up racing debts, which our dear Grandpapa paid with drafts from Charlotte's dowry."

Gerard winced. "Charlotte is gone."

You little toad. "Yes. I've examined the family records. Had she lived, she would have had no dowry to recommend her."

The boy sniffed. "Barbara has quite a bit. Mama says so. Do we know how much Barbara has?"

Kendryck seethed. "What? Do you think I would raid Barbara's dowry to fund your London expedition?" With great restraint, he did not rise or curse. "This brings us to your attitude toward women, and in particular, your treatment of Mrs.

Wallingford. You will never again exhibit the kind of disrespect we witnessed last night."

The boy looked straight ahead as he pursed his lips at Kendryck's reprimand.

"The lady is to be my wife, and if you wish to remain in this family's good graces, you will never again intimate by word or deed such behavior toward her."

Gerard said nothing.

"*Is. That. Clear?*"

"Yes, sir."

For such disrespect, his grandfather would take the boy out to the horse barn and use the whip on him. "Leave. And know I want that letter by four."

"Or what?"

Defiant cuss. "Or I will send you to another place, another land! There, no Albions exist, nor do gaming tables or public houses. His Majesty's government needs men to clear the forests on the Canadian frontier."

The boy's sharp brown eyes went to slits. "No."

"Refusal is not an option. Today, you have one choice, Gerard. School or Canada." He watched the boy grit his teeth. "At four, tell me which it is to be. Now get out."

WHEN KENDRYCK CAUGHT sight of Tynley along the forest path an hour later, he allowed the satisfaction her company brought him to drive out his distaste for the scene with Gerard. He was even more pleased when he saw her maid, Seren, accompanying her.

At sight of him, Seren stopped and turned back toward the house.

Jericho and Dick trotted along beside Tynley. Both dogs, tongues out—he could have sworn—smiled at their good company.

Kendryck held out his hands to catch her waist and help her down the drop.

Tynley looped her arm through his, and they headed down the path. "Tell me what happened with Gerard."

"He needs to return to school." He told her about the fight at university and the student who was so badly injured. "He will apologize in writing, but he will also go to that family and make amends for his behavior. I will not allow anyone in this family to act as he has. We've had enough of thieves and scoundrels. We don't need more."

"He must learn that a man or woman's worth is not based on what they think they are but what they have done."

"Self-importance irritates you," he said with satisfaction.

"Just as it does you," she said. "You would be surprised at how many actors are blown-up blasts of wind."

He chuckled. "Impressed with the applause they get, eh?"

"And why, I ask you?" She whirled in front of him, and the wind toyed with her awful hat. "The words they recite are not their own. The scenery they work before is not of their hand. The facility of the other actors is not their doing… Well, not entirely."

"And yet their self-indulgence pricks you."

"It does. I have known such self-important people that they come to a dinner or a party, and all they do is blather on and on. They never ask how you are, where you are, what you do. They just fill the air with their knowledge, their experiences, their overblown pride!"

This was the first outrage he'd heard from her, and it was intriguing.

She went on. "I do dislike those who waste my precious time with the arrogance of their conceit."

"I have known a few like that."

"Ridiculous, aren't they?"

"What brings them to mind now?"

"Nothing in particular, except that…" She rolled a shoulder. "You asked."

"I see." He pressed his lips together and walked on.

Presently, she said, "And you?"

"What makes me angry?"

She nodded.

He stopped and picked off a few dead leaves from an oak. "You have heard some of it."

"I have. I liked what I heard." She grinned. "I want more."

"I dislike those who have a sense of entitlement. As if they are owed every good thing for no good reason. I dislike those who belittle others whom they think are not worthy, but have no idea why, other than their self-possession. I can become very angry at those who belittle others."

"I see," she whispered as she came into his arms and brushed back his hair under his top hat. "How noble you are, sir. I like you."

"Do you?" He lifted his hat away. "A lot, I hope."

Her green eyes widened. "Enough to marry you, and soon."

"I've told Carter we go day after next to Cardiff. I've written to my friend William Drummond and his wife to tell them of our visit. While we are in Cardiff, I thought we would stop at a seamstress and milliner."

"Is that so? For you, perhaps?"

He loved the plushness of her breasts against his chest. Would that he could strip off his greatcoat and enjoy her more.

"For me and you. I thought you would do me the honor of seeing a milliner so that I might buy you a new hat to walk here with me each day."

The wind picked up, and her awful leghorn hat caught the gusts. She caught the hat as auburn tendrils of her hair came undone from its pins. "You do not like my hat, sir?"

He picked it from her fingers and glowered at it. "No."

"Why?"

His dark brows inched higher. "The brown of your coat alone is satisfactory. But not lovely. Combine the brown with the teal of your hat, and your complexion drains to dishwater."

"I have no other hat as warm."

"As I thought. We shall buy a new one. Or if the milliner has none you like, she can make one to your specifications. Then, when you receive the new one, bring this teal contraption to me."

"Why?"

"We will bring it out here and burn it."

She stared at him. "That bad, is it?"

"It is. I know once you and I are wed, my dear, I will always prefer you in nothing. Not a stitch. Not a ribbon. But when we are out and about, I will thrill to see you attired in all the colors that enrich your beauty. I had good training for those colors and fabrics that complement a woman. For you, my darling, it will always be greens and jade, purples and gold."

She took it in as the flattery he meant it to be. "You are man of many surprises." She kissed him then, a soul-searing meeting of her mouth with his.

He could love her. How well he would, too. All the days of his life. The knowledge came upon him like a monsoon, destroying all in its path. Doubt, reluctance, fear—gone.

Chapter Nine

"I'M SO GLAD you allow us to introduce you to the modiste Barbara and I favor." Kendryck's stepmother Madeline regarded Tynley from her carriage seat. Barbara sat beside her. The two women were trying to make polite conversation after the conclusion of an argument they'd had with Kendryck minutes ago. They objected once more to Gerard being left out of this trip. Kendryck had ordered the boy to prepare to visit and apologize to the parents of the boy he had hurt at school.

In truth, they had been excited to be invited by Kendryck to come along to Cardiff. He planned for them all to stay three days in town, and had sent ahead to reserve three rooms in a carriage inn for the four of them. Gerard, whom Kendryck ordered to Canterbury to see the Cramdon family, had stayed at home to prepare.

"I am grateful for your ideas, too," Tynley told them, hoping to alleviate the tension. "I know nothing of the town. I would never know whose shop to visit. Nor can I say I know much of current fashion."

"Madeline and Barbara know well Madame St. Claire's talents," Kendryck said, a note of irritation still in his voice from the argument he'd had minutes ago with the two women. "She does lovely work. And lovely prices, too."

"We will be prudent in our choices, Strade." This from Barbara was an olive branch to Kendryck. This morning, in addition to her support of her mother's position about Gerard, Barbara had argued with Kendryck about the Hollens family jewels that she wanted to wear during her debut in London in the spring. Kendryck had refused, saying he would not allow them to be worn. In fact, he was going to sell them—all of them—and give the proceeds to an orphanage in Cardiff. The two women had exclaimed in horror at his decision and pleaded with him not to do it. He, however, had not been moved.

The silence in the cab had been deafening for many miles. This new topic promised a relief from the tension.

"Never fear, Kendryck," Madeline piped up. "We will not allow Madame St. Claire to overbill Mrs. Wallingford."

"I want only two items," Tynley said. "A new winter pelisse and a new gown for the wedding. That is all." She widened her eyes at Kendryck. "And I shall pay for them myself."

He heard that with the arch of a dark brow. "You did not tell me that."

"No. Until I am your wife, I pay my own bills."

"Very well. But not for that new hat. That is my gift to the bride."

She winked at him. "I will have it in a new color. What say you to chartreuse?"

"Ugh!" Barbara slapped a hand to her bosom. "Poison green. Please don't. No lady should wear that. It's like…those plants Charlotte would lug in from her days in the forest."

Tynley stilled. *Like the item in that pouch in my bed.*

"I quite agree," Kendryck said, gazing at his half-sister. "She did bring those inside."

Then he turned away from them and, with a hand to his chin, considered the landscape passing by.

"What color do you think will be best for your wedding day?" Barbara asked—and Tynley saw this as her attempt at diversion from the last topic that had soured. Since Kendryck's announcement of their engagement, Barbara had displayed enormous enthusiasm for the details of their coming nuptials. So this inquiry was nothing new from her.

"I favor a sea green or a crystalline jade."

"Silk," Kendryck added, coming back to the conversation.

"From India, sir?" Barbara asked.

"I have about forty yards of it that I bought in Calcutta in the bazaars and brought home. I had the footmen load the boot earlier," he said, and tipped his head toward the back, "with ten yards of it in different colors."

"So that's what they were struggling with this morning." This was news to Tynley. He'd said nothing of that before, and she had not seen any bolts of silks among his treasures in the half-timbered Tudor part of the Rambles. He must store them elsewhere.

"Choose what you like from it, my dear. Or not! Buy French if you wish. But do know that when we return home, I will open the rest of it all, and, Madeline and Barbara, you may choose a color or two and have them fashioned as you wish."

His stepmother blinked in surprise. "That's a very fine gift, Strade. Thank you."

Barbara was just as stunned. "Very generous, too, Strade."

"You are both welcome."

"We will have to visit Madame St. Claire more often!" Barbara chirped.

"I would say we will," Tynley agreed. "I have never been devoted to fashion. I loved most of the costumes I wore when I acted, but that was years ago. For our wedding I want a gown simple in style. In the past four years, I have had only one new gown, and I can say I am unused to the thrill of it."

That last gown was the dress that had been cut by scissors. She'd repaired it days ago as best she could, adding a woven passementerie braid along the hem. She had put it on a few days ago, but immediately taken it off. The aura—so like that which affected her after the rotting plant had been in her bed—sickened her. Last night, she had tried once more to wear it for dinner, but she could not shake the dread that fell over her after she donned it. She simply could not wear it.

Seren had noticed Tynley's reaction to the gown. The girl worried and wanted to ask staff who might have noticed anything that could indicate who had cut the gown. Tynley had cautioned the girl against it. The servants were already on alert after Kendryck had interrogated them in his bedchambers the night of the discovery of the rotting plant. No one claimed to have noticed anyone going in or out of Tynley's chambers.

Tynley had not expected anyone would admit to the ruin of the gown or the plant, either.

She forced her attention back to the conversation in the carriage.

"Whatever you like best, my dear, is what you must have." Kendryck regarded her with a twinkle in his blue eyes, as the family carriage idled in the courtyard of a handsome carriage inn. A weathered sign swung on a pole announcing this was *The Old, the Famous, the Beautiful Black Gander.* "Come now. I will register all of us. We shall have our tea and a good rest. And tomorrow, we begin our calls."

THE NEXT DAY at eleven, Kendryck and Tynley set out to call upon Kendryck's friend, the vicar of St. Michael's Church and the young cleric's wife. They were to meet in the church at noon.

Barbara and Madeline had taken the day to shop. After a late breakfast in the common room, they happily went off, assuring Tynley they would inform Madame St. Claire of her visit on the morrow.

"The church," Kendryck said as his coachman took them off into town, "is from the twelfth century. The same period as our curtain wall and some of the castle at the Rambles. The blue stone is the same as much of that of the main house."

This, she noted later as they stepped down to enter the church, gave the building a lighter motif. The stained-glass windows were dressed in a white stone that offered a more cheerful mien than the brooding Rambles.

They strolled inside the cool, quiet nave. Above, the arches met in charming symmetry atop the honeyed stone walls. The floor was of old slate, breaking at the altar for inlaid patterns of colored stones.

"I like this church very much," she told Kendryck. "I am so glad you thought of it. I like these stones, too. What do they mean?"

"Those," Kendryck told her, "are reminiscent of a Templar's church in Acre in the Holy Land. My friend, William Drummond, whom you will soon meet, is a scholar of the Crusaders' fight for Jerusalem. He can tell you in detail what these stones mean. I, sadly, have no idea."

William Drummond arrived minutes later in a hail of hearty greetings to his old friend and a warm welcome to Tynley. His wife Samartine, who insisted Tynley call her by her given name, was as cheerful. Drummond looked like a ragged angel, all bushy, pale blond hair that stood out in massive curls. His wife had wild black hair that she had barely tamed into a chignon. Both had laughing blue eyes, bright as the sky at dawn.

They strolled the old chapel while Drummond held forth on its history. Then they all adjourned to the vicarage down a stone path and into a cozy timber and beam house. The vicar told how Kendryck and he had met.

"Our mothers had attended the same finishing school and visited each other often," he told Tynley over tea in his cozy parlor. His adoring wife, petite and jovial, sat beside him. "We children came along to visit, too."

"We struck up a friendship that has lasted nearly three decades," Kendryck added. "It has been a saving grace to me. Drummond, you see, has the ear of those greater than ourselves." He pointed toward the heavens. "And I was pleased to have the benefit of insight of those above to my troubles."

Drummond rejected so much praise. "Kendryck exaggerates. I assume he has told you what happened to him in India?"

"Indeed, he has."

"Has he also shown you the gifts so many gave him for good service to the people?"

Tynley confirmed he had shown them to her.

But Kendryck was not proud of the gifts. "Hardly service to them, sir. I did my duty."

Drummond gazed at Tynley. "Had he done any less, had he rejected the presents, the Company would have shipped him home. In disgrace."

"I was able to avoid all that and resign in my own time and for my own reasons. If Owen and Charlotte had remained healthy, I might still be in Calcutta trying to figure out how to leave without attracting attention."

"All heartache under the bridge, Kendryck," said Drummond. "Now you are here, and ready to marry. I do congratulate you in that. Both of you."

Tynley thanked him. "We know we are fortunate."

"You are. So then you must tell me, why do you wait?"

"The banns," Kendryck said. "I wish to give Tynley weeks to make certain she knows whom she marries."

"I know now, Mr. Drummond," she added. "Make no mistake."

The vicar knitted his bushy brows. "You know what he wants to do with those items, Mrs. Wallingford? Use them as proof of misconduct by the Company. Create a storm."

"I do, sir."

"I worry about you, Kendryck," Drummond said. "That will cause a great deal of notoriety. Not just for you, Kendryck. But also for you, Mrs. Wallingford."

"I am aware of that." She nodded and swallowed her own fears for Kendryck's reputation. Did Drummond know that Kendryck wished to make a bigger statement by writing a novel and giving speeches describing the problems in India? "People must learn this. I am certain Kendryck is not the only one who knows of the challenges there."

Drummond shook his head. "Officials have come home from the Subcontinent for five or six decades reporting to Parliament and changing the order of things there. Every time there has been a new inquiry or a new scandal, many have vowed reform. Some have called for abandonment of that country. But how can we when those in trade and banking demand the goods keep flowing, and at cheap prices?"

Kendryck would hear none of his friend's advice. "Things change for the worse, William. Even though many try to cut the corruption, they do so in a manner that separates the British from the people they govern. When first I arrived as a lad, most British showed honor to the Hindu and Muslim cultures. They learned their languages, ate many of the same foods, and wore loose clothes, so useful in the heat. Now that is increasingly not so. British officials give no reprimand to those who disparage the religions and the food. British are banned from going to any religious ceremonies other than Christian. They cannot wear sandals and must not wear pajamas. A true separation of the British is taught by the Company officials. Tolerance is dead. You know what that brings, William. Fear and hatred of those who are so different, of those we do not understand or appreciate."

"Can you fight that tide, Kendryck?" his friend pressed. "And take Tynley with you? One man—and one woman—against the force of the British East India Company and those at home and abroad?"

Tynley stilled. That she and Kendryck might become so notorious they were outlaws was her greatest fear.

"Are you saying," Kendryck said, staring at him, "I fight a losing battle?"

"I say you fight a long and hard one. You know, my friend, once you begin this, many will disown you as a renegade and try to prove you a traitor."

"There is no evidence to prove that I have committed any crimes, nor that I plan any coup of the government. That would take an armed militia of ten million men."

"Or a rabble of barefoot men and women who, in any other time and country, might be called rebels."

"That will not happen here," Kendryck said.

"I agree. Cromwell tried that," Drummond said. "He failed."

"William, do you think we fought Napoleon for so many years because we disliked his belief in equality?"

"We wanted him to fail because his basic attitude was that all the world should be French."

"Exactly. And ours is now that all the world should be British."

Drummond smiled sadly. "We shall see how long that idea lasts."

KENDRYCK AND TYNLEY prepared to leave after an early supper. Samartine Drummond hooked her arm through Tynley's as they walked toward the front door. "Do not be dismayed by the men's sharp talk of politics. They have done that always. There is no harm in their disagreements. Tell me, instead, that you will come visit me often after you are married. I have few true friends."

Tynley found that hard to believe. "I would love to be yours. Of course I will visit. And know that you must come and visit us often, too. Stay a few days, if you can."

All of a sudden, Samartine's blue gaze turned skeptical. "I doubt I will be welcome by Kendryck's mother. She never liked me."

Tynley sighed. "She did not seem to care for me at first, either. But we are more comfortable with each other now. Do reconsider."

"I will, though I must tell you that I am not up to my best

lately."

"Oh, no. I do hope it is temporary."

A spark lit Samartine's large eyes. "A few months, at most, I think. I hope."

"Ah, I see. Well then, I extend my congratulations and my best wishes. When you are up to travel, you must come. In the meantime, I will visit you as often as I can. I do look forward to putting my hand to the workings of Strade Rambles. Still, I must say, I think it runs well now." Tynley paused as the thought of her torn hem and the terrible pouch in her bed crossed her mind.

"Does it?" Samartine was wide eyed with concern. "I'd say from the look on your face, the house does not run well."

"A few small problems. Kendryck has dealt with them."

"His younger brother?"

Tynley was taken aback by the woman's suggestion of Gerard's poor behavior. "Yes."

"A troubled boy. Kendryck will take him in hand, I am certain."

"How…how do you know Gerard?"

"He made a few ungentlemanly remarks to my sister last year. He was at a garden party she attended, and he was—shall we say—relentless. Suzette was, at first, insulted. But he cornered her outside a ladies' retiring room and laid hands on her in a most unbecoming way. He tore her gown. She escaped by crying out. He let her go. But it was a near thing."

"Did she tell your parents?"

"Our parents are dead. My maiden aunt is her guardian, and that lady is not very forgiving of rude behavior. If she heard the story, she would assume Suzette had flirted with Gerard. I am the only person Suzette told about the incident."

Tynley's gaze traveled to the two men who stood near the door, joking like the old friends they were. "Did you tell your husband?"

"I did." Samartine followed Tynley's gaze. "My husband is a man of the cloth, Mrs. Wallingford. He does not spread disparaging stories about others."

"I think Kendryck needs to know this."

"If you are asking me to ask William to reveal this to Kendryck—?"

"I am." Tynley took Samartine's hand. "Gerard must reform. Kendryck is home only recently. He wants to see the boy on the right path. He can do only so much if he knows little."

Samartine looked at her husband and bit her lower lip. "I don't know."

"Give me your permission to tell Kendryck."

She took her time responding. "I will think on it. I will write to let you know."

"If you decide it is proper to share this, would you write a description of it for Kendryck?"

She pulled back. "Oh, I…would have to tell William."

"I understand." Tynley took Samartine's hand. "I enjoyed meeting you, and I look forward to many years of friendship."

"Yes. You will return here for your wedding, and I would like to invite you to stay with us the night before. The Old Black Gander is a graciously appointed inn, but when I think of a bride going to her wedding, I think she should have the comfort and joy of her friends."

Her kind invitation put tears in Tynley's eyes. "I'd like that, yes. Thank you so much."

Samartine hugged her. "Wonderful. That's settled. I will tell William that we each have a friend now."

Chapter Ten

DAYS LATER, THE four climbed down from their carriage to the front steps of the Rambles. Eager to find her own room and peace, Tynley bade Carter hello with a smile and hurried up to her rooms. Sinking back against the closed door, she rejoiced at the solitude. She'd had that at night in her own room, of course, at the Old Black Gander.

But the ride home today had been irritating. Barbara had revealed the price of two new gowns she had ordered from Madame St. Claire, and the cost was nearly double what Kendryck had decreed was her budget. The girl had pleaded and sulked, never apologizing, to try to smooth over Kendryck's displeasure with her extravagance. Her mother had tried to defuse the tension, but Barbara's sniping at Kendryck had not made for a pleasant ride home.

Kendryck had contained his anger, dealing quietly but firmly with both his stepmother and his half-sister. His failure to equal their ire only made them frustrated and more cantankerous.

Tynley had made polite conversation for a while, but ceased when Kendryck shook his head and, in essence, implied she needn't try to make up for the other ladies.

Alone at last, she vowed to push away all the problems of the family and concentrate on her wedding in a few weeks. She had been fitted for her gown—and insisted on doing it privately. She wanted her gown to be a surprise, and asked Madame St. Claire to show it to no one. The fabric Kendryck had brought for her was an exquisite silk in an iridescent shade of blue-green. She had thought it ever so appropriate to wear the fabric he had bought in the bazaar for their wedding. The style of the gown was to be a simple Grecian bound, with satin ribbons of the same color on the pouffy sleeves and at the hem. Madame had taken measurements of Tynley's feet and promised that her brother, a cobbler, would make matching slippers. All would be ready for Tynley days before the wedding. Madame would also make a new heavy coat for Tynley. All would be sent to the vicarage of St. Michael's, where Tynley would spend the night before her wedding.

A footman knocked on her door, and she admitted him and Conway. They both bade her good afternoon as they carted in her small trunk and her valise, and she told them where to place them. Her maid Seren appeared and asked if Tynley would like a bath. She readily agreed, and the girl went off to order the hot water brought up to the boudoir.

An hour later, Tynley dressed for the evening and went downstairs, praying there would be no more discord over dinner.

Carter was in the main salon talking with Kendryck, and both appeared overwrought.

"Come in, my dear." Kendryck beckoned. "I will tell her, Carter. But do go and bring them in."

"We have visitors?"

He stared at her. "We do. Two."

"Two. Who are they?"

"One is the cousin of Mrs. Hammond."

"The publisher of the *Fleet-of-Heart Chronicle*? But...her cousin?"

Kendryck walked to the window and looked out upon the front lawn. "I met him when I first arrived in England from India. I had gone to London. You remember, I wanted to change my plans and meet you both in London, but..."

"I know the rest. Why did you have to meet with a Bow

Street Runner?"

"Because the first applicant was missing. Lady Peregrine met with me and Mrs. Hammond because the first applicant had written to me that she was coming here."

"Here?"

"But she never arrived."

Tynley noted Kendryck's tense posture. "What happened to her? Where did she go?"

"Her parents had not received word from her. And she had promised to write as she went from town to town. Also, when she arrived here."

"I really do not understand…"

"Neither do I, Tynley. But now we receive Mr. Jack Shaw, Mrs. Hammond's cousin, and another Runner. Hopefully, they have news to tell us."

His frown boded ill tidings.

Carter appeared on the threshold. Two young, taller, lankier fellows stood behind him. They were dressed in smart black serge and simply tied cravats. "My lord, Mr. Shaw and Mr. Thynne."

"Do come in, gentlemen. Allow me to introduce you, my dear. This is my fiancée, Mrs. Wallingford. Please sit down. Tea, Carter. A bracing one for our guests. And if I am not mistaken, I could offer both of you gentlemen a brandy to warm you after your cold journey."

"Aye, milord." The first fellow came forward, a slight limp in his gait, and shook Kendryck's outstretched hand. He was fit, broad-shouldered, with rich sable-brown hair and eyes to match. Tynley recognized his likeness to Germaine Hammond.

"Mr. Shaw, I hope I might say it is good to see you," Kendryck said.

"I am glad ye are inclined, sir," Shaw said, but gave only a polite nod to indicate this was no social call. "Though our news will not be welcome."

Tynley prickled with fear. Why were two Runners here? Why was *one*?

Shaw continued, "This is my friend and colleague, Mr. Frederick Thynne."

The second man so resembled his name that Tynley thought he could be blown away on a gust of wind. But he was congenial, with flashing, bright blue eyes.

Kendryck invited the men to take seats. Each chose a separate chair beside the other. They faced Kendryck and Tynley, who sat on the settee.

"We've come, my lord, with news that Thynne and I must tell you. It is not good."

Kendryck nodded. "I am eager to know. What have you learned?"

From his frock coat inside pocket, Shaw extracted a few news sheet clippings. He handed one over. "Have you seen this article, sir?"

Kendryck took it in hand, but rose to get his glasses from a far table. He returned to the group, reading as he came. His face lost all color. Removing his glasses, he looked at Shaw with concern. "No, sir. I have not seen this before. What paper was it in?"

"A few. The *Chester Chronicle* and *Bristol Mirror*, for two."

"I would not have seen it, Mr. Shaw. We take Cardiff papers here at the Rambles. The London *Times* and *Lloyd's List*, too, but they come by post seven to ten days later than their release." He handed the scrap of news sheet to Tynley.

She took the paper and began to read.

"I am horrified, Mr. Shaw," Kendryck went on.

Tynley skimmed the piece. Her heart in her throat, she tried a second time.

Miss Mary Ann Roundbridge, missing.
Mrs. Nora Roundbridge begs the assistance of all to notify her
Of any knowledge of her daughter's whereabouts. Miss
Roundbridge, age 23,
Is a comely lady, blonde hair and blue eyes, last seen dressed in
Green serge gown and pelisse. She told her mother she booked

*A seat on the mail coach in late September from Southampton
to Bath, and hence to Bristol.*
*Her mother offers a reward to any one who will give
information about her.*

"Aye, sir. I knew you would be dismayed," Shaw said. "Moreover, sir, since we met a few weeks ago, I have investigated the passengers who took various mail coaches and found that a young lady of Miss Roundbridge's description did take a coach to Bath and on to Bristol. We have one driver who tells us he thinks he had a lady of her description on his run from Bristol through to Cardiff. After that, we have only a few indications she might have gone on to Cardiff. Not one is very good."

"I see." Kendryck took the news with a frown. He glanced at Thynne. "Will you both please tell me what you do know?"

Thynne spoke up. "I was in Bristol three days ago when Mr. Shaw arrived. We met by happenstance at an inn where we Runners take a room when we are on assignment out of London. Shaw shared with me the details of Miss Roundbridge's disappearance. It so happens that I had been investigating a report by a family in Bristol that they witnessed a young lady being accosted in the streets near one of the carriage inns. I found the two men who attacked a lady that night. Sad to say, they did not know her name, but they did say she was young, pretty, with a lot of blonde hair. I took both men away into the custody of the local constabulary."

"Was it a robbery?" Tynley asked, hoping it was only that and not worse.

"She appeared an easy target," Thynne said. "They thought to take her money. A robbery. She fought well, so they cried off. In gaol now, they will hurt no one for a while."

"I am horrified, Mr. Shaw," Kendryck went on.

"The past two days in Cardiff, we investigated among the mail coach drivers. Of course, we have not spoken to all of them yet. Many are en route, and we do return to complete the list.

One driver thinks he may have had Miss Roundbridge in his coach. This was, give or take, two to three weeks ago. This lady had been crying, and she had a bruised lip and cheek. He assumed she fled an angry husband and said nothing to her. Thynne and I have speculated that the woman he saw may have been Miss Roundbridge."

"And you have come here to see if she journeyed on to us at the Rambles," Kendryck concluded.

"We have, sir," Thynne said with a sharp examination of Kendryck.

"We have had no visitors."

"Has everyone in your household been at home for the past three weeks?" Shaw asked.

"We have. Until four of us went to Cardiff four days ago, no one has gone anywhere except to the village to buy groceries."

"Who were those who went with you to Cardiff?" Shaw asked him.

"My stepmother, my half-sister, and Mrs. Wallingford."

Shaw's dark eyes flashed. "We understand your grandmother is in residence."

"She is, sir. She is elderly and not of complete awareness. She goes nowhere except her rooms."

"I see. And in Cardiff, where did you lodge?"

Tynley found the questioning thorough and unnecessary. Did the two men suspect that any of them knew the missing woman's whereabouts?

But Kendryck was not put out and answered easily. "We stayed in the Old Black Gander. Do check with the inn keep."

"And you, sir?" Shaw eyed Kendryck critically. "When did you arrive here from London?"

"October ninth."

"And you have not left the vicinity of your home here, since then, sir, except for this trip to Cardiff?"

"No. I have been here the entire time."

"And you, Mrs. Wallingford?" Thynne swung toward her. "I

heard Lord Strade introduce you as his fiancée. When did you both decide to marry, ma'am?"

Kendryck took her hand. "Mr. Shaw knows all the details of how I advertised with his cousin in the *Chronicle*. He also knows of the mixed mails and misunderstandings."

She regarded the two Runners with a serenity born of the truth she'd tell. Or rather, part of the truth. She doubted that they needed to know so personal a date as when she had decided to marry Kendryck. "I journeyed here to Wales on my own. Yes, I know you look at me askance, sirs. It sounds so similar to what Miss Roundbridge did, but my route and timing were different. I set out from London via mail coach. Then I booked passage on the *Irish Boston* out of Southampton to Cardiff. From there, I came to Rhoose in another mail coach. From Rhoose, I journeyed up to Lord Strade's house in a private carriage, which I hired myself."

Both Runners looked at her long and hard.

"In your travels here, say in Cardiff," asked Thynne with a nonchalance that rung false and forbidding, "did you hear of any rumors of a lady mysteriously disappearing?"

"No. I did not. I kept to myself, Mr. Thynne. A lady out and about alone is a target, I know. I did not speak to anyone except those I had to. I heard no tales, either."

"When did you arrive here, ma'am?" Thynne persisted in his inquiry.

"It must be almost two weeks ago, now."

"Which day?"

She had to think back. "A week Thursday. In late afternoon."

"Did you retain the ticket for your berth on the *Irish Boston*?"

"No." Thynne wanted proof she had sailed when she said she had. "I saved none of my chits."

"And you came to Lord Strade's house immediately in this coach you hired in Rhoose?"

"I did." *I did not tarry in Cardiff or Rhoose.* "I hired the carriage for a quick journey, and the coachman brought me right to the front door. I am certain he will be easy to find to confirm my story."

"And that I will do," Thynne said with an efficiency that rang bells of alarm in her head. He did not trust her. "Once here, did you stay?"

"She did." This was from Kendryck. "Mrs. Wallingford came and did not leave until she left with me and my family for Cardiff days ago."

Shaw checked his partner's gaze. "We wish to speak with the members of your family, my lord."

"Of course, Mr. Shaw. I will have my butler call them down for you."

"One by one, if you please," Thynne added, a long, thin finger in the air.

"As you wish," Kendryck agreed. "My younger brother is not here. He left early this morning for a trip to Canterbury."

Tynley did not know that. Gerard had left days earlier than he and Kendryck had planned. She wondered why, and would ask Kendryck later. If, indeed, he knew. Gerard could be such a surprising lad.

"Why has your brother gone away, sir?" Thynne inquired.

"For personal reasons. He visits a student he knew last term."

"I see," Thynne said, but from his expression, he was mulling that over. "When does he return?"

"He will stay only a day or two, then journey home. That journey over and back can take as much as two weeks total."

"We will need to talk to him."

"That's fine. He will be available to you," Kendryck said.

For some reason, Thynne stared at Kendryck.

What had Kendryck said that inspired his curiosity? Tynley had no idea.

Shaw broke the impasse. "We wish to talk to your staff, too, my lord."

Kendryck nodded. "They are at your disposal."

"Thank you, sir," said Shaw. "We know this is an inconvenience, but Thynne and I must pursue every aspect."

"I am glad you do, sirs."

"Do you know, my lord," asked Thynne, "if any of your staff have left the house in past few weeks?"

"Not to my knowledge. You must ask them yourselves."

"We will, sir," he said.

"Now." Kendryck took up the point of the discussion with a wary eye at Thynne. "My butler will return shortly with a hearty tea for you. Do please remain here in the salon—"

"Sir," said Shaw, "we can go to the servants' quarters."

"But you wish to interview my family, Mr. Shaw, and they would prefer that to occur here, I do assure you."

"Of course," Shaw demurred.

"Do refresh yourselves," Kendryck continued. "You have had a trying time of it."

"You are kind, sir," Shaw said with a nod of thanks.

"Do know, gentlemen, that I am very interested in Miss Roundbridge's welfare. I feel responsible for her venturing out in such a manner, alone. I abhor the possibility that something terrible may have happened to her."

Shaw nodded. "Good to know. sir. We both will remain in this area to learn what we can about her actions."

"We will stay at the carriage inn in Rhoose," said Thynne.

"The Fine Duck," Kendryck added. "A good accommodation. I am most anxious to learn of Miss Roundbridge's whereabouts. I do commiserate with Mrs. Hammond and Mrs. Roundbridge. Had my communications been better, Miss Roundbridge would not have undertaken her journey here."

"Ah, sir," said Shaw. "Do not ask what might have been."

"Useless talk." Thynne was less agreeable. "Know, sir, we may have more questions for you as our investigation proceeds."

"Very well." Kendryck stood. "Do return."

Both men rose, too.

"Thank you for your help, sir," said Shaw.

Kendryck gave them a strained expression. "Do notify me of

anything I can do to assist you. Now, if you will excuse Mrs. Wallingford and me, we thank you for your help. I hope to see you again, gentlemen, with better news."

He took Tynley's arm, and she went with him, silent and shaken.

Chapter Eleven

KENDRYCK AND SHE had retired to his study upstairs off his bedchamber, far away from the salon.

Tynley went into his embrace as soon as he shut the door. She did not care that they were not being proper to keep it open to the world. All the others in the house would soon feel the same shock and dismay as she and Kendryck. They needed time alone. The door could remain closed.

"Would you like a whisky?" He rubbed her arms and kissed her forehead. "I have a bottle here."

"Yes. A jigger. I need something bracing."

"It was a blow."

"What was especially shocking was the way their questioning went from causal to"—she rolled a shoulder—"intimidating."

"They were doing their jobs."

"But, heavens, they can be objectionable. Thynne especially."

"No one likes to see a Runner on their doorstep."

"And we have two."

Putting a warm hand to her cheek, he nodded toward the far chair. He went to his desk and pulled open a bottom drawer. Then pulled out a bottle of Scotch whisky and two small glasses. He poured a generous amount in each.

She took her drink to one of his leather wing chairs and settled into its voluminous cushions.

"They have little real evidence that she has come this way," he said to her.

"She really wished to be married," Tynley responded, understanding the woman's motivation. "You must have written very lovely letters to her. You did to me."

"I did not try to influence either of you, so much as describe who I am."

"You are, as you said, an excellent writer."

He winced and took a long draft. "But to think that my words have brought her to a dubious end…"

"I know. She came, took a chance, and trusted that she could make the journey."

"As did you." He stared at her with awe and sorrow. "I am delighted that nothing went amiss for your journey. What would we have done had we not met each other?"

"I hate to think of it," she said with the sadness of it flying through her. "A golden opportunity missed."

He grew pensive and sipped at his whisky.

"Traveling is so uncomfortable and so very hazardous," she ventured. "For a woman, it can also be adventurous. Most women live cooped up in a cage. But travel can be too full of new experiences. I do give her credit that she tried. Perhaps she took ill. Do you think? If so, she may recuperate somewhere between Bristol and here."

He pondered that a moment. "If that is so, I hope they can find her in time to call in a physician."

"I hope she was not attacked." That horror seeped into Tynley's blood like ice.

Kendryck put a hand to his temple and rubbed a spot there. "We must realize that there are many ladies with blonde hair. Many who may have been on a coach. Perhaps a few with a bruise or two. It's very little to go on."

"How many carriage inns are there between Cardiff and Rhoose and the village of Rambles?"

He looked off. "Five. Six? I am not certain. I did not count them as we went to Cardiff. And it's been so long since I've been at home. There could be dozens."

"Shaw and Thynne need to investigate each one. In case she's there. Ill. Hurt. Without any coin. Oh, all useless to speculate."

Kendryck gave her a consoling smile. "I am certain both men will realize that and take it on themselves to visit each inn. Miss Roundbridge could be in any one…or none at all. In a farmer's cottage or…"

"Heaven knows where." She sighed and took a drink. "I hope your staff take the interview well."

"They will. Carter will shepherd them like a father. I will talk to him later and learn. As for Madeline and Barbara, I worry."

"They will survive. You may need to bring that bottle downstairs for them to partake of."

He snorted. "I'll be happy to do so, too. You are right. The two women will get through it. They are resilient. Thank God Gerard is gone. He would not have taken well to them."

"Why do you think he left early? He was not supposed to go until after we returned. And how did you learn he'd gone?"

"A note from him. He left it here on my desk. He said he wished to do his duty quickly, which is an improvement." He took a drink and savored it a moment. "Whatever his reasoning, I am grateful for the respite. Also happy he's gone to do justice by that boy. Hopefully, I can get Gerard to the straight and narrow soon. It is tiring to deal with one so stubborn."

Tynley pushed aside the temptation to discuss Gerard's abuse of Samartine Drummond's sister at a garden party. She would wait for a letter from Samartine. If none came within a few days, she would tell Kendryck about the incident. He deserved to know. Even though Gerard had gone to Canterbury to make apologies to the boy he injured, they had no proof yet that Gerard was reforming beyond that simple measure.

To be honest with herself, Tynley did not believe he could. At that, she took another swallow of her whisky.

"Mr. Shaw will be respectful during his interviews," Kendryck said with a glance to the hall, worry lining his brow.

"Your stepmother and Barbara will take to him. However, I am not so confident that Mr. Thynne will please anyone."

"He was almost impertinent with you."

She frowned into her empty glass. "I agree."

"You handled him well and told him all he needed to know."

"But he asked questions in circles."

"He did."

She met Kendryck's concern with a worry of her own. "He knows something."

"And he's not telling us."

"I wonder why."

"I CANNOT BELIEVE that those two men would approach us to ask such ridiculous things." Madeline sniffed, picking at her dinner. Her reaction to questioning by the Runners was insult.

Tynley sighed inwardly and took another bite of her potatoes. She had hoped Madeline might be more compassionate about the fate of the missing woman.

Kendryck clenched his jaw, one sign he was irritated at his stepmother.

The four of them sat at dinner, and this was the first conversation among family only. Because all the servants had been with the two Runners for most of the late afternoon, the family supper had begun later than usual. Served well after eight, they all had declared they were hungry and sad as they took their places at the table. Kendryck had given Carter the signal to leave them while they ate their main course.

Frustrated, Tynley pressed her lips together.

"Those two were rough fellows," Barbara said, aimlessly pushing her food around her plate. "I disliked them both. No respect."

Kendryck blew out an exasperated breath. "They do their jobs. They deserve your respect, looking out for the put-upon, the missing, and the dead."

"Oh my, Strade!" Barbara went pale, dropping her fork to her plate. "You think this Miss Roundbay is dead?"

"Roundbridge, darling," her mother corrected her with wide eyes at Kendryck, who set his jaw, frustrated with the young woman for her mistake.

He put down his utensils and looked at his relatives one by one. "I hope you cooperated with those gentlemen."

Barbara scoffed.

"Despite what you think of their backgrounds," Kendryck said, focusing on her, "they do the government's work to keep this country safe from thieves and murderers and all kinds of ne'er-do-wells. You will not disparage their work. Without them, we would be left to the animals who would overrun us with their heinous acts."

Barbara had the temerity to cock a brow at Kendryck.

To that, he served her a daunting look.

Barbara wisely went back to her dinner. But at once, her pretty oval face contorted with tears. "I did not like them here, sir. How can they think we know anything about this lady? No one has come here. Or… Well, I don't think so. We don't know what staff had to say to them, do we? And we should learn. Don't you think, sir? Mama? Shouldn't you tell us, Kendryck? I mean…I am sorry, I mean, Strade. Strade! Oh!" She put her serviette to the corner of her eye. "I always thought of Owen as Strade. I am not used to such changes. Poor Owen. Gone from us, and he was my sweetheart. I loved him. I loved him so. Forgive me, Strade." She jumped to her feet. "I cannot go on! This is all such horrid news. I hate it. I am undone. Goodnight!"

Madeline gaped at her daughter as she fled. "She means nothing. Nothing. Disregard her."

Tynley watched her go and thought, *Oh, that means something. But what?* Plus, that little scene was pure bravado. She had seen seasoned actresses do worse. Yet Tynley was left with the impression that not all Barbara's words were an act. There was truth in there. *But which ones conveyed it?* She would memorize it, pick it apart later.

Madeline had gone white, fidgeting with her serviette, her chin trembling. "I am disturbed that this...this Miss Whatever-hernameis has gone missing. It's a shame. A shame. Really, it is. Traveling is a...a boon, a change of tempo and...and scenery, good for a person. That anyone should simply disappear is no benefit to our coaching system."

She too rose, excused herself, and rushed away, her serviette to eyes that did not shed tears.

Tynley tamped down her urge to call her back and call her out. A woman was in trouble, missing, worse! And Madeline reacted more mildly to Barbara's failure to mourn the missing lady than she did to the ruin of the British coaching system.

Absurd.

Kendryck sat back. "I have no idea what any of that really meant."

"Nor I. But I predict we will learn."

Kendryck sighed. "Please may it be sooner rather than later."

THEY HAD PEACE in the house. For the next week, no visitors came. No Runners, either. Gerard did not return, but had sent Kendryck a letter from him to say that all went well with his apology to the Cramdon family. The injured boy recovered well. His father had forgiven Gerard his misstep and invited him to remain a few days. Gerard had accepted.

Kendryck told Tynley he replied and said Gerard should begin his journey home next week, as Kendryck wished him to present himself at university to commence his apology to the school administrators. He wanted the boy's future settled before they were wed. "He should be in attendance for our wedding, but after that, I want him enrolled for the new term next year."

Samartine had written within the first week to Tynley that her husband had agreed to write to Kendryck and tell him about Gerard's behavior with her sister. Tynley awaited some word from Kendryck during their breakfast hours that he had gotten a letter from his friend. So far, however, none had come.

In the mail did come two very welcome letters. The first came from Tynley's best friend in London. Elpseth Taunton had arranged for her second to take her place in her nightly performances of *The Taming of the Shrew*. The theater owner had not been happy about it, but Elspeth had told him she needed the rest. When she said she would attend Tynley's wedding in Cardiff, the fellow had relented and even offered his congratulations.

The other letter that came was from Aunt Juno. The lady wished to attend, but feared her health would not permit it. She wrote that she had recovered much of her stamina from her poor spell when last she and Tynley met, but it was not enough to bear the weight of such a lengthy journey.

Kendryck had seen the delight on Tynley's face at the acceptance of one of her friends. "They love you, my darling. Lady Peregrine would be here were it easier for her to attend. But I am so pleased Elspeth can come to wish you well. She values you as I do."

She took his commendation with good humor. He had not said he loved her, but she could see in his gaze and in his deeds and words that he cared for her.

Such regard confirmed her own instincts about his nature. She could say he loved him for it, but she waited for the fullness of that feeling. She was most certain it would be the day she married him. All else paled in significance.

Tynley knew what love could do. She'd had the privilege of it before, and she thanked her good fortune that she would soon have it again. She could weather the challenges she and Kendryck faced with his family members.

As for his attention to Indian affairs, she wished not to address it yet. In her heart, she needed time. She would need to feel her way forward into any controversy his actions would raise. It was one thing for a man to become notorious for his political and economic views. It was another for a woman to become notorious for any reason at all.

She shied away from imagining a future of chaos. Instead, she focused on the easier challenges to fix. Family seemed one of them.

Since her outburst the night of their return from Cardiff, Barbara had become demure, almost timid. She came to dinner respectful and mute. She took her tea alone or with her mother in that lady's room. She came down to breakfast, Carter told them, but she came after eight, and dined alone.

A nervous Madeline took it upon herself to fill her daughter's perceived void, and conducted polite but innocuous conversations with Tynley and Kendryck at tea and supper. Other than that, she too stayed away.

As one week turned to two, they all speculated on Gerard's return. Tynley wondered why William's letter had not arrived.

Mid-month came, and Gerard did not return.

William did not write to Kendryck. Nor Samartine to Tynley.

On their walk ten days before their wedding, Tynley resolved to tell Kendryck about Samartine's sister. Before she could start, he raised the matter of Gerard's failure to return home. "I am worried about him. So much can happen on the road, as we know. But I fear he's in deeper trouble."

Tynley could not contain her own concerns. She did not like the boy, but she did not wish him ill. "Do you think he told us the truth?"

"That he will return?" Kendryck considered the clouds scudding along the horizon. "No. In fact, I begin to doubt he went to humble himself before Viscount Cramdon and his son. I would wager good money Gerard went to Canterbury to post the letters. Perhaps he stayed for a few days. Or he even paid someone to keep a letter and post it for him. Then went on his merry way."

"He would try to fool you like that?"

"Oh, he is wily enough," Kendryck responded.

"How could he afford to pay someone to do that?"

"Before we left for Cardiff, I gave him money for travel. It was a generous sum, as I did not want him stranded for lack of funds. But he has been gone so long now that I surmise he could be gambling to fund his way. Visit his friends. Make a right spree of it all."

"What will you do?" she asked, seeing the toll this took on Kendryck's good nature.

"I'll not hire a Runner to find him. We have enough challenges with the two Runners we know. Besides, the kind of trouble Gerard gets into would infuriate a good man of the law. They have more important things to do. I wrote yesterday to Viscount Cramdon. I need to know when Gerard left, if indeed he ever arrived. But I also asked Cramdon to help me by asking his son the names of any of Gerard's school chums. I will use that list to inquire if any of them have heard from him or seen him. I know not what else to do. Part of me fears for his safety, yes. But another part of me assumes he is well, thriving at whatever mischief he is up to. I do know one thing: Gerard will come home when he wishes—and he will as soon as he runs out of money."

"Stop a minute." She put a hand to his chest, her choice about Samartine's secret clear now. "I must tell you something about him that Samartine told me when we were there."

"She knows Gerard?"

"Her young sister does, or did. Gerard was at a garden party the girl attended, and he accosted her. Samartine told me the story the day we visited with her and William. I asked her if William had told you. She said no."

Disappointment in his friend showed on Kendryck's face. "It is true. He hadn't."

"I don't want you to think ill of William. Samartine told me he is not inclined to tell stories secondhand. But I wanted you to know. She said she would ask him to write. I asked her if she would write to tell you what her sister had said, but I fear both of them have decided against it. Or perhaps they wait until we go for the wedding because they wish to tell you in person. I am sorry to be the bearer of bad news."

He cupped her cheek. "You must not take this as anything I criticize in you. You have done me the favor of full disclosure of Gerard's behavior. I value you all the more for it."

Tynley went into his embrace and put her head on his shoulder. "I value you more each day. I want you to be happy. You have had so much to overcome since you've arrived home. Even I have added to your list."

"You are the joyful item on that list. I marvel that you have not fled this place and me to seek a more peaceful existence."

"I want a peaceful existence with you," she whispered against his lips. "I want it for you."

"We will create it together. All the days of our lives." He kissed her with all the hope of tomorrow in his lips.

Her eyes closed, she imagined what they would have together for decades to come. "I want our wedding to be a happy day."

He lifted her chin. "It will be, my darling. Never fear. And after, we go to a restful honeymoon."

Her eyes popped open. "Restful? I never thought of that word to describe it."

"Trust me. You will enjoy it."

"And you won't tell me where we go?"

"No. A surprise is a surprise. And I am as anxious as you to leave here and enjoy it!"

Chapter Twelve

AFTER TEN O'CLOCK the night before all of them were to leave for Cardiff for the wedding, Kendryck grabbed his greatcoat and beaver hat, called to Jericho, and strode out the front door into the December evening. He could not sleep. He had tried. Finally, he gave in to the restless urge, summoned Jericho with a whistle, and walked down the road to the main thoroughfare to the village.

He had not gone on a nighttime walk since he had arrived home. A mark of his distress over any issue, nightly walks had been a habit of his since he was a boy of ten. At his various posts while in India, he had not walked far, most often in circles. Many parts of many towns were forbidden to him. And in such locales as the residency in Hyderabad, he had to be sure to avoid going anywhere near the women's quarters. Such areas were strictly forbidden to all men.

Tonight he had given in to his stress and thought to walk it off so that he might enjoy the approach of his wedding. The past week had been filled with his worries over the missing woman, but also with his delight in Tynley's gaiety over their nuptials. He had only to watch her laugh with Carter or her maid Seren, and he absorbed her happiness. The two of them had promised each other to put their festivities foremost in their minds.

The event was marred, however, by Gerard's continued

absence. This morning, he had received a letter from Viscount Cramdon. The viscount had received Gerard's first letter to him declaring his intention to appear, but as Kendryck suspected, Gerard had never arrived. The viscount's son had offered the names of two friends of Gerard's whom Kendryck might contact. Kendryck had dashed off an immediate letter of thanks for the information and ended with his own apologies for the problems his brother had caused. His best wishes for the recovery of the man's son went with a promise to write to him with any news of Gerard's return home.

He had little to go on to find his brother—and the question of his fate kept Kendryck and Tynley from complete happiness about their marriage. The only answer now was to hire a Runner to find the boy. Shaw would be a good man for it, but he was already working to find Miss Roundbridge. Working with Thynne did not appeal. Tomorrow morning, Kendryck would write to Bow Street to commence the search. Any Runner would be acceptable.

That decided, he felt freer, but he stopped as he came in sight of the village. He was glad of the late hour that negated the possibility of seeing anyone he might know. They would ask how he was, and he was not inclined to lie to them. He would discuss his marriage, his bride, his hope for the future. But after that, he anticipated anyone he met would have that light in their eyes that insinuated they knew as much about the doings up at his house as he did. He had servants, all of whom had friends or relatives among those in the cozy little cottages. He did not wish to add fuel to their gossip about the goings-on at the Rambles.

He stepped through the brush and brambles, the panting of Jericho and the crunch of dead foliage under his boots the only sounds that met his ears. He much preferred to stroll in the daytime, and to do it with Tynley. Even though he had settled his plans about Gerard, he was still bedeviled by others in his family whose behavior unsettled him. His grandmother continued to worsen, her escapes from her rooms more and more of a problem. She had fallen the other day on a rug in the upstairs hall, and in her delirium had blamed Madeline for moving the runner. Madeline had argued with the lady, her fist in the air. Kendryck had intervened, recalling how monstrous that lady's wrath could. He had demanded Madeleine retire peacefully while they dealt with his injured grandmother.

Madeline had not been congenial since then. In fact, neither she nor Barbara had recovered their normal selves, cool as they normally were, since the two Bow Street Runners had visited and questioned them all. They seemed to blow hot and cold with Tynley, who took it all well. But the two women grew more churlish and petulant each day. Barbara especially so—she even requested once more to wear their grandmother's sapphire parure to a neighbor's holiday house party.

She had come to him this morning in his study, opening the subject again.

"Your mother has jewels she brought with her when she married, Barbara. I'm sure there is something suitable among them for a debut."

"Mama says you have a large box filled to the brim with a Hollens family collection. Why can I not have them?" She had tossed her head of long strawberry-blonde curls as she wailed at him.

"I have good reasons to forbid you to wear that parure."

She stuck her nose higher in the air. "Because you are mean."

"Because those sapphires were paid for by the blood of other people."

"Oh, don't be silly."

"Silly? I suppose I am if you consider that the money came from Grandfather's investments in trade of forty years ago."

"Ha! Rum or sugar? What's the problem?"

He vowed not to yell at her. "Barbara, would you like to sit on the floor?"

"What?" She glared at him.

"Sit down."

"No."

"Do it."

She had collected herself, and wrapped her gown, as well as her hauteur, around her as she sat on the carpet.

"Extend your hands out to each side of you as if you hold hands with another."

Confused, she did it anyway.

"How would you like to sit like this for weeks?"

"What? No!"

"Put your hands back out on the carpet, Barbara. This is how black men, women, and children sat shackled together in the holds of ships for eight or more miserable weeks as they crossed the Atlantic Ocean. Our grandfather gave money to construct those ships and invested with others who enchained those people and transported them to the New World. Our records, there"— he had pointed to the wall where logbooks were stacked up— "detail the profits. Thousands of pounds we earned off the misery and suffering of innocents who were sold into lifelong slavery. No, Barbara, you will not wear any of those jewels."

Affected by the tale, she had sat mute for a minute. "You will sell them?"

"I have not decided." If he did, would he not be profiting from them just as the rest of the family had?

She had scrambled to her feet. "I am innocent, too. I did not do any of that. So why let them sit in a box where no one can see them? You are just being ugly. I want to get married. Leave you. Leave this—this hideous house! You want me gone. I know you do."

"I want you married to a respectable man who cares for you, and you for him. But I cannot allow you to decorate yourself in those things bought with pain and death!"

"Oh, you hypocrite. I know you earned a fortune in Calcutta!" She leaned toward him, spitting out her wrath.

How had she gotten that idea?

"But you are so overblown with your fake dignity and your

counterfeit piety. You are spiteful. You don't want me here. The only one who ever did was Owen. And he's gone too. But never fear—sapphires or not, I will go and never darken your precious Rambles again!"

She had stalked off, slamming his door on her way out.

She had also left him with the hideous fear that she would bind herself to the first man who took her fancy and condemn herself to a hellish existence because he was strict and had denied her the damn sapphires.

He paused and inhaled. The wind off the sea was particularly brisk tonight. It was, after all, the end of November, and he really should not be out here. But he was not ready to return to the house.

At the path toward the front door, he turned for the one that he and Tynley took each day. Tree limbs obscured the way, and he picked his way along, relying more on memory and instinct than light to guide him. Jericho loped beside him. He got to the spot where Tynley usually allowed him to lift her down into his arms, and he smiled at how happy he was to be marrying a vibrant, charming woman. One who had been a stranger when they met, but who had become his confidante, his sparring partner, his laughing, smiling fiancée. Whose very presence presaged a bright future for them both.

He was thrilled that her friend, the actress, was coming to Cardiff. Perhaps she was already there at the Old Black Gander. Two friends of his and of William Drummond's had replied to Kendryck's invitation, saying that they would attend with their wives. The four men had been tender ten-year-old lads when first they were sent away to boarding school. With so many guests, Kendryck had sent a missive to the innkeeper of the Gander to ask for rental of a private dining area above the common room for the night before the ceremony. He had ordered a dinner party for all the guests.

Jericho came running back to him, his huge tongue hanging out as he danced around. The dog was one to frolic, and he had

Kendryck laughing at his antics.

"Shall we go in?" At his words, the dog spun, as if Kendryck had fired a gun, and ran ahead. Instead of following the path to the house, he veered off toward the old curtain wall to the castle.

Kendryck grumbled to himself. He was not about to chase after the animal. He was done for the night.

But the dog came barreling toward him to dance around once more.

"What is it you are so happy about?"

The dog charged off, back where he'd gone, and disappeared. Within a moment, he reappeared at the maw of the gatehouse and yipped at Kendryck.

"Very well." Kendryck flapped his arms. If the dog had felled some woodland creature and wanted to preen over his prize, Kendryck was about to grant the dog his wish. "After I praise you, we'll go in," he said when Jericho circled him again and did his little jig.

At once, the dog was off toward the ruined gatehouse. He paused at the entrance, looked back to ascertain if Kendryck followed, and scampered off into the bailey.

"Where are you?" Kendryck said to the dog, who had disappeared into the mist of night. Moonlight filtered through dark clouds now and then, so Kendryck finally spied him milling about the entrance to the Tudor half-timbered house. Sniffing, licking bits in the dirt, Jericho would look up at Kendryck as he approached, wag his tail, then return to his perusal of the ground.

Kendryck stepped over the debris and stumps of trees in the old courtyard with a note to himself that one day soon, he must order his groundsmen to clear the mess.

Jericho sat on his haunches right in front of the door to the Tudor house. The door was closed. Kendryck thought nothing of it. But the dog sat quietly, his tail still thwapping the ground, a scrap of cloth hanging from his jaws. As if to influence Kendryck to make note of it, the dog nudged his hand.

He took it from him. But the moon was once more behind

black clouds.

Curiosity had Kendryck lifting one hand to bite the fingertips of one glove. He slid it off and shoved it in his coat pocket.

The moon and clouds conspired to grant him a fleeting ray of moonlight.

He sucked in air.

The cloth was small, rectangular. It was dark and soft, the nap of the fabric clumped with dirt and water. Rain, most likely. He could not tell much in the faint light. But he did not have to see its fullness to realize what it was. Velvet.

It was the vermilion velvet pouch from his collection. Once, in a chest behind two three-hundred-year-old wooden doors. Locked by two sizable, if equally old, keys.

He rubbed the small velvet bag between his fingers. Its cord was ragged, broken, dirty. It was empty. And it was here.

Here.

He pocketed it in his greatcoat, took a step closer to the door, and pushed. It was locked. He put his shoulder to it and shoved. It did not give.

He stepped back, and his gaze went around the outline of the doorframe. Not trusting the light, he ran his hand around it. Intact. Not jimmied.

He bent to the lock. In the hazy glow of the moon, he saw the outline of the large, old black faceplate. In light relief, a blacksmith had centuries ago burned a chevron between two rams *passant*, the family crest. The two stood, proud as ever, unmarked. There was no sign that it was damaged.

Someone had found the bag, emptied it, and had the audacity or carelessness to throw it away here in the dirt. They had not assaulted the door with hammer or sledge. They had not ruined the ancient faceplate. Nor had they used any tool to mark the integrity of the lock.

They had used a key. Most likely two keys. He would confirm that when he went inside the house.

They had used *his* key. Which meant they had walked into his study, taken the huge iron key from its antique wooden box in the back of the bottom drawer of his desk.

They had also taken the second key, smaller, sitting beside the larger, then used that to open the door to the old buttery.

They had assessed what was there and decided that, for their purposes, the contents of this pouch would be best. Easiest. Valuable. Transportable.

Diamonds, hundreds, thousands. He did not know. He had never counted them. But he had valued them greatly. They were to be, like the other goods in that back room, the treasure that he would showcase to the world. The items he would put on display, notate, offer as the proof of a culture of a people who deserved to be honored, not conquered. Not ruled. Not ridiculed.

Whoever had taken his diamonds had robbed him of part of his goal. But they had not stolen his ambition. Only made it stronger.

"Let's go in, Jericho." He slapped his thigh, and the dog fell in with him.

His diamonds were gone.

But the person who took them would have no peace. No joy.

I will see to it.

Chapter Thirteen

TYNLEY THREW THE blankets and coverlet off and rose from her bed. As nervous as a first-time bride, she drew on her quilted robe and slippers and padded into her sitting room. She lit a candle and sat for a few minutes. The light was too pale by which to read, and she knew not what else to do but the one thing her mother had taught her when a child. *Count your blessings, my girl.*

If you can't, she'd say, *count your troubles and leave them at your feet.*

Of late, privately, so as not to add burden on burden to Kendryck's, she had kept her worries to herself. The fate of Gerard was the biggest among them. She wondered how the boy could be gone so long. She did not see him as adventurous. Only with his friends. She did not see him as one to hie himself off to contemplate his future alone. She saw him only in trouble. Deeply in trouble. In gaol. Or in a ditch. Somewhere. Forgotten.

She shivered and pulled her robe around her.

Her troubles mounted. The past few days with Gerard's fate unknown, Madeline seemed to become surlier toward her each day. She sniffed at Tynley's gowns. Glared at her when she attempted conversation at dinner.

Barbara was worse, barely talking to Tynley when they were in the same room. Her one thread of decent conversation occurred the day before yesterday, when she asked if Tynley planned to wear any jewels with her new wedding gown from Madame St. Claire.

"No, I have no jewels, Barbara."

"I thought all actresses acquired them," the girl had said, her gaze drifting down to Tynley's throat.

"Famous ones, yes, they do. I was not on the stage for long. I did not earn that much money, and I bought no fripperies. Nor can I say I was very talented."

Barbara met her gaze with the very devil in her eyes. "Talents have nothing to do with success in Drury Lane."

"You are wrong, Barbara."

The girl huffed. "Don't all actresses live by allowing men to support them?"

"That is not true. You will meet one in a few days who has made her name and her fortune only by honing her skills on the stage."

"She has no paramours?"

"None."

"Hard to believe." Barbara looked down her nose at her.

"Ask her."

"I will." She had put down her fork and, in an effort to appear nonchalant, twirled a tendril of hair at her cheek. "How many men did you have?"

Kendryck dropped his fork and knife. "Barbara, this is not acceptable."

The girl tipped her head and narrowed her eyes at him. "Don't you want to know how many she's had in her bed?"

That was too much, even for Madeline. "Really, my dear!"

"Oh, stop, Mama." Barbara was undaunted. "You want to know. You said so yesterday."

Kendryck shot to his feet. "You need not come to our wedding, Barbara."

"Oh, I wouldn't miss it, brother dear." She wiped the corners of her mouth with her serviette and demurely rose to her feet. "I will enjoy meeting your bride's actress friend. I need to learn a few tricks to keep a man, don't I?"

"Barbara! Leave here!" her mother spat.

"A prudent idea," Kendryck said. "Do not return to this table unless you plan to speak in polite and cultivated ways."

The girl was becoming more hateful as the days wore on. As if she took the place of Gerard, she made minutes with her pure hell. Madeline could not contain her. Had she even tried to train her?

Tynley was eager for her wedding for a change of atmosphere. To give Kendryck and herself something wonderful to enjoy and celebrate. Moreso did she welcome a honeymoon. Time apart from others. Time with Kendryck alone.

The past weeks with him had only strengthened her desire to marry him. He was prudent. He was kind. He had ethics…and a noble goal. He tried to navigate the challenges of family strife with a deft touch. And though he and Gerard had not had a friendly relationship, Kendryck still sought to lead his young brother toward a useful life. To be an educated man. A gentleman. If, indeed, the boy came home and, pray to God, arrived soon, unscathed.

He would. He had to. Where else would a boy of twenty-one go with little money? His friends might help him for days, weeks. But Kendryck was right—eventually, Gerard *had* to come home. If not for succor and affection, for his daily bread.

A cry rent the air.

Tynley cocked her head.

Another came. A shout of alarm. From the hall.

"Come back here!" a woman shouted.

"No, ma'am! Do not!" That was Conway, who slept out there on his pad. Protecting Tynley from…

Something or someone thudded against her door.

She sprang forward to open it.

Two people tumbled inside.

Tynley jumped backward to escape falling into them. One was a woman. The baroness!

The melee went on, one rolling over the other.

"Stop! Stop!" Conway shouted at the old lady. Conway got the better of her and rolled the woman to her side.

Tynley gasped at the pitiful sight. Kendryck's grandmother lay flat upon the floor, screeching at the footman. "Beast! Beast, let me go!"

"What in God's name?" Madeline raced up to them and stood gawking.

But the elderly lady struggled, incensed, her rheumy eyes wide with fright. She waved a hand before the face of Conway. And in her hand was a pair of scissors.

"Grandmama?" Barbara ran up, her oval face contorted in distaste. "Her again. Old silly thing." She walked away, a hand securing her robe over her shoulder.

"Stop, ma'am!" Conway was having a terrible time trying to capture the scissors the woman waved before his face. "Ma'am! You give me those."

"You've got to stop her," the old lady blabbered, dribbling the words.

Kendryck came bounding down the hall. Oddly for this time of night, he wore his greatcoat and boots. "What is wrong here?"

Tynley answered, "Your grandmother is frightened."

"She came running out of her room, sir." Conway managed to press the old lady's two forearms to the floor. "She was yelling that a lady was going to kill her."

"Aye, aye," the lady moaned, and focused on Madeline. "That witch. I shall kill *her*!"

Conway raised his eyes toward Tynley.

"My boy," the old lady pleaded with Kendryck. "She's for me. *She is.*"

"Lucy!" Angrily, Kendryck summoned his grandmother's maid, who hung back against the far wall. "What happened here?"

Lucy scuttled forward and muttered, "Mrs. Hollens visited to see if her ladyship was in need of anything."

"She's evil!" The baroness, now flat to the hall floor, began to sob. "She'll kill me. She will. She will."

"Never, Grandmama," Kendryck promised, but addressed the lady's maid. "Did you check that she went to bed?"

"I did, sir." Lucy wrung her hands.

"At this hour of the night?"

"Just minutes ago. She was awake, sir. I do go, sir, at any hour I think she might need things."

Tynley went to her knees and ran her fingers through the old lady's tangled hair. "No one will hurt you, my lady. We want you to be happy and warm. Does anyone have a handkerchief?"

Kendryck pressed one between her fingers as he knelt beside her.

She dried the old woman's tears. Her skin was parchment. Her eyes soft with apologies, brighter and clearer with each of Tynley's tender touches. "Come now. Sit up. You will be well. No one will hurt you. Can I have a glass of good brandy, please?"

"My study, Conway," Kendryck said.

"Yes, sir." Conway shifted the woman totally into Tynley's embrace and pushed up from the floor.

She crooned to the lady soothing words a mother told a frightened child, and pushed her matted, tangled white hair behind her ears. The woman's condition was deplorable, and the maid Lucy had to be corrected.

"The baroness needs a soothing bath." Tynley rocked her in her arms. "Warm. Tonight. Now. Her hair washed, too. Clean clothes. This night rail… Burn it. Her slippers too, please." She braced the lady, so slight, in her arms. "I think you need hot soup. Does that sound good? Yes? And tea. Very well. We shall have that, too. After the bath. Ah, here you are, my dear. Sip this."

The lady took the crystal glass as delicately as if she were in a ballroom. "Oh, lovely." The old woman sighed after the first taste. "You are good to me, Mama."

Tynley glanced up at Kendryck, her heart in her throat. "She has been sorely neglected."

"Lucy." Kendryck did not look at the maid. "If you value your position, you will take care that when I inspect my grandmother's rooms tomorrow morning at nine, she has fresh linens, clean clothes, and a spotless bedroom and boudoir. Conway, you will get Peters, and the two of you will build the biggest fire possible in the baroness's rooms. Then you will draw a bath of generous proportions. You will both wait, and afterward, you will have all items promptly removed. The two of you sleep until noon tomorrow."

"Yes, sir, but my post here—?" Conway tipped his head toward Tynley's door.

"You are done for tonight. You are released to see that all is done for my grandmother."

Conway blew out a breath and scowled at Lucy. "Lead on."

The maid spun and scurried down the hall toward the servants' stairs. Conway trudged behind her.

Kendryck took one of his grandmother's hands as she sipped her brandy. "Like that, do you, Grandmama?"

"I do, boy. I've not had any. They don't give it me, you know."

"I know. We were wrong in that."

"Waste of good brandy." A sound of disgust came from Madeline, who spun and strode toward her bedchamber.

The baroness leaned forward out of Tynley's arms. "You know she tries to kill me." Her eyes followed Madeline down the hall. "She does."

Tynley sucked in air.

Kendryck tucked a hank of hair behind the lady's ear. "She would not, Grandmama. She would not hurt you."

"She does, she does! She—she comes in to my room at night and pinches me and twists my fingers." She lifted a shaking hand, and Tynley winced at the sight of two gnarled fingers and huge bruises on the old woman's wrist.

"Oh, sweetheart." Kendryck's bass voice caught as he kissed her fingertips. "That will not happen. I promise you."

The old lady licked her lips. "Can I have another?" she asked, her mouth hanging open in anticipation.

"You can," he said with a smile. "Every night before bed. Now, can I help you to stand? Let's try, eh? And I will take you to your bed."

The lady stumbled to her feet with both Kendryck and Tynley aiding her. Then, as Kendryck caught his grandmother up in his arms, he said to Tynley, "I will put her to bed, but afterward, I must talk with you."

IN HER ROBE and slippers, Tynley had gone downstairs and helped herself to brandy from the dining room sideboard. Climbing the stairs with her glass, she let out a huge sigh as she rounded the landing and looked down the length of the hall. All on the second floor had retired to their bedrooms. From the far end of the hall, where the baroness had her chambers, Tynley detected the sounds of movement of furniture. Perhaps the two footmen were still bringing up hot bathwater and situating the tub. Hopefully Lucy was properly seeing to the needs of her elderly charge. Barbara and Madeline kept to their rooms, as they should after the disgraceful scene they had made in the hall.

Tynley sat in her chair near the fire, yearning to see Kendryck.

Minutes later, a knock came at her door.

She hurried to open it and fell into his open arms.

He caught her under her knees and walked with her to her settee. "I should not be here, but I must speak with you." After settling her near him, he combed her unbound hair back from her cheeks and graced her with a tormented smile.

She caressed his stubbled cheek. *My heavens.* She loved him. Had for weeks, and never more than now. The revelation felt like freedom. Tonight when he saw to his grandmother and, by deed more than words, reprimanded the neglectful Lucy, she had known.

"I'm so glad you've come to me," she told him. "You and I did not walk today, and we need to talk before we wed. I was, and I still am, so thrilled that the time is nigh for us to do that."

He caught the wealth of her wild red curls and lifted her mouth so close, so sweetly close to his. "No, no. You must listen to me, sweetheart. I have thought long and hard about this engagement of ours."

"As have I." She put her lips to his in a tender kiss. She did not change his scowl—but she had good intentions. "I am glad it is near. The month has been long, too long."

"And there has been enough time for you to see what you truly would walk into, were you to marry me."

She threaded her fingers though his abundant black satin hair. "I will marry you."

"There is too much against it, Tynley."

"Too much *for* it, my darling man."

He caught her hand and dragged it from his hair. "No. You listen to me. You wanted time. You've had it. This family is too addled, too corrupted, for someone who is so rational, so balanced, to become a part of it."

"You think you can scare me off?" None of his family's behavior was his fault.

"We all should." His sorrowful blue eyes absorbed her.

"You do not see me running, sir."

He clamped her body nearer. The touch of him—so endearing, so enthralling—flooded her body with need of him. "You should. To save yourself, you should go. Tomorrow, you can. With ease."

She gave a laugh. "No."

"Before we say vows. Before we see our friends. You can leave me. You will say I am to blame."

"I will not."

"But you must, my precious woman. There is no hope for

this family and the troubles we have."

"There is hope, and I am looking at him." She pressed closer to him. His allure was a magnet to her soul. She wanted him as her friend, her husband, and her lover. And like so much else she had decided she wanted in her life, she would have him. No matter the challenges of his family. "There is always hope, Kendryck. You bring it here. Whether they recognize it or not at the moment is their problem. But you have clear sight of who each one is. And I've seen you work tirelessly. I have seen you tame your anger and instead use logic to set them in the right direction."

He shook his head and rose to pace before her fireplace. The embers burned low, throwing red lights to his glistening hair. "You do not know the full of it. I sense the bitterness in Madeline and the stubbornness in Barbara are characteristics I do not have the power to change. My grandfather, my father, and my older brother Owen oppressed those two women with their chicanery and their licentiousness."

She rose, determined to make him see the alternative. "An ethical man can be a model of manhood. I am certain all three of them see it in you."

He raked his hair and spun toward her. "How can you believe that?"

She arched her brows. "I've lived it. I've seen it as my mother influenced my father to stop drinking and gambling. If she could not influence him to change his strict ways with me, she succeeded in some ways. And she changed as a result. When I wanted to leave to become an actress, she helped me by trying to persuade him. She let me keep some tender feelings for my father, which otherwise I would not have to this day."

His gaze seared her with longing. "Your heart is so pure, my darling—of course you would change. I doubt the same can happen with Madeline and Barbara."

"Other men neglected them, perhaps even disregarded them."

"They belittled them!"

She nodded. "You do not. You give them what any woman needs."

"A new dress? A new hat?"

"A renewed integrity. The honor of your public regard. You plan for Barbara's debut. You take both on holiday and welcome them to our wedding. You invite them to meet your friends and mine."

"I refuse Barbara the family jewels."

"As is your right. It is for her own benefit that she not show them off. To wear them only indicates to any prospective beau that she tolerates or even welcomes similar dastardly invest-ments. You will not have her life so tainted. That, my dear man, is wise of you."

"That may influence Barbara to change. But Madeline is beyond management. She is…vindictive. I've considered sending her away. She brought with her in marriage settlement a dowry for Barbara. A widow's portion for her own retirement. And a small cottage in Milford Haven. To my knowledge, she has never been there."

Tynley got to her feet and wrung her hands in dismay. "To her, that would be the end of the earth."

Kendryck braced a hand to the mantel and stared into the fire. "I think Grandfather and Owen forgot about the property entirely. It's not much. It might even be in need of repairs."

"She would hate it," Tynley said, imagining the fire of Made-line's wrath should it become her home.

"Yes. With every bone in her body." He took a massive inhale of breath. "And then there is Gerard."

"He is redeemable."

Kendryck spun and gazed at her with limpid eyes. "Oh, my darling. I doubt it. I hurt for him, and I worry about him."

She went to him and wrapped her arms around his waist. "He is young. Hurt. Acting out his rage. He can be turned."

He pulled her into his arms. His lips against her ear, he

crushed her close. "Oh my, how I wish you were right."

"I am. We must try. Again. Harder."

He sank his fingers in her hair. "I think he has stolen from me."

"What?"

"I went for a walk tonight. Unable to sleep, Jericho and I took a turn about the grounds. The dog found this." From his inside vest pocket, he removed a small pouch. Dirty, splotched by rain, the red velvet was ruined.

"It is empty." She bemoaned every word.

"The two keys to the two doors have been used, replaced in a careless manner. I checked when I came in. I was in my study when I heard the ruckus in the hall with my grandmother."

"We don't know it was Gerard."

Kendryck let out a huge breath and stared at the ceiling. "No. But who had opportunity? He did. Who had motive? He did."

"Who put those items in the Tudor cupboard?"

"Conway and Peters."

The two footmen, then. "And you trust them?"

"I do. They are good boys, cousins, the sons of good men in Cowbridge, not too far away. They are also under oath not to discuss what is hidden there. Furthermore, they have no idea where I keep the keys."

"How would Gerard know what's in that storage room?" she asked herself more than Kendryck.

He rolled his shoulders. "I don't know how, unless he saw us that day I showed them to you. Plus, to be fair, I have no reason to suspect him more than any others. Only that I assume he thinks in devious ways, and that he had opportunity while the four of us were gone to Cardiff."

She nodded, unhappy about what she would say. "Also that he was gone when we returned."

"And that he has not returned home since then." He sagged, forlorn.

She drew him into her arms. "We can do no more tonight.

You are weary, and so am I. We have a journey ahead of us tomorrow, and I am certain you will have much to say and inspect tomorrow morning before we leave."

"I must see if Peters is finished helping Conway. I shall leave Conway in charge with my grandmother, and Peters will be your new guard."

She caressed his jaw. "No, he won't. Come, be my guard tonight."

A hint of a smile brightened his strained features for a moment. "We are not married."

"What difference can a day make?"

"I will not have you subject to ridicule."

That thrilled her, for Kendryck knew that people's good opinion mattered to her. "I know who I am. And tonight, you are tired and in need of tenderness." She pressed her lips to the corner of his tantalizing mouth and drew him backward into her bedroom. "So am I. Come to bed."

"You are very persuasive, Mrs. Wallingford." In his whisper was surrender.

She took him to the side of her bed and unraveled his cravat, then unbuttoned his frock coat. "I want to take your cares from you. Please come, take mine."

"I won't—"

"No. That is for the night we are one. Tonight we are two, sharing what has hurt us. Giving to each other the comfort that can once again make us strong to face each day."

Chapter Fourteen

KENDRYCK LEFT TYNLEY before dawn, well before the upstairs maid came around to light the fires. His departure early would not stop the staff from gossiping about his presence in Tynley's rooms all night long. An hour would not matter. He knew what had happened there. Nothing. And everything. She had lain down in his arms, and they had held each other and slept. The hours had brought him oblivion. It was the best night's sleep he'd had in weeks. Perhaps in years.

Leaving his valet to complete packing for his wedding trip, Kendryck took the stairs at a jog. Carter was ready, standing at the breakfast room door to the kitchen.

"I'll eat now, Carter. Quickly, please. Whatever Cook has ready."

"She anticipated you'd be up early, sir." The butler set a plate of eggs and creamed potatoes before him a minute later.

"I imagine you've had word of the doings last night."

Carter continued his duties. "I have, sir. Conway was down early this morning to tell me. He has gone to bed, sir, as you instructed. Peters, too."

"They are good lads, Carter. I appreciated their help last night."

"I understand, sir."

"Tell me, Carter." Kendryck toyed with his coffee cup. "Have you had any challenges with Lucy?"

Nervous, the man wiggled in his dark serge, and his bushy brows rose high. "Occasionally, yes, sir."

"Such as?"

"She complains, sir."

"About her work?"

"About the baroness."

"I see. And have you been inspecting her work, Carter?"

"Not regularly, no, sir. I am remiss."

"And is there a reason for that?"

He locked his pale blue eyes on Kendryck. "His lordship, your brother, sir, said Lucy did a good service to the baroness, and I never questioned him."

"And since my brother has passed away, how have you gone on?"

"I relied on Mrs. Hollens. She told me the baroness was being well taken care of by Lucy and by she herself, sir. She said she loved the lady."

Kendryck swallowed his fury. Love had never been the attitude of Madeline toward his grandmother. "Carter, you realize this is not true."

The fellow shook with his dismay. "I do, sir. Now I do."

"I expect better from you, Carter. From Lucy, too. Most of all, I expect more from myself, as I should have known. I should have perceived the conflicts there." *Now because of my grandmother's lack of acuity, I cannot say if her accusations against Madeline are real or fantasy.* "I want you to do daily inspections. Impromptu. When my wife and I return, I will begin the same myself. But you are not to notify any of the staff."

"No, sir. All mum, sir."

"In the next few weeks while I am gone, I expect all of you to work up to my expectations. In regard to Lucy, especially, if she is not treating my grandmother with all the courtesy and respect she so deserves, you will sack the woman on the spot."

The butler colored a deep shade of pink. "I agree, sir. It will be done."

"I would hate for any other of the staff to be dismissed. But if necessary, I will do it."

Carter was forewarned. "Yes, sir."

"Good morning." Tynley stood on the threshold, her cheeks aflame, as if she'd run down the stairs and right into his reprimand of Carter.

"Good morning, my darling." Kendryck rose, got her chair, and set it within inches of his. "Come and dine. Carter is about to get you your breakfast."

"I am, sir." He gave a wan smile and a tip of his bald head toward the kitchen door. "I am off."

"I heard part of that," she told Kendryck as she took her chair and reached for his hand. "He seems very upset."

"He should be. I understand his taking orders from Madeline. She was in charge after Owen died and before I arrived home. Still, she is not the most compassionate person, and he ought to have inspected my grandmother's quarters or circumvented Madeline's orders to the extent that he could."

Tynley dropped her serviette to her lap. "No more of that. I want to tell you that I slept like a child, and I thank you, sir."

"Likewise, madam." He lifted her hand and kissed her fingertips. "I look forward to more of the same."

She wrinkled her nose at him. "I expect to get a lot of sleep in the next few weeks."

He pulled her hand closer and nipped her wrist. She snickered, the imp, and he loved her. He loved her quite beyond anything he had planned. Beyond any love he had known. "How disappointed will you be if that is not so?"

She fluttered her lashes like a coquette of eighteen. "With just that in mind, I have ordered Seren not to over pack."

He chuckled. "Wise of you. I am eager to get away. But I must tell you, I will take my time this morning looking into my grandmother's condition."

"Do. If we arrive a bit later in Cardiff, I am certain the innkeeper will have it all in hand."

"There are a few other tasks I must accomplish."

"Do them. We are ready when you are."

He frowned. "There is one thing I did not tell you last night. With so much amiss, I did not have presence of mind to do it. But I have decided to hire a Runner to find Gerard. If he does not come home soon, we must know where he is and how he is."

"A fine idea. We know so very little. I worry too."

"I will write to Bow Street today to hire a man. I hope Shaw and Thynne are at the end of their search for Miss Roundbridge and the former is available to start to look for Gerard. If not, I will take who I can."

"I wish we had some news of their investigation. It would put our minds at rest before our wedding."

His countenance darkened. "Yes. Both men promised to inform us of any progress to find that lady. Any news would be good. The disappearance of Gerard only compounds that of Miss Roundbridge."

KENDRYCK LEFT HER a few minutes later. Tynley finished her breakfast alone and hurried up to her room to finish her packing for her wedding trip. Her only new gown was to be the one Madame St. Claire had made for her, and that the modiste would bring it to her, along with her new winter coat, on the morning of their wedding at the vicarage. As she took her good green gown from the wardrobe, she paused to run her fingers over the hem she had repaired a few weeks ago.

Meanwhile, Seren stood over Tynley's bed and folded the last of the chemises into the trunk. Her hazel eyes clouded. "I wish you to be happy, ma'am. We are all so glad you are to be our mistress." She fumbled in her apron pocket for a handkerchief.

Tynley put her arms around the girl and hugged her close.

"Thank you, Seren. No tears. This is a happy occasion. Know too that I will be delighted to lead the household. I hope I do as well as Mrs. Hollens." In truth, Tynley had seen that the house and staff were ordered, efficient, and very clean.

"But we've not been happy. She can be—begging your pardon, ma'am—mean." Seren wiped her nose. "You're not. And we're happy for it, we are."

"I tell you what we will do. After Lord Strade and I return home from our honeymoon, I will call the servants to a meeting, and you will tell me anything you wish changed. All for the better, mind you. Though I must say, I have thought all of you did a very fine job."

"One thing you'd do for us? When we're sick, you let us rest up."

"I will. Anyone recovers more quickly that way. Has there been a lot of illness among you?"

"In the cold months, yes."

"And why is that, do you think?" But Tynley had a good idea of the reason.

"I'd say we need more warm clothes. Woolens and scarves." The girl imparted that in a hush, as if she might be overheard.

"Never worry. We will ensure everyone is warm and cozy."

"Thank you, ma'am. I…I want to serve you when you come back."

"I see no reason why you won't." Tynley noticed her sheepishness. "Why would you think that?"

The girl gulped.

"Tell me."

"Miss Hollens says I'm to return to her to serve. That you'll bring back a new girl because you're not happy with me."

Tynley had no idea that Seren had previously been Barbara's maid. She hadn't thought about the matter, but now she understood another reason Barbara had been churlish lately. But that did not excuse her lying about Tynley's opinion of Seren. "I never criticized you or your work, Seren. I am very angry with

Miss Hollens that she would tell you such a thing. Believe me, it is not true."

"Oh, ma'am." The girl twisted her handkerchief. "I am so glad, I am! I did not want to go back to Miss Hollens. Sorry, ma'am. I should not say such, but yes…" She dabbed at her tears.

"No more crying now, Seren." Tynley put her arm around the girl and patted her shoulders. "All is well. Say nothing, if you wouldn't mind, to Miss Hollens. I will speak with her."

"Yes, ma'am." Seren bit her lip.

Minutes later, Tynley gathered her pelisse, her gloves, and her new hat. The girl looked pensive. "Is there something else that bothers you, Seren?"

"I wanted to ask about last night. We talked about it in the servants' hall this morning. Well, I mean, I hope you don't think it awful that we did, but…"

"No, it was a terrible scene, and I think it appropriate that you all know what happened and how, so it does not happen again. What about it did you wish to discuss with me?"

"When the baroness was rambling, she had a pair of scissors in her hands."

"She did." Tynley had noticed, indeed, she had.

"Mrs. Hollens says the baroness steals them from Mrs. Hollens all the time. Lucy says it too. The baroness says Mrs. Hollens hurts her, and she takes them to fight her off."

Tynley was aghast. "And she uses the scissors in defense of herself?"

"Do you think that's true, ma'am?"

"Do you?" Tynley asked.

"Some folks do. Lucy does."

Tynley had to think logically here and not pass judgment. "I don't know what she used the scissors for or how she got them."

"But do you wonder if she was the one who cut your gown?"

"I do, Seren. But we have no proof. And so you and I will make no accusations, either. The baroness is not clear in her mind, and we will not demean or criticize her."

"No, ma'am. Never."

"Do finish the packing," Tynley told her with a smile. "I shall go down. Rest assured, I will begin to monitor what goes on between the baroness and Mrs. Hollens."

"Thank you, ma'am. I am wishing you a happy wedding day, ma'am. And a happy honeymoon."

"Thank you, Seren. That's wonderful of you to say."

"I'm glad you are going away to get married. And glad for your honeymoon trip too. The house is not…"

Tynley took the girl's hands in her own. "We will make the house a happy place for weddings and holidays and birthdays. Every day. For everyone who lives here."

BARBARA AND MADELINE were already in the carriage when Carter opened the door for Tynley to climb in.

"About time." Madeline sniffed. "It's freezing out here."

"A terrible time of year to marry," Barbara muttered.

Tynley appreciated the warmth in the floor from the hot bricks. But she did not appreciate the venom of the two women opposite her. "Do vent your spleens now before Kendryck arrives. I will not respond, but he well might, and I doubt you will wear so smug a smile when he does."

Both women huffed and sank their hands deeper in to their muffs.

"We had fitful nights." Madeline pursed her lips and shifted among the squabs.

"We all did," Tynley replied with a sigh.

"I understand you had a delightful night of it!" Barbara said with venom.

That fried Tynley to a crisp. That they knew Kendryck and she had spent the night in the same bed did not mean that there was any more reason to castigate the two. But she would not lower herself to share any of the details of what had been a glorious respite after the fright they had all experienced in the hall with his grandmother. Still and all, this nastiness, on top of the other ugly things these two said and did, would not go unremarked upon. Or, if they continued, unpunished.

"I am on my way to my wedding. I would like to think that a woman, even if she is a widow and somewhat of a stranger to you both, is entitled to serene companionship on her journey. I would hope, Madeline, you might extend me the courtesy you should have had at your own wedding."

The older woman caught herself up in outrage.

"I know not all they deprived you of when you came to this house as a bride, but I was not responsible for it. I will not pay for it. But I will ask for your kindness in my hour of felicity. And Barbara"—Tynley swung her attention to the condescending girl—"know now that I would certainly give you a joyful time in your coming months. Indeed, I would recommend it to his lordship. But he needs no recommendations, you see, because he plans to give you a commendable debut and a wedding worthy of a baron's sister." She lifted her chin, giving them the air and grace they understood—and lacked. "Unless you would like me to recommend less?"

The girl's brown eyes flashed with hatred. "You wouldn't."

"I am very efficient. When I return, I will take charge of the household. The accounts. The menus. The servants." Tynley brushed at her skirts that needed no refinement. "Ah, here is his lordship."

Kendryck appeared at the door, said a few words to Carter, and clapped his top hat on his head. Then, with a smile wreathing his face, he strode down the steps and nearly leapt into the cab.

She had not seen him look so happy in weeks. "What is it?" She took his hand.

"I have good news for all of us."

Madeline and Barbara glared at him, unimpressed.

"Gerard comes home. I had a letter from him this morning.

He was in Richmond when he wrote it. Yes, he did visit a friend on his way to see that boy Cramdon. They went riding, and he had a mishap."

"No!" Madeline put a hand to her throat.

"He broke his arm. Right arm. Twisted his left leg, too. The physician thought it might have broken, but sent him to bed with splints. He was in terrible pain."

"Poor boy!" Madeline was beside herself. "He must be horribly upset."

"And could not bear to lift a pen, I suppose." Barbara toyed with a smile.

"Broken bones are no joke," Kendryck said.

"I am so glad he has written," Tynley said, though she wondered why Gerard's friend could not have written to alleviate their concerns.

"Home alone, evidently. He and his friend. So they did not think to write sooner."

"Stupid," Barbara put in.

"Oh, don't be so peevish, Barbara." Her mother was having none of her sour words. "Gerard is alive and well."

"He says he may have an impediment, Madeline." This from Kendryck had the woman going white.

"How so?"

"He says he walks with a limp."

"Piffle! That will heal." Barbara patted her mother's hand. "It's Gerard. Really, Mama. He gets through all kinds of scrapes."

Kendryck squeezed Tynley's hand. "I am thrilled to have heard from him. I still have questions about why he did not write, and other things. But I am very pleased he is safe."

"Oh, so am I, Strade." Madeline had never looked so enthused. "When does he arrive home? When did he leave? I must go to him. Richmond is not far from London. I do long to go. I have not been in so long."

"Madeline," Kendryck said, "he comes home. Soon. If you went, you might miss him on the road."

"I'd like to go straight from Cardiff. After your wedding. I could catch a boat back to Dover." She was rhapsodizing. "Then up to London."

"Ma'am," said Tynley, thinking the woman daft to want to run after her son, "I do not recommend it this time of year. A boat on the waters around Penzance and eastward toward the Channel? No. My trip was not pleasant. Have you sailed before?"

"Oh, you just don't want to see me nurse my son!"

"Ma'am!" Tynley could not believe the vindictiveness of this woman.

"Please! Mama!" Barbara pleaded with her mother, while her eyes slid from Tynley to Kendryck. "Don't think of such a thing."

Kendryck shook his head at both of them. "Do as you wish, Madeline. Do go with her, Barbara. We could all have a fine respite from each other."

Tynley did all she could do not to yell at their coachman to stop and let the two women walk home. Fighting with herself, she cupped Kendryck's hand and prayed for a new level of forbearance.

He held her hand more tightly. "Nothing else matters now as much as the fact that we are getting married tomorrow morning."

She met his gaze and marveled at his resilience. "You are right. We are headed in the right direction."

Chapter Fifteen

THE FOUR OF them arrived at the inn just as Tynley saw that William and Samartine's coach circled into the courtyard. Kendryck offered his hand to Tynley as she alighted from the coach. She waited as he instructed his coachman to transfer Tynley's reticule and small trunk to the vicar's carriage. "She'll be spending the night with our friends," he told his man.

Tynley, eager to greet their guests, wound her arm through his and steered him from his two relatives. She wished him to focus on their future, not his family and their impertinence. "Forget them. This is the beginning of our new life together, Kendryck. They will enter into the spirit of things or not. They are the ones who will lose."

He regarded her with a look of gratitude. "I am in awe of your resilience."

"Thank you, sir. I have a wealth of it to spread around." She hoped that was true. Yet she felt the prickle of distaste and the question of how to shore her spirits up to survive Madeline and Barbara's onslaught. But these were her wedding festivities, and she was determined to make a show of her good intentions. Acting as if a feeling were true could often bring that emotion to life.

Kendryck took a breath and stepped with her toward William and Samartine Drummond. That couple's hired coach was idling in the courtyard. Directing that coach's groom to carry the luggage was another man.

"Good evening, Samartine, William. Tynley and I are very pleased you were free this evening to come to our little party."

"We would not miss it," Samartine told him, then leaned over to kiss Tynley on both cheeks. "Madame St. Claire sent your gown to the vicarage today. In fact, she sent four boxes. I was to open only one, your wedding gown. She sent me a note, as well as one for you. The one for you she told me to keep for you to see tonight when you return home with William and me. I opened my letter, and she recommended that I unpack the box to allow the gown to drape well. I did as she instructed, and oh my!" She gave Tynley a broad smile and lifted her shoulders in a typical little French sign of her approval of the gown. "It is *magnifique!*"

Tynley beamed. "I'm eager to see it."

"So am I," Kendryck said with a twinkle in his eye.

"Tomorrow, sir," Samartine chastised him with a grin. "That is soon enough!"

"My wife was exclaiming over it so," added William, "that I thought she and I would have to visit the dressmaker for a new gown and get married again ourselves."

His wife patted his hand. "What a fine idea, William."

"She is joking," he said with a wink.

"No, I am not! He tells me he was so nervous the day we wed, he does not recall our ceremony at all. I'd say we could do for renewal of our vows…with a new gown, too. What do you think, Tynley?"

Tynley gave Samartine a knowing eye. "Madame St. Claire will have ideas for you, too."

William rolled his eyes. "We are all in readiness for your stay with us, Tynley. Nothing like a bride in the house. Ah, now. Here is a gentleman I hope you remember, Kendryck."

"Leonard Haverford!" Kendryck reached out with both hands to grasp the man's shoulders. "I cannot believe it!"

The fellow was as blond as Kendryck was dark. He was also

as tall, as fit, and as ruggedly featured. His skin was bronzed by the sun, and his honey-colored hair was streaked white by it. If Tynley were a younger woman who was impressed only by looks, she would have found the fellow spellbinding.

The two men embraced and laughed. After their greetings, they spoke of having been at school together and being apart for decades.

"You went off to India, Kendryck," said Haverford, "while I was sent to Boston."

"The colonies!" Kendryck remarked. "I do remember. You went the same year I was sent to Calcutta. How does a British man fare in the new United States?"

"I experience no hardship now, although I was very careful whom I talked to and what I did a few years ago when Farmer George sent troops to us," Haverford said with disdain. "I recovered easily, though, and so did my business."

"Leonard runs a profitable tannery," Drummond informed them all.

"We have tanneries up the Charles River. We recently set up outposts for fur traders into New Brunswick and Ontario, and we do well."

"And how is it you are here in England and with William and Samartine?" Kendryck asked.

"Since I trade in dollars and pounds, my father suggested I come to London to make new friends with bankers here!" Haverford made a face. "You know how that is. One's father is not to be denied."

"I do indeed know that," Kendryck said with severity. "Are you in Wales to see to bankers here, too?"

"No. I am charged by my older brother to close the house in Cardiff before I sail on to London. All my family are moving to London. The house here is so old and in need of so many repairs, it is not worth it to repair it. Or so he says."

"That often happens here," said Drummond, "now that the war is over and London grows by leaps and bounds."

Kendryck stepped to one side as Madeline and Barbara came upon them, and after they had all reacquainted themselves, he began introductions to Haverford. "Allow me to introduce you both to an old school friend of mine. Let me amend that—a friend of Mr. Drummond's and mine. My stepmother, Mrs. Hollens, Mr. Leonard Haverford. And my sister, Miss Barbara Hollens, Mr. Haverford. A friend of mine from boarding school, home from America."

"How good of you to attend my brother's wedding, sir." Barbara had not let go of the man's hand. Her brown eyes did not part from sight of him, either.

Tynley had never witnessed such coquettishness from Barbara, and the view offered her a new perspective on the young woman's ability to change. She was interested in Mr. Haverford. That was no surprise, as any red-blooded girl of marriageable age would take to the handsome fellow. Tynley hoped Mr. Haverford did not keep a wife in Boston, or Barbara would be very disappointed.

The man's response showed that if he had a wife, he had completely forgotten about her. For he bent over Barbara's hand like a smitten courtier. "Miss Hollens." His baritone was reverent. "I am delighted to meet you."

"I heard you say something about being in business. Furs, was it?"

"Leather goods and furs. I began the tanning of leather goods when I first went to Boston in eighteen hundred."

"Goodness, sir!" Barbara truly was astonished. "You've been away from home for many years."

"I have." He appeared pained and yet proud to add, "I began it from nothing. Two thousand pounds was what my father gave me. I am a third son, you see, so I must make do by myself. Just like your brother did in India."

"You were young. Sixteen. Alone in a foreign land, and you made your business in a noble way, Leonard," Kendryck declared with admiration for his friend.

"As did you, I am certain, my friend."

To Haverford's statement, Kendryck opened his mouth to reply.

But Tynley tapped her fingers on his arm and smiled winningly at him. "I hate to interrupt." In Kendryck's praise, Tynley had heard his comparison to his own work. In years to come, she would find ways to help Kendryck correct his negative self-impression of much of his time in India. He was a noble man who had worked hard and long, seen the error of others' ways, and sought to pave a new way for others to value other cultures. "We should go in and greet our other guests. It is late, and I am certain many are here."

SHE WAS RIGHT.

While all of them stood talking outside, assembling inside were Kendryck's other two school friends and their wives, as well as Tynley's dear friend, who had taken a leave of absence from her play to attend the wedding. Kendryck could identify the lady as an actress the instant one gazed upon her.

Elspeth Taunton was a woman meant for the stage. Nearly as tall as Kendryck, she had the elegant carriage, high brow, and hollowed cheekbones that seized the glow from a thousand candles and defined her face in a million emotions. Tynley had told him that Elspeth had been a new sensation in London productions when Tynley first auditioned for a role. To a frightened, green girl, Elspeth had been kind, demanding, and motherly. The actress had been instructive not only about how to stand and walk to catch the light, but how to spellbind every member of the audience. After hours, she'd shielded Tynley from the men who preyed upon the innocents who sought a profession and protection, but tended to receive only manipulation and money in return.

"We are very happy you have come so far to be our guest, Miss Taunton." Kendryck attempted to be the perfect host for so renowned a lady.

"Tynley could have been a raving success, Lord Strade." Elspeth drank an ale and told Tynley's fiancé her version of the truth.

"Oh, Elspeth, really. I was not so talented."

"On the contrary, Lord Strade—she fell in love and submerged her own ambition to do it."

This surprised Kendryck, and he focused on his intended with a question in his eyes. "I have not heard you say this."

She shook her head. "There is more to the story."

"Indeed there is!" Elspeth had the rest ready, and appeared not at all deterred to state it. "You gave in and should not have. Tynley does not tell that abroad. She is too humble."

"I am too prudent," Tynley put in. "I have said this before. I gave up acting because all of the work was too much."

"Too much?" The woman cast a skeptical look Tynley's way, then took another draft of her ale. "Too much for whom? Eh? Know, my lord, Tynley had more talent in her little finger when she left than I have in mine." And at that, she raised her mug in toast to his intended.

Tynley swallowed hard.

He watched her and discovered the element that could rise to complicate his plan…and change their relationship. She had the force of character to support him, but did she really wish to? He hoped so, because now he wanted her. Wanted her gaiety and warmth. Her positive approach to life. All of which he so dearly admired…and badly needed to cultivate for himself. Could those needs balance each other? He was committed to her as a loving husband. And so he would devote himself to promoting that balance. He cared for her. Cared quite a bit. And he knew he could love her deeply. Beyond all his rules against entanglement, beyond his past disappointments and failures, he could love her. And he did. He did! He would commit and make their life together all that love could bring.

Resolved to love this precious woman who came to him with such belief in good outcomes and happy days, he took her hand in his and met Elspeth's assertion with one of his own. "I see in Tynley a strong woman who will succeed at whatever she sets her mind to."

"That," said the actress, "is true. Never forget it, sir."

THE WOMAN'S WARNING repeated in his head all through the dinner party. So as the party came to a natural close when the tables were cleared, it was clear to Kendryck that the guests looked weary. All had traveled to Cardiff in long or short distances, and it was time for Tynley and him to signal the end of the night.

Kendryck rose and thanked everyone for their kindness to attend. "You are most kind to honor Mrs. Wallingford and me with your presence."

Murmurs of respect and gaiety went round the cozy room. Many thanked Kendryck for his hospitality. Sitting next to each other, Haverford and Elspeth spoke as if they were long-lost friends. Across from Haverford at the circular table, Barbara wore a sad expression. It was the first time Kendryck had ever seen his half-sister with disappointment upon her visage. Was this so significant that Barbara would turn her attitude toward more positive notes?

Many of the guests rose in anticipation of removing up the stairs to their quarters for the night.

Kendryck and Tynley stood at the far door bidding them goodnight.

When the last few people were departing, Kendryck turned to her. "Will you come talk with me for a few minutes?"

"Of course. I was hoping for a chance to converse with you

before I left with William and Samartine."

"Good." He took her arm and led her down the stairs to the common room of the inn. The two main fires at either sides of the grand hall were blazing. Locals who frequented the inn took to singing in one corner, and a fiddler accompanied their renditions of shanties.

"Let's go over here," he suggested to her, and led her to a warm corner where no others took up the long, broad tables.

They sat next to each other, and he regarded her with a long, lingering look into her eyes.

"That dinner was wonderful," she told him as she reached for his hands. "I am so glad we did it. The guests enjoyed it. So did I."

"I'm happy to please you, my dear."

"I saw that you had fun, too. The arrival of your two old friends from school, but most especially of Mr. Haverford, made the evening special."

"As did Elspeth Taunton's presence for you."

Tynley got a faraway look in her eyes. "She attended my first wedding. My only friend who came. I will always remember that. She's been good to me."

He ventured to state what he had felt when the woman was so blatant in her remarks. "She embarrassed you by being so frank about your acting career."

True to Tynley's sterling character, she locked her gaze on his. "Not embarrassed, no. Dismayed. Her words did not convey the whole truth."

He grasped her hand. "Will you tell me all of it?"

She nodded.

"I feel it is vital to our understanding of each other. Am I correct in that?"

"You are." She licked her lips but did not look away. "I left acting not because Graham demanded it. Elspeth always concluded that was the reason, but it was not. I always corrected her when she implied it or told parts of the story abroad. But she never accepted my word for it. The truth is I left because I was with child."

He cupped her cheek. "Sweetheart."

She gulped, and tears flooded her large, lovely eyes. "I was pregnant and I was ill. Very ill. Nauseated and unable to eat. That's when I took up writing plays. I lay in bed and amused myself with stories I could portray on stage. Graham thought them silly little things. Not worth a penny. But I knew them to be good. Strong and useful for the stage. Elspeth has read them, and she knows their worth. She has tried over the years to get a theater manager to produce them." She winced. "No man will produce a play written by a female."

"Oh, my darling." He brushed tears from her cheeks. "So much and so many worked against you."

"Yes! How can people be so cruel to each other? Why? For sport? For power. That's what it is. And then I find you, my dear man. You, who see how barbarous men can be to other men. You, who fight for justice for those in India." She shot to her feet and wrung her hands in anguish. "You who see so much. Do you see what is true here at home? Here in Britain, women are not equal. We are as chattel. We cannot write. We cannot publish. We cannot vote or even have rights to our own children."

She shook back a sob. Then, with a look around at those who turned their heads to view her outburst, she ran to the door and threw it open.

He was on his feet. The wind was brisk, the night dark. A thousand stars sparkled in the black velvet sky as he followed her.

She had run to the entrance to the stables. Under the eaves, she huddled against the walls and shook with despair.

He removed his frock coat, wrapped it around her shoulders, and took her against him. His lips buried in her fragrant lavender hair, he crooned soothing words to her. "I understand. I do. I remember my mother saying the same things. Look at me."

She shook her head and burrowed into him.

He was not dissuaded, and spoke softly in her ear. "Listen to me. I have been focused too closely on prejudice and inequality on one group of people. You bring me to task. And rightly so, my darling. I should be fighting for all those who are prohibited, limited, denied, or driven from their rightful place on this earth."

She raised her ravished face to look at him and sniffed. "There are so many who have so much to contribute and who are so hurt."

"You first among them."

She swiped her tears away from one cheek.

He cradled her close and brushed her other cheek free. "You will be first in my heart."

"I would like that. But you wanted a friend, not a lo—"

He brought her infinitely closer. To avoid speaking of his deep affection for her, would he deny her and himself the joy of a perfect union? "Tomorrow when you are mine in the sight of God and man, you will come first with me. First to help. First to favor. First to make happy."

She regarded him with awe and a bit of shock. "You would do that? For me? Oh, Kendryck, you must not. You have a mission to complete, and I—"

"Tomorrow, you will be my wife. My life. To be first with me, is that not what you are worth? To yourself? And to me? I say it is so, my darling. I say it is so."

She surveyed him with reverence. "You are an extraordinary man."

He snorted. "Never."

"You are. You would fight against a company controlled by the most powerful people in the land. Men who are wealthy, titled, and well appointed. You would fight against an economic trend to dominate what goods are produced and at what price. Now you would add to that load, that burden, that task, one to save half of mankind?"

"For the betterment of all." He nodded and sought to soothe her with a smile.

She tipped her head. "Weeks ago you asked me if I would consider leaving you. If I could accept the conflict and the controversy of what you wish to do in the coming years."

"You did not leave me then."

"Nor will I ever."

He hugged her close. "Then it's a fine thing we do tomorrow to wed."

She kissed his cheek. "Very fine."

He drew her closer. Her lush figure filled his arms, and his mind was flooded with scintillating images of how he might have her…or rather, how they might have each other tomorrow at this time. "We fight together for others, and for each other, we win all that we desire."

"Tomorrow," she whispered as she rose on her toes to speak on his lips, "it is only you I desire."

He cupped her nape, feeling her chignon cascading over his fingers, her hair wild satin to his touch, her breasts flush to his chest. He took her mouth in a full claiming. He hungered for her, and he had held himself in check. He fantasized of her in his bed, naked and writhing and wanton—and he had chastised himself for his rapacious appetites.

She was tender. A widow who had lost a husband and a mother who had lost her son. But she deserved a kind lover, a respectful one, a man who took her slowly and reverently. Yet he had visions of sampling her, sipping from her skin, laving her nipples, tasting her belly, and sucking her plump lips into his mouth. He had nights when he wanted her beneath him in his bed or atop him in a chair. Her legs spread wide, her heat pressed to his, him inside her, and she—oh yes, she—panting for him. Never wishing to rise and leave him.

He kissed her and could not stop. He crushed her lips beneath his. She grabbed his shoulders and groaned, dragging him close. He sent his tongue inside the cavern of her mouth, and she mewled, then opened wider to take him in. He lifted her and whirled to place her against the wall of the stables. Her legs wrapped around his hips. If only they were naked, she'd be his.

And he'd be a damn fool to ravish her now, like this, in the cold night air against a paddock wall.

He'd spoil the trust they had built, diminish the principles and goals to which they had agreed. "Tomorrow we will consummate the vows and seal them with more than kisses."

She broke away with a cry. "I want you now. I do."

He dropped his head and pressed his lips to the bare, gossamer skin of her shoulder. "Heaven knows I would take you here. But you are more precious to me than this rough handling. I want you to marry a man of whom you can be proud."

"I have been from the day I met you."

He grinned, but set her away from him, though his blood burned in his veins to make her completely his. "Then we are two of a kind. Tomorrow, I marry a woman I am proud of."

Chapter Sixteen

THE NEXT MORNING, the sun blazed though the panes of the vicarage windows. In her bed last night, Tynley had nestled into the eiderdown and dreamt of her little son beckoning her into an enormous, colorful, flowering garden. She awoke with a start, smiling at the poignant memory of his chubby cherub's smile and his laughing invitation. He was as joyful as she today, and he wanted her to take this journey into a new life with a man she revered.

At once, she knew one thing to be true. Freddy would have loved Kendryck. Looked up to him, as he should. As he had with his own father.

She swirled to her side and pushed up to put her bare feet on the thick carpet. Samartine had prepared her room for her with all the attentions a bride would savor. She had stacked the large dress boxes from Madame St. Claire on the far window bench. The delicate pink paper boxes were tied with a wide ribbon of fuchsia, and she knew why. They contained items especially ordered for her by her groom—more than she had expected to be made. The modiste's note sent to the vicarage with Tynley's gowns had detailed the fabrics she used to make all the garments.

The muslin night rails in one box are made of the softest,
lightest fabric I have ever touched. Lord Strade told me he
purchased the lengths from Dacca weavers in the bazaars before

he left home. The fabrics were bought with his new wife in mind. Wear them, Lady Strade, in good health and happiness.

The two gowns in the second box are both day gowns, meant for you to celebrate your marvelous complexion. Woven by the weavers of Varanasi along the Ganges River in the north, says your husband, this fabric is created from threads woven by Mulberry silk worms. The weavers spin gold thread in patterns to complement the natural color threads of the silk in the gown.

The item in the third box, I leave for your husband to describe to you. These threads of silk are woven in a special ways to create the shiny charmeuse fabric. It flows over the hand like water.

Your husband requests that you not open these boxes until you reach your honeymoon destination.

It has been a pleasure to serve you. I hope I may have that honor again.

Madame St. Claire

Tempted as Tynley was to open the gifts, she folded up the notes and tucked them into her reticule. Taking her mind from the lure of them, she glanced about the bedroom. Fragrant sachets of orange and persimmon hung from the door handles. A large Delft porcelain basin stood at the side table, and a pitcher nearby was filled with washing water. Fluffy toweling sheets stood upon another side table. Her reticule, brought in last night by William's footman, lay open to her personal toilette items. Her lavender soap, her French body powder, her half corset, and the finest muslin shift she had chosen for today sat within, awaiting her. To the other side of the room stood her small trunk filled with two older day gowns, walking boots, and a pair of white satin slippers.

The last time she'd worn them had been to the premiere of one of Graham's plays. She'd brought them along here to her next wedding, thinking that it was her way to bring along her past and her first husband to bless her new life.

Then she turned to the garment meant for the moment when she truly began anew. She caught her breath at its beauty.

Her gown hung from a hanger across the broad beams of the cottage roof. She gazed at it in awe. Its beauty astonished her, the celestial blue-and-white-stripe satin sarsnet, trimmed at the hem with white satin. With a heart-shaped neckline, it was lower than a morning gown, but nonetheless modest. The sleeves were long and loose, with deep four-inch cuffs of Chantilly lace at the wrist. Madame St. Claire had ordered a tiny French bonnet to match it. The hat tied beneath the chin with glossy blue ribbons. Madame had delivered it to the vicarage late this morning. Wearing the gown and hat, Tynley would feel as if she were a young and virginal bride.

Though truly her thoughts were far from virginal. Last night, the urge to kiss her fiancé and take him to her fully had nearly overpowered her. While Kendryck had surprised her with his declarations of helping her in her desire to write plays, that had been only one impetus to show him her appreciation and desire for him. She had not sought any of that aid from him, and did not expect it, ever, to be so. But he gave his devotion freely, instantly, and she could be naught but grateful to him. Devoted to him as she had been before, she was now doubly so. She would be more than his willing bride today—she would be his enthusiastic one. Given her body's sensual response to him last night beneath the stars, she hungered to become his willing partner in their bed.

"Do go on, my girl," she chastised herself, and got busy with her ablutions. She would be perfect today. For him. For herself. For their mutual goals, ever would she devote herself.

Two hours later, she took the stairs down to the parlor. Those who had been at the inn for supper last night chatted together, waiting for her to appear. She greeted them, nodded, smiled, and searched the room for the one man she would always seek.

Kendryck stood apart, his gaze trained on the doorway to the hall. He beamed at her approach. At his welcome, at his eager joy to see her, her head swam. He was too delicious for her to comprehend. He wore an azure frock coat of brushed velvet. His waistcoat was a sky blue that matched his adoring eyes and the blue in her gown. A cravat of frothy cream framed his square jaw and contrasted with his swarthy skin and onyx-black hair. His trousers of fine black wool fit his long legs and lean hips like a second skin. This man was to be her husband, and her flesh tingled at the prospect that he was to hers in spirit—and soon in body.

"You are divine, my darling," he said to her beneath his breath. "The gown is nothing to your beauty."

"And your clothes nothing to your good looks, sir."

"Come." He arched a brow and tried by a shake of his head to live down the blush in his cheeks. "You are the moment I have lived for. Time to become Mrs. Hollens."

Within minutes, she was. Truly now, a wife once more in the murmurings of a few words.

"My best wishes." Barbara was one of the first to step up and congratulate her and Kendryck. "How does it feel to be married once more?"

"A thrill. An honor," Tynley told the young woman. She gazed at Barbara, who had a question upon her lips. "What is it?"

"You do look different."

"Do I?" A hand flew to her cheek.

"As if you are transformed." Barbara seemed puzzled and shook her head, even as she smiled with a glint in her eyes. "Are you?"

"I am very happy, Barbara." Though Tynley sought other

words to answer her, she was astonished that the girl seemed to care about her, or that she would even remark on such a transformation.

Kendryck wrapped his arm around Tynley's waist and drew her near to him. The warmth of his hip against her sent shivers through her veins. "She looks like a bride. New and pleased. My wife and my baroness."

"I meant…" Barbara drifted in her thoughts a moment. "You care for each other a lot, don't you?"

Tynley gazed at Kendryck, and a realization had them both grinning at each other. "We do," they said in unison.

"I want the same for myself," she admitted to them.

"It is possible to find a true mate, Barbara," Tynley told her, and regarded her husband once more with a reverence she reveled in.

"If one is careful and honest," Kendryck continued as he looked deeply into Tynley's eyes, "you can be very happy."

Barbara tried to smile but failed as Haverford and Elspeth came forward to congratulate the two. "Excuse me, please," she said before she left.

A footman approached with a tray of white wine.

Kendryck took two glasses and gave one to Tynley, just as his friend and hers did the same. The four shared a toast and felicitations.

"I think we will speak with the other guests quickly, wife," he told her at length, and excused them from discussion with Elspeth and Haverford.

She hugged Kendryck's arm. "I am eager to be off."

"My sentiments exactly."

THEIR TRIP TO Kendryck's mystery honeymoon site, he told her as they departed the vicarage, would take perhaps only twenty minutes. He had hired a carriage through the auspices of the owner of the inn. The Strade family coachman and groom he had ordered to remain in Cardiff at the inn, to take Madeline and Barbara home to the Rambles the next morning. Madeline had given up her idea to go to Richmond, but would go home, she told them, to await Gerard's return.

"Both ladies will be so pleased you allowed them the family coach," she praised Kendryck as they climbed into the sumptuous gold-and-black lacquered coach he had hired for them alone. The cheerful sun had climbed overhead to noon, and the wind of last night had died. She was on her way to bliss in a comfortable conveyance with a man she yearned to enjoy. "And where in the world did the owner of the inn find such a well-appointed coach to hire?"

"In Cardiff, there are public stables where many are now selling their carriages."

She settled into the worn but clean and comfortable leather-upholstered squabs and sighed in happiness. "This is grand. Why are people selling their carriages? Can they not afford the upkeep?"

"I would gather, yes." He took his place beside her and helped her remove her winter coat. The bricks in the floor had heated it to a sweet temperature, and outer garments were definitely not necessary. "I am not privileged to know the details. I have few friends here in Wales, or even in England. But I specified I wanted a comfortable ride for you and me. And here we have it!"

His first words struck her as sad, but he had come around to a happier note at the end. She took his hand, and he drew her close into his embrace as the coachman snapped the reins and drove away from the vicarage.

She settled her head against her husband's shoulder, but then shot up and took the pins from her little toque. She liked her new little hat that matched her wedding gown. This would be one more to replace the one Kendryck disliked so much.

"I like this hat better than that old teal thing," he told her. "But I am glad you have taken it off."

"Why is that?" She was ready to ignore their problems and have fun with him.

He sank his fingers in her coif and kissed the tip of her nose. "I love your wild red hair, my darling."

"Thank you." She snuggled up to him once more, and, toying with the buttons on his waistcoat, she counted his rapid heartbeat. Hers had its own tattoo. She lifted her face to the man she had married and admired his handsomeness. "I had a lovely time at our wedding."

"Hmm." He arched his dark brows in a sly manner. "Would you do it again?"

"For the fun? With you? Of course, sir!"

He ran his knuckles across the arch of her cheek. "Have many men wished to wed you?"

"Ahh. I was an actress. Many thought I was fair game for their dalliances. Only one man wished to wed me. And I married him. Happily. Now I have been fortunate enough to do that a second time with a man who also wished to wed me. I am, Kendryck, very happy."

"I promise to be a kind and loving husband."

She ran her hand over his strong jaw up his cheek, now rough from his growth of beard from the morning. "I see it in you."

"Your trust in your insight is remarkable."

She pressed her lips to his. "I feel it in your kiss."

"But just now, *you* kissed *me*."

She pressed her thighs together, stunned by her need of him, dying for his hands on her. "Then kiss me, husband, and let me feel the power of your touch."

He shot a hand into her hair, and, as if on cue, it all fell down around her shoulders. He paused in surprise. "Did you not do your hair up tightly just so that curtain of red might easily be mine to have and to hold?"

"There," she crooned to him. "Proof you know me so well

already."

He brought her up to him, and upon her mouth he whispered, "I adore you."

"How much?" she taunted him.

He groaned. "More each moment." And then he took her. Took her mouth in deep kisses. Took her breath in irresistible assaults on her mouth. Took her imagination as his tongue parried with hers in a dance of temptation. "You are so willing."

"You are so tantalizing."

He kissed her once, then twice so fiercely that she thought she'd die of ravishment—and love it.

He drew back. "We must not do this here."

"Why not?" she asked him, forlorn and naughty as a child deprived of sweets. "I have wanted you forever."

At that, he quietly cursed, scooped her up from the seat, and positioned her on his lap.

"Oh, sir. If you wish us celibate, this will do us no good." She chuckled and rubbed her nose against his.

"You think not?" He cocked a brow at her.

"I know not. You—"

He anchored his hand behind her head and held her there while he claimed her lips with the tender fury of his desire. His mouth was firm. His lips parting hers. His tongue searching the cavern of her body with an insistent probe that had her grabbing for the silk of his hair. Then slowly, as he gave her drugging kisses, he sank his fingers into the gape of her décolleté of her wedding gown. His fingers tickled and stroked. At first near her throat, then lower, across the swell of her breasts. Finally, inside, between them, where her heart beat madly and her nipples beaded to diamonds.

He put his two hands to her cheeks. "I told myself I would not take you like a villain."

"Hmm," she said as she considered that with a tip of her head this way and that. Then she pulled at the end of his beautifully tied cravat and said, "You aren't."

He took her by the shoulders. "Not against the stables and not in this carriage. We must be in a bed."

"I do agree." She sank to lick the skin of his corded neck. "But one must have a few bites of bliss before the main course." She undid the button of his soft linen shirt and kissed the hollow of his throat. "Otherwise, one's appetite is not prepared."

He laughed, he groaned, then he pressed her flush to his chest. "You should have told me you were a tease."

She rolled her eyes. "Why? Isn't this more fun?"

He hooted. His grip on her was mighty and seductive. "What should I know, my darling?"

"About…?"

"Making love to you."

She bent to his mouth and licked his bottom lip. "That I will be as needy as you."

"Thank God."

"That I will want all of you as mine."

"I rejoice at it. And? Anything else?"

"That I am yours completely, and you may have me at your will," she whispered, and took one of his fingers and nipped the end, "as long as I may have you at mine."

Chapter Seventeen

"WHAT IS THIS place?" Tynley asked her husband as the coachman brought their carriage to a stop. The slanting rays of brilliant winter sun cast the white and flint stone of a charming cottage in shades of gold. The roof was thatched like those described in children's fairytales, and Tynley felt the enchantment of the place and time fall over her like a fable full of romance. She took his hand. "How did you find it?"

"'Tis my grandmother's cottage, inherited from her mother. Old and graceful, I thought it a good choice for our first days together. I employed one of my mother's former retainers who lives in Cardiff to air it out and prepare it for us this morning." His smile upon her and upon the frontage of the peaceful little place was one of utter contentment.

She followed his line of vision.

The aged, white-haired coachman set down one small trunk on the small front stoop with a grunt. Then he fumbled with the large, old iron key that Kendryck had placed in his hand a minute ago.

"I have visited here often as a child," Kendryck said, "twice before I left for India and once as I returned home to the Rambles in October. The beach is not far."

"I can hear it." She closed her eyes, listening to the gentle rush of waves across the sands. "I can smell the salty winds."

"You like it all?"

"I do. Very much."

"I'm glad." He did a once-over of the cottage with a look of remembrance on his face. "I always felt great peace here."

The coachman trudged back to gather more of their luggage, but Tynley did not care that the man would see her bestow on her husband a kiss on his lips. "It is a perfect choice for us."

He caught her against him. "For you, perfection is something I will always attempt to find. Come inside and check my skill at that."

She brushed her lips over his. "I know how superb your skills are already."

"No." His sky-blue eyes went dark with intent. His lips firmed. His voice grew gruff. "Not yet, you don't."

"Ah, but I've read Madame St. Claire's notes on the contents of my gifts from you."

"You opened them?"

She shook her head. "You wanted to be present. I would never deprive you of a thing you wanted."

He narrowed his gaze on her. "You wait not a moment to begin our real honeymoon, do you?"

"Should I?" she whispered, her body pulsing with need of him now that they were minutes away from being totally alone.

"No, by God!" He bent and, in one swoop, lifted her into his arms, then strode toward the front door. "Love does not wait patiently."

HIS WIFE CONSTANTLY surprised him. In his embrace, she was a laughing, affectionate treasure, her arm around his shoulder and her kisses decorating his cheek. Would that he could make her this happy always.

As he crossed the threshold, he was loath to let her go. So he stood with her in his arms and made a circle of the little gathering room. His heart filled with the serenity that always came to him here, and in his wife's appreciative gaze about the room, he saw the same tranquility suffuse her.

The crusty old coachman appeared at the door. "My lord, I have one more trip to bring in the lady's garment boxes. Is there anything else I can bring you or do for you?"

"No, Mr. Simmons. You have been very kind."

He looked confused. "But you…you have no servant to help you, sir."

Kendryck smiled down at his wife's knowing look. "We are well, Mr. Simmons. Quite capable of unloading the trunks and boxes."

"Food, sir?"

"Already provided," he said as he watched his wife arch a brow and nod.

"Water?"

"Done also. My thanks to you for your services, Mr. Simmons."

"Right you are, then. I bid you good day, sir."

"Good day to you," Kendryck said as Simmons took one last look around the room. As he had instructed his mother's man, the cottage had been dusted and swept, and goodly fire lit in the fireplace. He'd even put a kettle on the hook to heat. "Be hale and hearty, Mr. Simmons."

"Aye, sir. You and the missus too, sir." The kindly fellow tipped his cap and shut the door against the world.

Tynley snuggled closer into the crook of Kendryck's chin. "I would ask you to put me down. But I like this chivalry of yours."

"I like your cuddles, madam. But I do fear my back will not sustain the weight."

"Oh, pooh!" she shot back, chuckling. "I am not heavy."

He stared at her for a long minute, his heart swelling with pride and joy in her. "No. But the truth is, my darling, once I let you go from me, I will yearn to have you back."

"Have me in all other ways," she said upon his lips. "Have me before I die of wanting you."

"Don't die, my sweet. There is so much between us that needs expression, it will take decades to articulate it all."

She pouted, feigning a coyness she never possessed. "I am not patient, Kendryck."

He hooted. Then he set her on her feet and hauled her close as two could ever be. "Nor I. Not any longer."

He brought her up into his embrace one more time and kissed the breath from her. He broke away with a rush and threw back his head. "I know how to make love to a woman and make her cry and beg and plead." He set his jaw and gazed into her mellow eyes. "But, my darling, I fear I may gobble you up and give you naught this first time."

She put a hand to his chest and pushed herself away. "Then come undo me, my darling, button by button, string by string. And I shall do the same so slowly, you will think it all a dream."

She whirled around and presented him with her back. Covered buttons down her the back of her wedding dress had him praying for deliverance. He stepped forward and undid the tiny things in frustrating little jerks of his fingers. But soon, the sarsnet gaped and he brushed the fabric from her shoulders.

Her skin was perfection. Her hair, which had fallen from her pins in the carriage, dipped down the hollow of her spine and spread like a dark red waterfall over the points of her shoulders. He brushed it over her arms and let it drape down to her breasts. The gown swished to the floor and puddled around her. With a hand to her forearm, he helped her step from the circle of fabric. Then before him was the hated corset. Today, she wore only a half. Her foresight to do that brought forth a smile—and a hesitation to his fingers. Slow seduction was the best way to lure a woman. And he knew not how to quell the raging need inside him, save to go at the laces with a forced deliberation.

As if she perceived his torment, she stepped backward into his outstretched hands. She trusted him, and he rejoiced. He would not fail her.

He found some grace about this process of ridding her of her next layer, and to his shock, the corset fell away. She caught it and dropped it to one side to a chair.

He had only to work on the translucent muslin petticoat tied at her waist. That fell so easily, so quickly, that he caught his breath. Now all that remained to keep him from revealing all she was for him was her shift.

He took hold of the thing that hung on her shoulders and did her no justice. For he could detect that, beneath the fine diaphanous muslin, she was shapely. He had known it. Of course he had. She had been in his embrace. More than once, she had pressed the wealth of her breasts to his chest. But this lithe flesh beneath his fingertips, this supple movement of her muscles as he touched her—this showed him how feminine she truly was. Not just a female draped in yards of shapeless cloth, but a woman with a delicately curved back, graceful arms, a trim waist and hips that flared to give her drama, form, and the ability to hold a child, and hold a man within her generous flesh.

She turned her head to one side, her gaze in search, he surmised, of his hands, which had paused in their unveiling of her charms. He cupped the points of her shoulders and moved forward to mold himself to her back and her derriere. Her feminine physique set his blood on fire. She dropped her head against his chest and took his hands to lead them to the small bits of cloth that held up her shift. With infinitely slow movements, she led him to slide the straps from her shoulders and let the thing drop.

His eyes slammed closed. She was all lissome, warm woman in his arms. His wife who sighed at the feel of him. Who settled her curves and hollows into the planes and valleys of his own.

Then, all at once, she was gone.

He blinked. She faced him, a step away, her lips sulky, her green eyes pleading with him. "Look at me."

Oh, God. He needed no invitation. He could not look away.

She was stunning. A Venus. A confection of flawless skin, large, round, dark pink nipples, heavy breasts, a gently rounded tummy, and hips that flared and beckoned. Her thighs were trim, her legs long, her clockwork stockings so white and held up by a damn delicious-looking pink bow around her lower thigh. Her shoes were little slippers. Her feet were long and shapely. How many could say their feet were elegant and appealing to their lover?

She could. He'd tell her all of her that drew him. All that called to him like a moth to flame. Bee to honey. Kendryck to the raving beauty who was his wife.

She smiled, no trace of modesty to deny that she liked that he saw her and reveled in her. He did not need a shy wife. Did not wish to pamper a reticent woman. He'd had that once. A different time and place and need. Now he wanted this woman, this adventure, this passion, this delight in the mingling of bodies and the thrill of passion.

She gave him a sultry wink. "May I remove your clothes now?"

He spread out his arms. "Do as you will." Heaven knew, his body did as it wished. Fully erect and ready to sink into all her beauty, his cock pounded with need of her. "I pray for patience."

She strolled toward him, her legs approaching him in smooth strokes, her hips moving in rhythm, her breasts swaying, her arms reaching for him. Her subtle lavender scent washing over him as she pressed her hands to the edges of his frock coat and slid off it off. As reward or punishment, he knew not which, she trailed the tip of her nose along his jaw and nipped at the corner. "Now your waistcoat."

She undid it and took it away. She'd undone his cravat in the carriage, but now, she slid it away, and the slither of the cotton sent his cock into spasms. If she did not hurry, he'd be done and she'd be waiting for long minutes.

In sharp tugs, she yanked at his shirt tails and moaned at their stubbornness. He grasped her hands and led her to the buttons of his flies. And there she made quick work of the garment that might give her the most satisfaction, were it gone.

His flies gaped. Cool air had him sucking in his breath. She noted it with a smile, and instead of whisking away his trousers, she cupped him.

Once more, he shut his eyes. This heat, this affection, this advance, was beyond what he had ever known. His first wife was a cloistered girl who knew how men's bodies joined with women's, but she had been taught to wait for the man's initiatives in all things.

This new wife of his was a different woman of experience and desires. He applauded her actions. In truth, he nearly sank to his knees in gratitude at her assertiveness. She was who she was. Bold and brave and now, with the fulfillment this night, she would be his. And by her claim, he would be hers.

She had paused with her hand upon his manhood, her head upon his naked shoulder. "Shall I continue?" she asked in a small and tender voice.

"Please." He took her chin and raised her face to his. "I would show you who I am, as you have done me the honor."

Her acceptance stood broadly in her generous smile. "Oh, Kendryck. We will be so good together."

"We will, my darling," he said, "as soon as you let go of my personals and take off the rest of my clothes."

As if she'd been burned, she let go of his cock and brushed at the fabric of his trousers. In a second, he stepped from his trousers, his shoes, and slipped off his small clothes himself.

"Your socks, sir." She waggled a finger at them.

"Come to bed, pet. Take them off me there." He led her around the large chimney and raging fireplace to the other large room of the cottage. There, the big, broad feather bed he remembered awaited them. "I plan to leave your socks on, however."

"And why is that?" she asked, clearly into his game now.

"I like them on you. And I have plans to kiss them away."

She giggled. "I want to see that!"

"You will!" He picked her up and threw her into the mound of quilts upon the bed.

"Oof! This is delicious!"

He jumped in beside her. Like children, they hit the feathered coverlet and mattress a few times. The old stuffed quilts bounced around their bodies.

He stilled at the view of her full breasts bouncing. "Oh my," he said in reverence, and reached for her to pull her beneath him. "I may die tonight loving you, my wife."

"Don't. Please don't." She froze and stared at him. "I need you tonight and always."

He could not take his gaze from her lips.

She slid down flat to the bed and reached up to bring one of his hands to cover the hot curve of one large, lovely breast. "Come have me, my darling. I need you."

Chapter Eighteen

"YOU ARE QUITE the loveliest creature, Lady Strade."

His gruff words were as much aphrodisiac as his big, broad hand upon her waist. She knew he was being gallant, but to hear him declare it with such charming words thrilled her to her bones. "I am glad that you think me so, my lord." She rubbed her legs along the length of his, and he settled between her thighs and planted little kisses along her chin. "Would that you always think highly of me. I will work for that."

"No work required, I do believe. You are already formed, madam." He lifted up and rolled to support himself on one arm as he let his eyes roam over her length. "And beautifully so."

His gaze set her aquiver. "I want your hands on me," she said before her desire for his claim would rob her of her voice.

"Like this?" he asked so faintly that she hardly registered the bass sound. But he sent his open palm down the length of her throat to the hollow between her breasts and rested it there.

She arched up. "More," she said as she stared at him.

His eyes reflected the flames of the fire behind the grate as he held her enraptured and covered one breast with his hot hand.

"That," she sighed.

"And this," he said as he bent, took her areola in his mouth, and licked her tender skin with his rough, demanding tongue.

She bucked higher. "Again," she demanded.

"All you want," he said, and sucked her into the cavern of his mouth with a force that had her mewling.

She grabbed at his back. Her nails sank into his brawny muscles and claimed him like a jungle cat.

He gave a laugh, but moved ever so slowly to take her other breast. At his wicked leisure, he laved her, nipped her, and, at long last, sucked her nipple inside the hot, moist depths of his mouth.

Between them, against her thighs, she felt the probe of his desire. She whimpered and, needily, clamped her legs together.

But he told her, "No," and spread her legs wider with his own.

She clasped him more tightly to her.

He slid down her body, skin to skin, silk to satin, kissing as he went. Her stomach, her belly button, both arcs of her hips, the line above her nether hair. With one hand beneath her derriere, he lifted her most intimate part to his mouth, and with the other hand, he parted her lips and sank inside to lick her to a hot, high keen.

She shook in his arms, a quaking mass of need and joy and hunger for more of the same.

But he lowered her to the mattress, a wicked gleam on his face. "Like that, eh?"

"Yes. And I am mad for more," she confessed.

His blue eyes seemed to glaze. But he sank two fingers inside her and, for a long, exquisite moment, played there. "Made for more, I am thrilled to say."

She swallowed, crazed with his caresses. "My darling man, if you do not do this soon, I come without you."

"Well, then, Mrs. Hollens, I think it's time we consummated this union." He hauled her to him, lifting her legs beneath her knees and pushing wide her thighs. "Lovely lady," he murmured as he sank inside her, "this is only the beginning of what we are together."

He slid inside her. One grand move that filled her completely.

One wild claim that took her breath and seized her imagination and shook her to the core of her heart.

SHE AWAKENED TO find Kendryck gone. The sounds of utensils clanking on the far side of the fireplace assured her that he was busy at some task. She rose and took a quilt to wrap around her for modesty that was irrelevant but wise in the November air.

He had donned his breeches and tugged his shirt over his head, then tucked it in. But his lustrous hair was mussed, and his ruddy cheeks were even more so with his nearness to the fire.

"I hope you're making us a warm drink."

He looked up at her, a grin of devilish delight spreading wide his lips. "A toddy. Rum and sugar and a sprig of licorice. Come over here and keep me company." He waved a spoon at the quilt around her torso. "No need for that. I've built up the fire, and if you think you are still cold, tell me. I can warm you up."

She strolled in front of him, deliberately giving him one of her best stage struts. She flounced onto the settee before the very fine fire and watched him work. "I will give you leeway to warm me later. I am more hungry and thirsty at the moment."

"Huh." He put one hand on his lean hip, feigning a frown. "Should I be concerned you were not satisfied?"

She toyed with a curl at the end of her hair. Her act of nonchalance was a poor one, but she teased him with it. "If you are, sir, you must have been blind and deaf to my reactions to your every breath."

He went quite still. "Not so, my darling. My breath was gone the moment I placed my hands on your sweet skin."

"I invite you to do it again, my lord, but first do give me that toddy you talk of."

He made up his concoction and handed her an earthen mug filled with fragrant liquid.

"This smells—and tastes—marvelous."

"Did you know that the word *toddy* is really from a Marathi word? They live in the western part of the territory. Such a drink is one many use to warm themselves in bad weather."

She took another sip. "You know so much of the culture. I have much to learn from you."

"I'm thrilled you are willing."

"Of course I am. Who you are, I want to know. What you know, I want to learn. What you wish to share with others, so too do I." She watched his face lighten as she spoke, and she was honored she could do that.

"You sound rather like that portion in the Bible about Ruth and Naomi," he said as he came to sit beside her. "'For whither thou goest, I will go; and where thou lodgest, I will lodge: thy people shall be my people—'"

"And your cause, mine." She ran her fingers through the shock of black silk hair at his temple. "My heart, yours."

He caught her hand and brought it to his mouth to kiss her fingers. "I told myself when I wrote my advertisement for a wife that I would not love again. That I wanted only a friend, a companion. I had learned in India that I like having a wife. A confidante, a person who is loyal to me, and I to her. I confess, my darling Tynley, that you are much, much more to me than a friend."

"I thought so," she said with compassion for how he had loved and lost. He was not prepared to declare such a profound emotion as love for her, but she could wait. She could. She pushed the challenge away and told him what she knew to be true. "When I answered your advert, I did not seek more than a friend, either. I had had a man I loved and known the value of it. I hoped that in time, with a man I admired, I could grow to care for him in many ways, and that he might do me the same honor. I married you, Kendryck, with that hope. I know you held the same one."

He drew her near. "I am overjoyed you are as free with me as you are. Your acceptance of me as your mate is an honor."

She swallowed the lump in her throat at his praise. "I feel the same."

"I enjoy the physical mating of man to woman."

With him today, she had found ecstasy she had never before enjoyed. She bit her lip, took a sip of her drink, then put it aside. "You may have seen that I relish it with you, too. I had a fond relationship with my husband, but he was not...as eager. Or..." She glanced away, then returned to face her new husband, who gratified her sexually more than was proper for a lady to say. "Or as inventive."

Kendryck took her in his arms and brought her up onto his lap. Like his move in the carriage coming here, it was a provocative act, sensual and seductive as not much else in her life had been before she met him. She'd fallen in love with her husband with kisses as preludes to more kisses. The physicality of what she had done today with Kendryck was eternities away from the nigh-unto-Puritan courting with which her first husband had wooed her. This melding of bodies in new and profound ways was ambrosia to her. Much more of this headiness and she could say she loved her new husband. Loved him quite dearly.

She froze. It was only for a moment. Yet she could see Kendryck took her stillness as modesty or surprise. But the emotion that rolled through her was that very one she had told herself she need not seek, need not acquire, need not desire in this second marriage. Just as he had not.

He swept her hair back, combing his fingers into the wealth on either side of her head and bringing her lips to his. In the move, her quilt slipped down, down, down, and she was naked before him. He gazed down at her breasts and her belly and sucked in a breath. "This freedom between a husband and wife, my darling, is a treasure to be honored and cultivated."

He lifted a breast and bent to take the tip between his lips.

She threw back her head to revel in his claim of her.

"Sweetheart," he crooned in a mellow bass voice, "I love that you can be natural with me. The teachings of our culture do not condone it. But I learned that this can be a welcome thing in a marriage." He held her breast in his hand and rubbed his thumb over her nipple.

She grew hard and hot and needy with his caress. "Do that more and we will not eat or drink for a long time."

"How long?" he asked her in a whisper.

At once she knew that was an invitation to once more have the man she married. "Hours."

He looked as though she had given him the most marvelous gift. Wrapping his arms around her waist, he stood with her, and she instinctively circled her legs around his waist.

"Where are we going?" She was laughing as he headed not for their bed but the nearest wall.

"Here," he said as he nipped her ear and put her back to the hard surface. "I cannot make it to the bed. I want you now, here. All of you."

Beneath her derriere, she felt him let down his flies, take his cock in hand, and position her above him.

Her mouth fell open as he thrust inside her, and in sure, strong strokes took her once more to a star-filled summit where they both cried out in perfect harmony.

TYNLEY SLEPT, EXHAUSTED. Despite what she would claim, Kendryck recognized that his wife needed a good rest. As for himself, he swept a hand through his hair and ignored the urge to wake her. She needed her sleep. He needed nourishment.

After tucking the quilts up to her chin, he rose from their bed. He picked up his clothes and dressed. In the main gathering room, he picked up his wife's clothes and draped her gown over a chair, then folded her petticoat and shift. He gazed at her half corset and wished he could throw it away. Corsets only bound a woman up, often very uncomfortably too. This one had not done justice to the generous curves of his enthralling wife. He sighed and turned away from the contraption's destruction. He had to get some sustenance!

He ambled to the small corner that served as the kitchen area. He had asked a friend who lived nearby to provide supplies for them this morning. The first item he found was a large, covered pitcher of water. He poured out a mug full and drank, then went to look for the jugs of water he had asked for. On the step of the back door stood four large jugs filled with clear water. He lugged one inside and carried it to the fireplace. There, a large pot stood empty. He filled it, hung it on the iron hook, and swung it over the flames. Tynley would want a bath, and he would happily give it to her. Himself afterward, as well.

But while he waited for the water to heat, he opened a larder cabinet to find a few supplies he had also requested. He took out a crock filled to the brim with a smoked ham. Another covered dish had a mash of potatoes and onions. In a smaller pot was a stew of squashes. The last two were still warm from the morning. So he dished himself a plate, found a serviette in the cabinet, then a set of knife and fork, and sat down at the small table in the gathering room to consider his very good fortune.

The sun was just setting, and the slanting rays of dusk gave just enough light through the windows of the cozy room. He ate, appreciating the delicacy of the food his old retainer had provided. Tynley would like it, too.

A surge of gratitude flooded him. He smiled to himself and stilled. He was not used to that. After the problems with his superiors dealing with their dislike of his Indian wife and his arguments with them, he had lost his belief in the goodness of mankind. Worse, he'd no longer thought that all things came right for those who were kind and dedicated, or even honorable in their dealings with others.

But from the first minutes he spent with Tynley, he'd begun to shed that disillusionment. He paused, his fork to his mouth, unable to recall moments or words that had caused that. Yet her attitudes toward others—his family, most of all—had changed him.

His family had not changed. He blew out an exasperated breath and frowned. Madeline had not changed. She was as silent, as curt and devastating, as a sharpshooter. That had always been her nature. It had set him against her when he was a child. In the past months, he had tried to find reasons to like her. He had failed. She was as self-centered as ever.

And Barbara? What of her? She followed the example of her mother. A sad choice for a young woman with little to recommend her other than her looks and a sound education. Still, Kendryck had noticed a difference in the past two days. Had she became more of a coquette in Haverford's presence? Was she jealous of the actress's appeal to Haverford? Heaven knew, Barbara would not attract many men with her condescending attitude. If she wished to marry a man she could live with in harmony, she might temper her lofty nature and become more congenial.

Kendryck sighed. Was that even possible?

Certainly, Gerard had not changed. Leaving home without notice, disappearing for weeks, his brother had been as irresponsible as ever. Meanwhile, Kendryck questioned if the young man had been the one to break into the old Tudor house and take the diamonds. Swallowing hard on the last bite of his supper, Kendryck hoped he'd be able to ascertain if Gerard was guilty of that theft.

But the boy is wily. If I ask him, he can deny it. I can ask all I want. What I need is some proof of someone's culpability!

He'd sat he knew not how long, pondering that, when it was clear to him the sun had fled with the day, and the cottage lay in golden shadows cast by the flames of the fire. He should get more wood from the shed and check the temperature of the water in the pot on the hook. He wanted to bathe his wife, see her skin glow pink with the heat of the water and the touch of his hand.

His gaze fell over the three large dressmaker's boxes that stood on a stool near the front door. They were pink, tied in fuchsia ribbon, delectable-looking packages for his luscious wife.

"Good evening." She appeared, marvelously tousled and sleepy-eyed, at the corner of the chimney. She wore her quilt once more, only her sweet skin beneath. She strolled toward him, leisurely licking her lips. She focused on him with seduction in the toss of her hair and the swivel of her hips. Then she sat down next to him and snuggled close, one arm going around his middle, her gaze on his empty plate. "You've eaten, I see. What is there?"

"Sliced ham. A potato and onion mash. Squash too. No, no!" He caught her hand and urged her to remain where she was. "I will wait on you. You must be starving."

"Thank you. Yes, I would love a serving of each. Tea, too, I think, if that kettle has hot water."

"It does. I can even offer you a warm bath with hot water from that larger pot."

"That sounds wonderful. All of it. I will eat first, bathe later," she told him as he reached the larder and began to carve the ham for her. "It is lovely and warm here. Your friend did a good job of preparing for us."

"He did."

"He used to work for your family."

Kendryck caught the question in her voice. He continued his preparation of her dinner as he told her about the man. "Johnson is his name. Robert Johnson. Good man. Former underbutler at the house. He worked for my mother. Came with her to the Rambles and left three years after I went off to India. He told me all this when I visited with him here in south Cardiff in October. Mr. Johnson and Madeline did not get on. Never had. He came here to work and came without a reference. Sadly."

"How did you know that, and how did you find him?"

"William told me. Johnson had gone to William for a reference when Madeline refused. William was here at the same vicarage, as curate, then. For a year, he worked for William while

William helped Robert find employment. He left, but they kept in touch. Mr. Johnson and his wife and family are parishioners of William's."

He came over and handed Tynley her plate.

"William is a very good friend to you," she said as she speared a bit of sliced ham. "He has been for many years, even though you two were separated by thousands of miles. That is a comforting feeling, and rare to have a friend so dear."

"Over the years, William wrote to me about many things of which I would have no knowledge, nor would I have ever been able to help." He paused to remember his vibrant, loving sister. "He was very friendly with my sister Charlotte. Went to call in the Rambles when she wrote to tell him she was ill. He kept me appraised of her condition. For that, I am indebted to him once, and for other felicities, many times over."

"Samartine and he were very kind to invite me to spend last night with them. I will write them my thanks for the night."

"It was good of them to take Madame St. Claire's work for you." He waggled his brows. "Wouldn't you like to open your presents?"

"A few more bites of ham, sir!" She licked the corner of her mouth. "And tea! Then the boxes!"

SHE WIPED HER mouth with her serviette and pointed to her shift that he had folded and placed on one chair. "Hand me that, would you, please? A lady should not prance about her salon in her altogether."

He shrugged. "Oh, I don't know. I rather like the idea."

She cast him a dubious but playful look. The scoundrel.

He got to his feet with a theatrical sigh and retrieved the thing. He shook it out and came before her. "Stand up and raise your arms."

Teasing him, she grinned and did as he asked, allowing the quilt to slither to the floor.

"I hate to cover you up."

She arched daring brows. "Not for long. Then you can remove this again."

He caught her around her naked waist and pressed her against him. "I hold you to it."

She lifted her gaze to the beams. "Indeed, you do so quite well."

He kissed her and left her swaying, wanting him despite decency and all else that might ever keep her from him.

He examined the boxes. "Which one will you have?"

"They all appear to be the same, though I understand from Madame St. Claire's note that they are not. Each holds different treasures. So you must provide the details on whatever I reveal."

His face took on that devilish look of expectation. "I do so promise, my dear. Which one?" He waggled a finger at the pile of pretty pink and fuchsia.

"The middle one." It was the biggest, and she assumed the two gowns would be inside.

He brought it to her.

She undid the ribbon and lifted the flimsy paper of the lid, then rifled through the tissue paper. Inside lay an eye-popping emerald silk gown with golden trim at the bodice and short, puffed sleeves. She clasped her hands together, not wishing to touch it to destroy the glory of the gown. "Kendryck," she murmured.

"Yes, darling." He came to stand behind her, two hands to her shoulders to look down inside the box.

"It is utterly…" She had no good word for the shimmering fabric.

"For you, who is utterly lovely, my wife." He bussed her cheek. "Take it out. Let's see it."

She lifted it up by the shoulders, and the fabric swished to the floor in a cascade. But beneath that gown was another, and it caught her eye. The second gown was of similar cut in the bodice. She would be displaying a lot of cleavage in it. But she could not care, because the purple color was that one envisioned for ancient royalty. It shimmered in a dense violet, trimmed in gold of a different pattern on the billowing sleeves.

"I have never had anything so breathtaking."

Behind her, he dropped a kiss to her hair. "Neither have I."

She whirled into his embrace. "You are so good to me. This must have cost you a fortune."

"No." He pushed one long red curl behind her ear. "I bought the silks in a local bazaar. They are the Varanasi, the very best. I have other bolts of different colors. Blues and jades, greens and teals. An orange that you may think you could not wear with your coloring, but you can. All are yours. To do with as you wish, whenever you wish."

"I will try them on for you."

"Later. You have other gifts to open."

She nodded, eager as a girl. "You spoil me, and you risk danger that I will want presents from you all the time."

He laughed. "On the contrary, I will spoil you all I want, and yet I know that you will never ask me for a thing. Open the rest and don't tell me I cannot dress my wife as I wish."

"So the rest are dresses?"

He gave her a wide-eyed look. "I might have forgotten."

She laughed and went to the next box. But that presented her with an item of two pieces in an embroidered, creamy silk.

"Indian charmeuse," he told her as she held up the silky, long-sleeved top and trousers that puddled to the floor. "The phoenix-es embroidered on the shoulders and the bottoms of the trousers symbolize life renewing. The set is for a woman. You. They are pajamas, meant to be worn in leisure hours by a lady when she is with her retinue."

"Darling," she told him, holding up the sinuous pieces, "you are my retinue. I wear them only with you."

"I approve. Now open the last box." His pale blue eyes twinkled with mischief.

She hastened to do his bidding. But the contents of this box had her speechless. She knew they were night rails. Madame St. Claire had said so in her note. Each one was different. One plain, devoid of complement, save for white hand stitching over the entirety of the breasts. One had lace, a delicate work that resembled the finest Valenciennes at the long sleeves and at the hem. One had short sleeves, caught by a silken white ribbon at the arm. The fourth was a confection with tiny butterflies dancing over the whole gown, and with it was a cape with a train fit for a princess, at least ten feet long. Each one was made of while muslin so thin it was transparent. In these she would be naked.

She clasped that last one to her chest and stared at him. "I might as well wear air. Kendryck, these are so ethereal, I would be no more than a phantom."

"You will never be a phantom to me."

She shook her head. "You do me great honor to give me such lovely gifts."

"You do me the honor, wife. I am beyond delighted."

She put away the delicate gown in her hand and went into his arms. "Allow me to thank you properly."

He feigned innocence. "What did you have in mind?"

She took his hand and led him around the fireplace. "I have a few ideas."

Chapter Nineteen

TYNLEY KNEW NOT how to account for her unquenchable desire for her new husband. The next day passed in a mist of kisses and caresses. He was a creative lover, sharing with her new delights and teaching her new passions in the most extraordinary positions.

All of them, he told her, originated in an ancient text of which his wife was familiar. "All are imitations of the mating of birds of the sky and animals of the earth," he said. "But many are absolutely impossible without practice."

"Many seemed impossible without breaking a bone," she said. But they laughed more at the attempts and returned to what they both enjoyed as natural mating, he above her, kissing her in oh-so-many places and making her the happiest of women.

In the hours they dined, they talked of their childhoods, their parents, and the ways in which each of them became the individuals they were.

"You and I were both cast out by our parents," Tynley said to him the second night after their simple supper. "You for your lack of worth to the family. Me because acting seemed too risqué for them to accept."

"Writing anything is not the normal profession for a woman," he said.

"Being a second son is a burden," she remarked.

"Especially when there is another male to follow…and funds are few."

"Astonishing what we learn, isn't it," she said, "from what our parents intend to teach us?"

"Attitudes, they can teach us. But they serve more as models, and it is our choice if we wish to imitate them," he replied.

"I see in Barbara," she told him, "the beginnings of her veering from her mother's path."

"Do you mean her interest in Haverford at the wedding?"

"I do. I think she saw in him a man she could admire and want. She valued money and position before. But now I think she can set her sights on a kind and thoughtful man with whom she can live a life filled with friendship and peace."

"Ah, well then," Kendryck said as he contemplated the fire behind the gate. "I think she has far to go. Haverford is an honorable man. I am sure of it. He was an agreeable boy. I do detect he is the same as ever he was. He would not marry for money or position. He and I talked the night before you and I wed. He told me then that his family press him to wed a woman for advantage. He told me he loved a young woman a few years ago. A Boston girl. Her parents forbade their marriage because he was British, and they were staunch rebels against the Crown."

"That is sad," she said, knowing she led her husband to a discussion of his first wife and their challenges among the British and the natives of India. "That people forbid others to marry those they love because of politics or all else is a difficult matter to solve."

He shrugged and picked up the poker to nudge the logs. "I doubt we know how. Other than to emphasize the importance of equality among all men and women."

"But we must learn."

"Agreed. As each culture comes to know others, we must emphasize tolerance."

She rose from the settee and went to put her arms around him and lean her head against his back. "Was it awful for you and your wife?"

"At first, no. I was in the country and responsible to a British official of the Company who had a wife and two concubines who were Muslim. He embraced the food, the clothing, and went to play chess each Tuesday night with the nawab. He went to celebrations and took his wife. He learned the language."

"Did he have children?"

"Yes. Four. All girls. He was wealthy and sent them back to his grandmother in Kent, and has had them educated in English finishing schools. They are, I am told, accepted. Soon of age to come out, they will try it. But I doubt the grandmother will put them out in London Society. Brighton, perhaps, where rules are more lax and those who come for the Season are not those who consider themselves to be the highest in the instep."

"And is this Englishman still in India? Does he influence others to follow his example?"

Kendryck turned in her arms, his eyes dim with sadness. "No. He died last year while on duty in his territory. The East India Company began to put out edicts years ago forbidding such fraternization with native Indian women. But those rules took a long time to pervade the Company. Furthermore, the Company has also ordered that half-caste children, as they call them, cannot join the Company army. A few years ago, all Anglo-Indians were discharged from the army. Being a sepoy could pay very well. Now those men have nowhere to go for employment, and they grow bitter. Others who were born of such unions and who have an education may work for the Company, but only at lower levels. They also receive base pay. It is the damning of those who had nothing to do with the nature of their birth."

"And your wife? What did she think of her choice to marry you?"

"She was gracious about it. I know she suffered in silence often when many in her family refused to acknowledge her or invite us to family celebrations. She felt ostracized. But she never complained to me. She was a loving and supportive companion.

Gentle and soft-spoken. Intelligent in the ways of humankind, but not educated in more than reading and writing."

"How did you meet?"

"She was the eldest daughter of a nawab. I saw her at a festival, and she was lovely. Petite, with big black eyes and long fingers. She spied me too and came to my residence one night with her eunuchs."

"No! She had servants? Male servants?"

He smiled. "She did. Mean fellows, they were, too. Three of them. As the eldest, she had three female hand servants and an amah. A nurse, that is, in case she became ill. She also had a dancing girl, in case she needed to refresh her skills in the art."

Tynley was awed. Curiosity about how well he had recovered from his grief at her loss merited her next question. "Do you miss her?"

He met her gaze directly. "I used to. Not now. When I think of her lately, I know she would be happy for me to have found you."

"To advertise?"

"To gain you by any means would be the finest one."

"You are eloquent, sir." She traced the outline of his square jaw. "I may ask you to read my plays and edit."

"Ha!" He shook his head. "I would never be so bold."

"But a good writer needs a good editor."

"Who said that?"

"Richard Sheridan."

"The playwright?"

"And owner of the Royal Theatre. He did not say it to me, of course. But the new owner often repeated it."

They cleared their dishes and washed them up, then he led her to their bed.

"Would you mind if I don't wear one of the muslin gowns?" she asked him.

He tipped his head. "You don't like them."

"I do. They are breathtaking, but when I put the first one on last night, I felt oddly…more exposed in that nightgown than in the nude.”

He smiled. “Never wear them.”

He understood, and she was relieved he was not insulted.

“I like you as God made you. And if you don’t wish to wear them, I agree. Might I continue to have you as God made you?”

“Always,” she said, and went to his embrace and the joy of being united with him once more.

SHE SLEPT LONG after him, and rose, tying the stash of her cream-colored pajamas around her middle. He sat on the settee, staring into the fire he had laid. It blazed brightly and warmed the small house well.

“Good morning.” She kissed his lips, and he took her down to sit beside him. “Did you sleep well?”

“With you? Better than ever.” He had a teapot on the table before them, and an empty mug sat next to her. “Shall I pour for you?” he asked.

She accepted and watched him fill the cup. “You look…very serious. Are you concerned about something?”

“Gerard’s return. The missing diamonds I told you about. Barbara’s future. I told her I would give her a London debut. The time to prepare for that draws nigh. What would you think of all of us going to London…say, at the end of February?”

“That sounds good to me. There is much to prepare for her if she wishes to come out this year.”

“You’ve no objection to returning to London?”

“No. Did you think I would?”

“I was not certain you would like to be in the city again. You were happy to come to Wales.”

“I was happy to come to meet you, nothing more or less. I like London. I have lived there all my life. I have friends there. I worked there. To return would be a thrill. To go with you would be a new and gratifying adventure. Do you not have to show yourself as the rightful heir to take your family's seat in the Lords?"

"I do." He grinned. "Not that I am so ready to go through all that folderol. Dressing up, applying, paying the fees." He rolled his eyes.

"Oh, pooh! Do not tell me you are not eager to do all that? To begin your crusade against ill treatment for other human beings, I would say to go sooner is the best idea."

"You like speed in all matters."

"That I do. Get to the problem. Get the job done. Whatever you need to do, it is best done by starting immediately."

"By God! A taskmaster!"

"Irrevocable!" She giggled.

"Irresistible."

They were chuckling as the sound of a carriage approached the cottage.

"Stay here," Kendryck said to her. "I will see who it is."

Tynley went to their bedroom and got her robe from her trunk. As she rounded the fireplace, Kendryck was opening the front door to admit his friend William Drummond.

"I hurried William inside," Kendryck said by way of explanation. "It is frightfully cold out there. Come, William, please. Tea? You must be chilled."

"I am. Thank you. Yes, I'd like that." Drummond went to Tynley and kissed her on both cheeks. He was cold to her touch and frowning.

"Please sit down," she said to him. "You've come a long way so early in the morning."

He unbuttoned his greatcoat and sat on the edge of the cushion.

"What's wrong, William?" Kendryck went right to the problem as Tynley strode off to get William's tea.

"I received a letter this morning from your butler, Mr. Carter.

It was addressed to me. I have it. Here. Read it yourself." Drummond dug from his waistcoat inner pocket a small, folded letter and handed it over to Kendryck.

Tynley returned with a mug and bent to pour Drummond tea. She waited, her heart in their throat. He would not have come to intrude on their honeymoon if it were not a serious matter.

Kendryck focused on the paper, his face going white at the message.

"Tell me," she said as his forbidding gaze met hers.

"Mr. Shaw called at the Rambles day before yesterday. He has found Miss Roundbridge. He came in search of us to tell us. The news is not good." He pressed his lips tighter. "The lady is dead. Found in the woods near the road leading up to the Rambles."

"No!" Tynley's knees gave way. She sank down next to him. "That's awful."

"We must go home."

"Yes. Immediately," she said.

"Wait, Kendryck." Drummond had his hand out. "There is more. I went to the inn to hire the carriage that brought me here."

Tynley had concluded that he did not have his own conveyance. When he or his wife needed one, he hired a carriage, just as they had for the supper party at the inn.

"Yes." Kendryck looked askance. "I understand, but…?"

"Your family carriage had just left."

"The inn?"

William nodded.

"But that's…not right. My stepmother and Barbara were to leave for home the day after our wedding."

"The innkeeper told me they didn't."

"What? But why?"

"The day after your wedding, your sister wished to go into Cardiff."

Kendryck sat back, confusion lining his face. "Instead of going home to the Rambles?"

"Yes. She ordered your coachman to take her in to town. She told him she had business there, and she arranged for another night at the inn for herself, her mother, and your coachman. She returned yesterday late in the afternoon. She had supper at the inn, and her mother and she left early this morning for home."

Kendryck narrowed his eyes and stared into the fire. "So Barbara knows nothing of this letter to you."

"Not until she gets home, and then only if Carter tells her about Miss Roundbridge and how he wrote to me to find you and give you the news."

Kendryck shot to his feet. "I thank you very much for this. Will you do me another favor, please, William?"

"Anything."

"Return with me to the inn. We will ask the keeper for a reference to anyone in his employ who might know where in Cardiff my sister went yesterday." He faced Tynley.

"I will pack for us," she told Kendryck, anticipating his need to return home as soon as possible.

"Thank you, my darling. I will hire us a good carriage to take us home, and I will return here as soon as I can. Then we will leave." His expression mellowed. "I am sorry, Tynley. This has spoiled our honeymoon."

She tried to smile but failed. Still, she hoped to offer some measure of reassurance. "We have many years to take many honeymoons. Go. Do this. I will get all in readiness."

Chapter Twenty

THE TWO OF them circled the road up the hill to the Rambles as dusk fell. The house looked dark, the windows as glassy, dead eyes upon the world below. Tynley winced, remembering her fears that first day she had arrived. Here she had fallen in love with a very good man. Here she had learned the age-old problems that lurked in the dusty corners of the mystifying structure.

She shivered and pulled up her collar of her coat, even as the coachman whom Kendryck had hired pulled up his old hack to the front portico. Candles glimmered in the windows of the main salon. The light was the only sign of life in the brooding house.

They bade good evening to Carter as he took their hats and coats. Ever gracious, the little man told Tynley how pleased he was at her marriage, and he hoped she would be very happy here.

"Thank you, Carter. I know I will be."

"Congratulations, sir."

With quick hands through his hair, Kendryck thanked the man for his best wishes and his letter to William.

"I knew not what else to do, sir. I only knew I had to inform you as quickly as possible."

"I am grateful you did, Carter. Ever will I be in your debt."

"No, sir. No need. You are a good man, sir."

A few barks and the sounds of nails on the tile floor signaled the arrival of Jericho and Dick. Tynley bent to greet the dogs, and her husband offered a kindly word to both.

Then Kendryck laid a reassuring hand on the butler's arm. "Am I correct that my stepmother and my sister arrived home earlier today?"

"They did, sir. A few hours ago."

"In our family coach?"

Carter looked at Kendryck oddly. "Yes, they did, sir. If you wish to speak to the groom—"

"No, Carter, that will not be necessary. At least, not yet. The man must rest and tend to the horses. Tell me, where are my stepmother and sister?"

"They have had their supper early, sir. They did not expect you, and so—"

"No, of course they didn't. What do you think, my darling? Shall we have a full supper, or…?"

Tynley took his hands in hers. "A full tea, instead?"

"Yes. Yes. I like that." He was weary.

"Carter," she said to the butler, "do bring us whatever is most convenient for a cold repast in the salon. We'd like also a good service of whisky and brandy with that."

"As you wish, ma'am." He bowed himself away.

"Let's go get warmed by the fire, shall we?" She led Kendryck to the salon.

The two dogs followed in their wake and took up positions by the warm fire.

Kendryck did not sit but paced, clasping his hands together now and then.

During the journey home, he had revealed much of his dismay about Barbara's odd behavior. Going in to Cardiff was an unusual act. Why had she gone? What had she done that was necessary and spur-of-the-moment, and yet so convenient while she had the comfort of the family carriage and Tynley and he were away on their honeymoon?

"I tell you, my dear, the three of them confound me. I realize

I have been away from them. They do not know me, and they have no reason to like me. But this, plus the mystery of the missing diamonds, Gerard's lies and failure to return home, plus the matter of poor Miss Roundbridge's death—all combine to make me question how we can all live together."

"You will *not* throw us out!"

The accusation had them both turning toward the threshold and the echoes of Madeline's shout.

Jericho and Dick shot up to bark at her.

"Ma'am," Tynley beseeched her, "there is no need to yell."

"I do as I will, *my lady*." She sneered the last two words.

"*No one*, Madeline," Kendryck growled, "*no one* is throwing you out!"

"Get these two monsters away from me!" She shooed the dogs and kicked at them.

Tynley cried out for her to stop. The animals left Madeline to circle Tynley.

"They have no manners," Madeline seethed. "Like you. Just. Like. You." She pointed a finger at Kendryck. She marched forward, her hands fisted at her sides. She wore a quilted robe and slippers of blood red. A virtual Valkyrie, she faced Kendryck, toe to toe, her red hair streaming over her shoulders, her brown eyes bugging out with her wrath. "I do not put it past you. Who are you? A spare. A mouse. Your head in books. So useless, your grandfather sent you thousands of miles away. And he sent you there to die."

She sashayed away from him, toward Tynley. "Why didn't he die, little widow?"

Tynley did not so much as bat an eyelash.

"He was nothing. Has he told you? Everyone else knows. Owen was told so in London. His little brother was a disgrace."

She turned back on Kendryck. "Like so many other silly English boys, you thought you could take an Indian doxy, a Muslim harem girl, and fuck her while you had babies. But they sneered at you, didn't they? Her family hated you, denied you their rubies and sent you back to Calcutta, your dick between your legs."

Kendryck's glare drained away. At once, he was calm, unreachable by her anger.

She saw it and went for him, with her nails out.

He caught her hands and forced them to her sides. "Sit down, Madeline. Here." He forced her to a chair near the fire.

"What's wrong?" That came from Barbara. She rushed in to skid toward her mother on her knees. "What's going on here? Did he hurt you?" She canted her head to one side and looked up to question Kendryck.

"Your mother," Kendryck said as a nerve twitched in his jaw, "needs to rest and recover her senses."

Madeline began to shake. Her hand covering her mouth, she cried. Quietly, but desperately.

"Come upstairs, Mama." Barbara urged her mother to her feet.

The woman kept her hand to her mouth, but as she stood, she sent a withering look toward Tynley—and she did not cry, but laughed.

Tynley stepped back. She'd never witnessed such deceit.

With a sardonic smile for Kendryck, off Madeline went in her daughter's embrace. She tossed her red hair, triumphant. Like a mirage of evil, she disappeared into the hall.

"Dear God, how false she is," Tynley managed, and dropped to a chair. "She could not hate you more."

He let out a huge sigh. "She may feel any way she likes. I won't tolerate her any longer. I will find a way to afford a house for her. Barbara can go with her, if she likes."

That would be the end of Barbara's hope for a debut. No man of good repute would accept her if she were put out by her own brother. Tynley understood Kendryck's feelings, and she supported him. Whether or not Madeline repaired her relationship with Kendryck, Barbara was the one who would have to change to survive this catastrophe. So too would her brother.

"And Gerard?" she asked her husband. "He needs a future,

too."

Kendryck came to sit beside her and take her hand. "That will be his decision. Before we left for Cardiff the first time, I told him his choice was school or Canada. A life of labor. He too deceived me when he told me he intended to go apologize to that boy he hurt. When he arrives home, we will see what he has to say for himself and what future he has chosen."

"He may want to go and live with his mother and sister."

"I will not give the women a living so that they can take in a boy who refuses to earn his own keep and yet will gamble their money away. They will force him, if I cannot, to make his own way in this world."

BARBARA APPEARED THE next morning in the breakfast room, her head high, her hands clasped before her. Her knuckles were white with tension.

"I need to speak with you, Kendryck." She stared at the ceiling as she spoke.

Tynley flinched. The young woman did not even glance her way. Very well. Barbara was intent on her purpose.

"Come sit down with us." Kendryck extended his hand toward a chair. In one hand, he crushed the note he'd just received from the village inn from the Bow Street Runner, Sergeant Jack Shaw. In it, Shaw told Kendryck that he and his fellow Runner, Frederick Thynne, would appear at the Rambles this morning at nine o'clock.

"No." Barbara cast Tynley a venomous look. "Not here. Not the two of you."

"You will speak with us both, Barbara, or not at all."

"I will speak about my mother."

"As long as you do not speak *for* her, I will listen."

Silence hung like a shroud in the room.

Barbara lifted her chin. "My mother apologizes."

Kendryck arched a long, dark brow. "To whom?"

"You."

He smiled. "She must come and do that in person. To both Tynley and me. That is how such things are usually done. You know it, Barbara. So why lower yourself to do her dirty work?"

"She is my mother."

"That is no reason for her to use you as her personal messenger for crimes you did not commit."

"I want to help her!"

"She must help herself."

"She is subject to fits!"

Tynley did not move a hair. Barbara was not far from the mark.

"Then we must find a doctor for her."

Tynley went numb with fear. A doctor who heard a description of Madeline's outburst last night could easily decide that the woman should be sent to an asylum.

Barbara stamped her foot. "No, Kendryck. You make this worse."

"Do I? How? By not allowing you to be your mother's whipping post?"

"She…she fears you took her words the wrong way."

He scoffed. "Does she? How would I take them? As compliments?"

Tynley shut her eyes. Madeline feared Kendryck would put her out the door. Perhaps with nothing. She could also fear he would not support Barbara, either. It would be the end of Barbara's hopes to have a debut and to find a good husband. Though at the moment, Tynley concluded, before any of that happened, the young woman needed to revolutionize her thinking about kindness and responsibility.

"Listen to me, Barbara." Kendryck shook his head, done with her foibles. "I will not continue this conversation with you. You tell your mother I refuse you."

"But…"

He rose from his chair, put his two hands flat to the table before him, and glared at the girl. "Go. Before I get a footman or two to haul you away."

In a flash of her red skirts and a pointed curse, she fled.

Kendryck dropped to his chair and put his head in his hands. "How much worse can this get?"

Tynley covered his hand with hers. She had no words to console him. They would soon learn the fate of Miss Round-bridge. The poor woman had died, and near the Rambles, too. The disintegration of Kendryck's family was just as doleful.

Chapter Twenty-One

SHAW ARRIVED AT the stroke of nine. He limped in, his lips white, his visage grim.

With him came his tall, thin colleague, Thynne.

Tynley was shocked at their appearance, as the two looked as if they had not slept well for days. When they were shown in to the salon by Carter, she invited them to sit down. "We will have tea served in just a moment." She had asked Carter earlier to have a tea ready for the men.

"That is kind of you, ma'am," said Shaw, "but unnecessary. Thynne and I have taken lodging at the village at the Inn of the Wolf, and we've had our breakfast."

She would not take no for an answer. "Nonetheless, it is cold out, Mr. Shaw. Mr. Thynne. You have come to us with news, and we appreciate your time and consideration. You must have something hot and nourishing."

Both men took separate chairs. Kendryck stood by the fireplace. Tynley sat opposite the two Runners on the settee.

"Please tell us what you can, sirs." Kendryck had told Tynley he wished to hasten this along. After the confrontation with Barbara, he needed as many details from the men as they could legally or ethically share. The Roundbridge family may have prohibited Thynne from revealing all. They had hired him to find her, and he was responsible to them first.

Shaw had been paid by his cousin, Mrs. Hammond, and by Kendryck. What he knew should be open to Kendryck and her.

Shaw took his time taking the measure of Tynley and Kendryck. "Thynne and I have been searching towns and villages from Bristol into Wales for weeks. We had no proof where Miss Roundbridge might have gone. In fact, we were about to abandon the search. Until last week. Thynne will tell you more."

Thynne appeared stoic as he examined Kendryck's face and form in his cold, methodical way. "I was lodged in an inn near Barry when a man told a tale of a woman's body found in a forest near the Rambles. I asked him how he had learned this, and he told me it was his cousin who lived there who'd heard it as rumor. I left promptly to investigate. I contacted the man's cousin, who led me to the place where he had found a woman's body in the brush. I asked him if he had moved it or touched it. He assured me he had not. He was too afraid."

Tynley folded her arms. She was trembling, but did not wish to display her nerves to the Runners. Still, she surmised, he knew.

"A lady in a green gown and pelisse lay in the brush. Her body was partly covered by leaves and rocks. Whoever did that knew she was dead. We saw no evidence she had moved from the spot. We did see that she had been dragged there, however."

Tynley swallowed bile.

Kendryck went white.

"Before I left," Thynne continued, "I told the man to keep watch over her body and not to allow any wild animals to approach. I went to the village, bought a large linen sack, and hired a cart to take her to the Inn of the Wolf in the village. Her body lies in the back room now. I await the coroner from Cardiff. I sent for him yesterday, and I hope he arrives soon. The body is not one I wish to keep above ground for too long—pardon my frankness, ma'am."

Her throat clogging with despair, Tynley nodded her thanks.

"How did she die?" Kendryck asked him.

Thynne pursed his lips. "That is what the coroner will tell

us."

"It is not evident, then?" Kendryck asked.

"My lord, even if it is," Thynne said, "I would not be at liberty to disclose that to you."

"Why not?" Tynley leaned forward. She had to know. "My husband and I are not involved."

"But you are, ma'am. Miss Roundbridge was coming to interview you, Lord Strade. You told us that." This from Shaw made Tynley's hair stand on end. "You said you had never seen her."

"That is true," Kendryck said.

"Nor had you, ma'am?" asked Shaw.

"No, never."

Shaw and Thynne checked each other's eyes.

What that meant had Tynley glancing toward Kendryck—and he nodded at her. He had seen it too. The two men definitely knew much that they were not sharing.

Both Runners stood. "We ask that you be available to us again after the coroner has done his investigation."

"Will he do an autopsy?" Kendryck asked.

Thynne fired a look at him. "Why do you ask?"

"I am familiar with a procedure when a coroner has need to determine cause of death. We have the same procedures in place in the East India Company in India when a man among staff dies suddenly or without known cause."

Thynne blinked, took that in, and seemed to relax. "I see. Well, sir, I do not yet know if the coroner will decide on one."

"Please let us know, Mr. Thynne. I do feel responsible in many ways for the ill fate of Miss Roundbridge. I will gladly aid you both or him in any way. And if the family needs funds to transport the body home, please write to tell them I am more than willing to see that done with all due speed and honor."

"Thank you, sir," said Shaw. "We will keep that in mind."

"We must be off," Thynne said. "Thank you for your time."

Then, just as Carter appeared at the door to the salon with

the tea service, Shaw and Thynne nodded in respect to Tynley and Kendryck and went around the butler to the foyer.

Tynley went to her husband and walked into his outstretched arms as they heard the front door close with a bang.

"THAT WAS HORRID," Tynley said to Kendryck when Carter had left and closed the salon doors.

"That she came all this way only to die is unbelievable," he murmured, and kissed the top of her head.

She looked up at him. "Who walks that stretch of forest? How would she have gotten there?"

"Anyone can walk there. There are paths by the dozens leading up from the village."

"So she took a carriage here to come see you at the house," she concluded. "That had to be her intention."

"We need to know how she died. Why she was dragged. If she was dragged… And if someone interrupted her. Waylaid her. God, it is unfathomable."

Shouts came from upstairs. Women arguing.

Kendryck sucked in air. "Dear heavens. What now?"

Sounds of someone running, then scuffling, had both Kendryck and her dashing for the hall and the stairs.

"Stop! Stop!" This was Lucy, the baroness's maid, trying to pull Barbara away from the lady. "You're hurting her!"

Kendryck got hold of Barbara around her waist and lifted her in the air. "Go to your room!"

She stomped on his foot.

He bared his teeth. "Now! Go!"

Tynley was trying to lift the old woman from the floor. "Come, come. Sit up. We will help you. You are not bleeding, are you?" She checked the baroness over quickly, her head, her arms and legs. No, there was no sign the lady had been badly hurt.

"You can sit up, can't you?"

Tynley sought Lucy. "What happened here?"

"She was calm as could be, staring out her window, she was. Then, all of a sudden, she points to the woods and starts yelling that she's seeing a ghost. I could not calm her. She was crying, and she wrenched away from me, mad like, she did, and ran out. I dunno if Miss Barbara was in the hall, but she—"

"My door was open!" Barbara spat. She'd not gone to her room, only stepped a few paces backward from the group.

Kendryck put up a hand. "I told you to go to your room."

"No, I won't. She was in my room!" She pointed a shaking finger at her grandmother. "She was in my dressing room, and she threw my clothes on the floor! They're ruined. Ruined!"

"Green is the color of the ghost," murmured the baroness. "It's her! It's her. I saw her, I did. You little snake."

Kendryck bent down to his grandmother. "May I help you up, Grandmama? Please? There you are. Take my hand, yes. You will tell me if you cannot stand, will you? That's good. Yes." He got her to her feet. "I will help you now to your room."

"No, no. I want to go with you."

"To my room?" he asked her.

"Your room." She pulled on his cravat to bring him near. "We can talk."

"Very well." He caught Tynley's gaze and winced. "We will go to my room. And we'll have tea and spirits. You'd like that."

"I will. I will," the old lady murmured in a litany of joy.

"And you can tell me what you saw from your window."

"I'll show you. Will I? Please. Green. That girl…that one! In green. Walking. Walking. Running, too!"

"From your window?" Tynley asked.

"Mine. You'll come to tea, too."

"I will come to your room, and you will show me. Kendryck too," Tynley assured the baroness.

She wondered if the lady were more coherent than anyone credited. Some visions, some thoughts, were not necessarily delusions. They knew that from the previous scuffle when the baroness had broken out of her room.

"Go talk to her," Tynley said to him. "I will get the tea brought up and have Carter bring whisky. We will all have a good chat, Grandmama."

It was the first time she had addressed the lady with such familiarity, and Tynley brought herself up short, ready to apologize.

But the lady leaned forward, patted her cheek, and said, "Tynley, girl, you are a treasure. Your hair is red, but you don't have that color of green gown."

Tynley's gaze flew to Kendryck's. Had the lady been rifling through her closet as well? She'd ask Seren, her own maid, if she thought ought was amiss. The girl was diligent, and Tynley doubted much got past her. If items in her closet had been rummaged, Seren would mention it to Tynley.

But other things, Tynley needed to learn. She would take tea with the baroness and take time to examine Lucy's behavior. Did the old woman's maid know or allow the baroness to continue to wander? What was her daily schedule, and how did Lucy cope with the spontaneity of the old woman's actions and words?

The greater question that intrigued Tynley was why her own auburn hair color and a gown of green were so important to the old woman.

After all, Madeline, Barbara, and she had hair various shades of red. As for gowns, what color green fascinated the old lady? Dark forest green, jade, seafoam? There existed a palette of different shades to intrigue her. Tynley now owned three of varying colors. How many did Madeline and Barbara own?

And who ran outside the baroness's window? Anyone?

Or were all of the older lady's words just fantasies?

THE NEXT AFTERNOON, Kendryck and Tynley sat in the library editing his first article he'd written about India. He regarded his wife, who sat in the one wing chair in the nook, her pencil in hand, a thoughtful look on her face.

That was all he needed to assure himself that she liked what she read. A good thing, too. He had written that first attempt slowly and painfully over the past few weeks. Writing a novel had taxed him, and he'd abandoned it to write the shorter piece. At her encouragement, he had put more words to paper this morning. But the task was a difficult one.

While his wife and he were away in Cardiff for their wedding and all-too-brief honeymoon, a small newspaper in London that focused on foreign affairs had sent a response to his inquiry and agreed to publish his work. As soon as the publisher received the first three, they would go to press. Kendryck was beyond pleased, and yet the conflicts with Madeline and Barbara, his grandmother's mental infirmities, and now the mysterious demise of Miss Roundbridge had stolen his concentration. Still Tynley had encouraged him to return to writing to take his mind off the matters at hand.

She edited the draft. In truth, she told him after reading the first three pages this morning, his work needed very little. What she learned of the organization and operation of the East India Company was more than she had known, and she surmised more than many in or out of government knew or understood.

Last night they had spent in each other's arms nearly sleepless. Their turmoils were so many that they had each risen twice to talk and walk the floor.

"If only Madeline would come and apologize," Tynley had offered.

"One can do that over and over again, but if her character does not change, what good is an apology?"

"I know. But it would help. If she would at least come to dine with us…"

He sighed. "In all of it, she could serve as a good example for

Barbara. I fear for the girl."

Tynley had assured him that would happen and curled close to him in bed. "She can change with a good man in her arms."

He kissed her palm. "You needed no change. You were perfect to begin with," he told her.

She had chuckled. "Not really. I have faults."

"I know not one."

She had stared at him in the dark…and for a long moment, he worried that she kept something from him. But then she kissed him, dare he say, almost in a desperate embrace, and he took her invitation to get lost once more in her charms.

For more than a day, she had been distant, her mind focused on some problem. He had asked her last night if she wished to discuss Madeline or Barbara more, but she had quickly told him no. Then she'd quickly brought up his grandmother.

"Tea today with your grandmother was full of her memories of her childhood. No green gowns and no ladies with red hair. She would not even stand by the window to describe for me what she thinks she saw."

So whatever had consumed Tynley was something else.

Kendryck himself often needed time to come to terms with an issue. He trusted she would come to him with it if and when she needed to.

God knew he needed time to digest all that had happened recently. No word came from Gerard, and Kendryck could only assume the young man was making his way home to the Rambles. His grandmother's condition was a worry, and so too the possibility that the baroness's maid Lucy was not doing her job well. If that weren't enough with Madeline being so belligerent and Barbara truculent, he had forgotten something vital, some fact he had to clarify. He drew a complete blank as to what it was—and he worried that his failure could have dire consequences.

He glanced up at a movement by the doors to the hall.

Carter appeared there.

Kendryck noted the man's dour expression and the letter he held in his hand. *More trouble. I see it coming.* "What is it, Carter?"

Kendryck had a good idea of the contents. He and Tynley had seen an article this morning in the *Cardiff Chronicle.* The coroner who lived in Cardiff had arrived in the Rambles village late afternoon yesterday and viewed the body. Then the man had gone to the place where Miss Roundbridge's body was discovered and examined the area.

Kendryck could recite the next three sentences in the newspaper article by heart.

He interviewed the owner of the Inn of the Wolf, who said the deceased had taken a room for two nights there. She told him she would meet a friend at the stables the first night. The identity of that person is unknown to the coroner.

"My lord," Carter said, breaking Kendryck's reverie, "this letter came for you a few minutes ago. It is from Mr. Thynne."

"Do give it to me, Carter."

Tynley stood up, her eyes wide as she came to his side. "Do you think they know how she died?"

Kendryck put on his glasses and read the letter. "By blows to her head. He suspects murder."

She gasped.

"The coroner has ordered an inquest tomorrow at noon in the Inn of the Wolf."

Chapter Twenty-Two

TYNLEY CLIMBED INTO the family coach and sat beside her husband. Madeline and Barbara had arrived in the foyer before either of them and took the seats facing forward.

Tynley folded her hands and told herself she could bear the two women's bad behavior. She had endured worse. Over the years of being cast out by her parents, her failure at acting, her attempt at playwriting, her husband's and son's illness and deaths, she thought she had suffered enough. Her abiding faith in the promise of wonderful tomorrows had lifted her up and kept her pointed toward finding a decent future for herself. Her answer to Kendryck's advertisement for a wife and meeting him, liking him—yes, growing to love him—had buoyed her. But this terrible possibility that the other candidate for his wife had encountered a horrible death by misadventure tested her good nature.

She did love Kendryck. Quite dearly. She would not deny it to herself now. And why would she? There was only that first intention that their marriage be one of aid and friendship. She would tell him soon. When the time was right. When her declaration could truly sound a positive note to their love affair.

When she could help him deal with the ordeal presented by the hatred of his stepmother for him and his half-sister's disaffection, she would tell him. Tynley had a few ideas how to do that. But she would wait to pursue that topic with her husband, until after Miss Roundbridge's last days were analyzed for all to hear and read.

Madeline had finally gone to Kendryck last night to make amends for her outrageous accusations the day they had arrived home from their honeymoon. She had been so crafty as to take Barbara with her to the meeting.

As if she needed an ally.

But in the act, too, she had shown her daughter that she must apologize for her rudeness. To a lesser extent, that she would do it for the sake of some peace in the house. And that, wily as Madeline was, she knew she had failed her daughter in the act and had to reestablish a detente to ensure that Barbara would have Kendryck's backing for a debut.

Yet now, though Madeline had made her bob to civility and Barbara had witnessed it, the two of them sat like ice queens in the carriage. For days, they had not appeared at meals, nor in the salon. They were one and apart, sanctimonious in their silence.

Kendryck bore it. He, too, had endured worse.

But Tynley was fast becoming furious about it. She had learned long ago to not permit her anger to rule her. She could destroy others with her rage. So could others, using their own. It was not a way to live.

But such perfidy as Madeline's and irresponsibility as Barbara's would not stand. Not with her. Not for her husband. Not in their house. And whether the two women liked it or not, Tynley was head of the household now. She would use her power, too. For her own good and the good of her husband, and if there were any future members of the family, for them too. Tynley had had enough of those who thought themselves better than everyone else. She would not bear it ever again.

TYNLEY TOOK ONE look at the tumble-down Inn of the Wolf and

recalled her first sight of it the day she came to the Rambles. It was a desperate little lodge in the center of the small Rambles village. Built of wattle, stone, and timber in only God knew what year, the main room could hold at most thirty people huddled near each other, the bar, and the fireplace.

Tynley led the way inside the gathering room. Behind her came Madeline and Barbara. Kendryck followed.

The day was chilly. Tynley could almost smell snow in the offing. The sky had that gray stillness, laden with storm clouds. It would arrive soon. Tonight at the latest.

Kendryck conferred with the innkeeper and led the three women to the second row of benches. The innkeeper had set up the room much as if the inquest were to be an entertainment. A few of the villagers came forward to doff their hats and shake Kendryck's hand. Three men welcomed him home and extended their sympathies on the deaths of those in his family. Two women came forward to do the same. Most villagers stayed away and eyed Madeline and Barbara as if the two were witches of the night.

For Tynley, they had more curiosity and came forward to smile, curtsy to her, and murmur their introductions. She took their offers of names and smiles as a hope for friendship. That, she could readily give. Everyone needed a new friend, and she was the lady of the manor now. She would gladly give it.

Kendryck had told her this morning that the coroner was a Mr. Silas Grant from Cardiff, and he remembered not only this name but the fact that the man had done certain favors for his grandfather. Those had been to perform abortions for ladies whom the old baron had gotten pregnant.

As Tynley looked at Grant now, she saw no hint in his manner of his dubious past. She could hope for his just rulings on this woman's tragic death, but Kendryck had readily told her he had none.

Grant was well nigh into his sixties, with a shock of white hair that stood like a brush straight up from his head. With a pair of coal-black eyes, he stood at a full five feet tall and four feet wide. He strode forward at sight of Kendryck and introduced himself.

Kendryck stood to greet him, and so did Tynley.

"Grant, Silas. My lord, good to meet you. I knew your grandfather when I was a doctor in Cardiff years ago. He had me help his friends often. My condolences on his loss, and the loss of your brother and sister, too. Anyone else you lost while away, hmm? I forget how long you've been gone to India, sir."

Kendryck accepted his apologies and condolences with cool grace, then turned to introduce him to Tynley.

"Happy to meet you, my lady. Not in these circumstances, of course, but you understand. I hear you are from London. That so?"

"Indeed it is, Mr. Grant."

"Like Wales, do you?"

"I have until now. Not in these circumstances, but you understand."

Her use of his words had his eyes twinkling—and not in a kindly manner. "Good, my lady. I heard word you were an actress."

"Yes. A playwright, too, sir." If this was an inquiry of her credentials for this inquest, he'd had them all.

"Unusual, that." He spoke with respect, but he turned to Kendryck with a gleam in his eye that was definitely lascivious. "How did you find such a lovely lady, my lord?"

So, yes. Grant was not fact-finding. He knew much already.

Kendryck took her hand and squeezed it. "We have many friends."

Not a lie, but not the truth to feed Grant's search for tidbits.

"Yes, well, my lord. I am glad you have come. As the leading gentry, we need you here."

"It is my duty, Grant. If you do not mind, my wife and I will sit so you can start. We wish to aid you in your attempt to establish order."

The man, shrewdness in his sharp gaze, bowed to Kendryck.

"We shall begin."

Grant strode to the front of the room. He looked straight at her and smiled in a sly way, then picked up his gavel. He banged it on one of the old, rough-hewn wooden tables to call the room to silence. Beginning with his gratitude that they had been prompt, he praised the citizenry and began a description of the proceedings.

"We will call various witnesses to establish what the deceased, a Miss Mary Anne Roundbridge, did while here. How she came here. Whom she saw. What she did. We will discuss who found her body. Where. How. When. Then I will list the details of what I saw when I first saw her body and when I went to the scene of her death. I did perform an examination of her body and an autopsy. Therefore, to decide on the merits of accidental death, death by misadventure, or intentional murder, I summoned all property owners for twenty miles in each direction. From these, I chose twelve men. Innkeeper! Bring them in!"

The innkeeper scurried away to the far door, and in marched twelve men, the door ajar as they filed out. A sickening, sweet smell swept the room.

Many coughed. Others grumbled. A few yelped or put handkerchiefs to their mouths.

"The body," said a few.

"Smells," murmured a few others.

Tynley recoiled. They had better finish this today so that they could do what they must to make Miss Roundbridge presentable and send her home immediately to be buried.

Grant confirmed from the jury that they had selected a foreman. Then he swore them all in.

"They have all seen the body of the deceased to their satisfaction. I did perform an autopsy on the body, and I shall describe that in detail. Miss Roundbridge's body was found five days ago in the forest approximately one mile from this inn. She lay on the forest floor for many days, perhaps weeks. Her body was facedown on the rocky ground. It was apparent she had fallen, face forward. I determined this because the debris in the skin of her face was embedded with such force that the only way she would have been so disfigured is by the force of her weight hitting the ground. Her knees showed, too, the impact. Miss Roundbridge's clothes showed that she had been dragged to the place where she was found. Then, too, she incurred other wounds on her body."

At this point, the main door of the inn opened wide. A gust of chilling air blew in, and with it came Kendryck's half-brother, Gerard Hollens. The young man swept off his top hat and unbuttoned his greatcoat with some difficulty. His left arm was in a sling. He searched and found those of his family assembled, then nodded at his mother, his sister, and Kendryck.

Tynley squeezed her husband's hand. "Home at last," she murmured.

Kendryck said naught, but followed closely as Gerard pulled the heavy inn door shut and strode toward the back of the room.

Tynley frowned. *So. Staying then. Interested, is he, in Miss Roundbridge's death?* Gerard was never interested in much but himself.

Scowling at Gerard's intrusion, Grant continued. "As I was saying, Miss Roundbridge incurred other wounds on her body. She received two sharp blows to her head. One to the side of her head above her right temple and another blow to the back of her head, left side. She had a severe head wound with extensive tissue damage. She must have bled profusely. Head wounds do.

"We have also found one large rock which may have inflicted this damage. I found this stone nearby, and it appears to have blood upon it. But, of course, the bloodstain is old, and only by its proximity to the body can we detect or surmise that the person who hit her used this item.

"The other result of my autopsy is that I found Miss Round-bridge was twelve to sixteen weeks' pregnant."

A gasp went round the room.

Tynley and Kendryck froze.

Next to Tynley, Barbara gasped and turned to her mother.

Madeline patted her daughter's hand. "Not to worry," she said to her.

Grant called the first person to testify. This was the villager, Thomas Davies. His testimony was brief and simple. He had found Miss Roundbridge's body in the brush when he was in the forest looking for a fox that had killed one of his chickens. Upon finding her, he had run for the innkeeper to help him.

The innkeeper came next, and he told of having met the deceased when she came to take a room in his inn. "She said she was going up to see his lordship, that she was to marry him and do it soon. The next morning, I served her breakfast, and she said she was meeting a friend near the stables later that morning."

"And did she meet a friend?" Grant asked.

"I don't know if she was a friend. But I saw a red-haired lady in a green coat talking with her that morning when I took out the slops."

Tynley's heart stopped. A red-haired woman in green attire sounded like the baroness's wild rantings. How wild were they? Tynley had questioned them before, and now…more so.

"Did you recognize that woman with Miss Roundbridge?"

"No."

"Can you describe her for us?"

"Had her back to me, she did. So, no, sir."

"Tall? Short? Fat?"

The innkeeper shrugged and shook his head. "Dun't know, sir."

"How long have you lived in this village, sir?" Grant asked.

"My whole life, sir."

"So…forty years?"

"Forty-five, sir."

"And the lady you saw with the deceased was no one you knew from the village?"

"I can't say, sir."

"Why not?" Grant pressed him.

"My eyes, sir." The man indicated his glasses. "They're not good."

Grant inhaled and winced, his attitude of one stymied. "One more thing—when Thomas Davies came to you with news of a body he found, did you think it might be Miss Roundbridge?"

"I did, sir. She went out that morn weeks ago, you see, and she never returned. Odd, that. I had the maid take her reticule from the room I rented her. And that was that."

"And after Mr. Davies told you about her, you had a look, and then what did you do?"

"I did go look at her. Poor lady. All covered in leaves and dirt. But I did what I should then. I took my horse to run to Cardiff and found a bailiff. That man told me where to find the coroner. You, sir."

The coroner dismissed him and called Kendryck to give testimony.

He strode to the front of the room and faced those assembled. He stated his name, his age, his position. "Late of the East India Company, for sixteen years. I am home upon the demise of my older brother, Owen, and I assume his titles, duties, estate, holdings, and responsibilities."

"How did you know Miss Roundbridge, my lord?"

"She answered an advertisement I placed in a London newspaper."

"For what?" Grant asked, feigning naïveté.

"A wife."

The crowd sent around loud whispers of shock and I-told-you-sos.

"Explain that, my lord."

"I wanted to be married. I knew no one in Wales. I was coming home, and I wished to be married."

"And you are married. Is that correct?"

"I am. Last week in Cardiff."

"To a woman from London?"

"That is correct, Mr. Grant."

"You must tell us how this came about. The relationship with Miss Roundbridge and the one with your current wife, a Mrs. Wallingford of London. Is that correct?"

"That was my wife's name before our wedding a few days ago, yes. I tell you in addition that I had no personal relationship with Miss Roundbridge."

"What did you have?"

"A correspondence, sir."

"Explain that to the jury, my lord."

Kendryck stared at Tynley. She understood he wished circumstances were otherwise, but Grant was a determined inquisitor. It appeared the man wanted to make of this woman's death a notorious incident that would smear Kendryck's good name.

She gave her husband a consoling nod. *Go on, my darling, tell them all. We will overcome all this. Together. I know we will.*

He told them all how he wrote the ad for a wife, of the time lapse for journey of correspondence to and from India.

"Six months is a very long time," said Grant.

"It is as fast, Mr. Grant, as a ship may sail from Bombay around the tip of India, south to the Cape of Good Hope in Africa, and north all the way to London."

Kendryck continued with his decision to meet in London and his missed opportunities to communicate with the lady about his decision not to have her come to Wales. He wished to meet her not at all.

"Yet your wife, my lord, did come to Wales to meet you. How is that?"

Grant was being argumentative.

Kendryck continued to explain about Tynley's arrival. Her subsequent decision to stay as his guest. Then their growing friendship and their subsequent decision to marry.

"A lot of words, my lord." Grant was testy about all the detail Kendryck had given. "During this time, did you meet Miss Roundbridge, sir?"

"Never."

"She never came to the Rambles?"

"No, sir."

"You are sure of that, sir?"

"I have never met the woman, Mr. Grant."

"And your servants?"

Kendryck cocked a brow. "What about them?"

"Had any of them ever met Miss Roundbridge?"

Kendryck frowned. "Not to my knowledge, no, sir."

"Would they have told you if they had?"

Kendryck met the man's black gaze with disdain. "If any strangers came to the house, yes, I would expect them to tell me."

"Why do you *expect* it of them, my lord?" Grant pressed, a nasty smile toying with his lips.

"Why, Mr. Grant?"

"Exactly."

"Because unlike my grandfather, my father, and my older brother, all my life before I sailed to India and now that I am home—I have treated each of my staff with the honor and courtesy they should have as human beings. I expect it from each of them. Furthermore, to my knowledge, I receive it from them."

"Very well, my lord. Thank you. That is all. Oh…one more question."

Kendryck waited.

"Do you know who the father of Miss Roundbridge's child is?"

"No."

Tynley could see her husband's mind work to ask the man, *Do you?*

"Thank you. That is all, my lord."

Kendryck walked back to sit beside Tynley. He took her hand, and she sighed, content. Beside her, Barbara fidgeted in her chair. Next to her daughter, Madeline arched her spine and sniffed. So much for her regard for Kendryck. Tynley wondered why the woman had bothered herself to come today.

"I call Lady Strade."

Tynley blinked. *She* was called? She looked up at Kendryck.

"It's fine, my darling. Grant is being thorough."

Grant is being an ass. She straightened her posture and stood. So be it. If Grant wanted her to testify, he'd get more—and much less—than he expected.

She approached the front of the room, cool as a spring flower, and faced the assembled villagers. She knew much about inquests. The procedure, the intimidation of witnesses. In fact, she had starred in a play about a Society murder and acted as the role of heroine. She knew how to charm an audience with her smiles and win them with a sharp show of defiance.

"State your name and residence."

She did.

"Tell us how you met your husband," Grant instructed her.

She repeated almost verbatim what Kendryck had said. Grant would get no new information from her.

"And you fell in love easily, my lady?"

"I do not see how my relationship's growth with my husband has any bearing on this inquest."

Tynley heard the audience hold their breath.

Grant cleared his throat. "When did you meet your husband?"

"When I arrived here in November."

"You came by hired carriage?"

Grant had done a thorough investigation of her. "I did."

"Why?"

"I do not own my own carriage."

A snicker went through the room.

"You stayed as a guest at the Rambles."

She nodded. "I did."

"Why?"

"A snowstorm came. I could not leave."

A bigger laugh went around.

"But you remained after the storm. Why?"

"Lord Strade and I became friends. He invited me to stay so that we might decide if we might care for each other enough to marry."

"And you did."

She smiled at Kendryck, who was beaming at her. "And I did."

"During any time at the Rambles, did you hear of Miss Roundbridge?"

"Yes. The day when two Bow Street Runners came to tell us that she was missing and they were tracking her."

"Did you ever walk into this village to meet someone?"

"No."

"No?"

"Lady Strade," Grant went on, "I repeat. Did you ever come into this village while you stayed at the Rambles?"

"No, sir, I did not."

"Do you own a green gown?"

"I own three."

"Did you ever wear a green gown and pelisse to come into this village?"

"No."

Tynley stared straight ahead. This was a point Grant was trying to make, and he could not. Originally she knew not any reason why her red hair and a green gown might be significant. Now she perceived that Grant wished to place her in a meeting with the lady. The frank look of outrage on Kendryck's face told her he understood as well.

She gave her husband a pointed blink.

His expression calmed.

"Lady Strade! Look at me!"

She slowly turned.

"Did you kill Miss Roundbridge?"

"I have never met her, sir."

"Are you left-handed?"

She froze. Her heart hammered as she controlled her expression. Left-handed? Left-handed because…to hurt Miss Round-bridge on the right temple when she was standing and left side of her head when down, the assailant was most likely left-handed.

Dear God. She knew who was left-handed.

"Are you—"

"No."

"Show us."

She faced him. "I need not prove that to you, sir. I am not on trial here. Furthermore, I can call witnesses who will state I did not leave the house."

Grant's nostrils flared. "Did you or did you not walk in the woods every day you were at the Rambles?"

"I did."

"Alone?"

"No."

Grant grumbled. "You are being very curt, Lady Strade."

"I answer your questions, sir."

"If you were not alone, whom did you walk with?"

"Lord Strade."

"And the two of you never met Miss Roundbridge in the woods?"

"No."

"And you never came across her body in the forest?"

"No."

"You walked on paths?"

"Yes."

"Which ones?"

She shrugged. "I do not know. I have had no map. I went on one path only."

"Her body was found adjacent to Lord Strade's estate."

Tynley merely stared at him. Yet now she knew she had to find precisely where the woman's body had been found. Which path was important. And did it converge anywhere so that Kendryck's grandmother would see who had taken that path?

Grant was red in the face. "You confound me, madam."

She said naught.

"Why will you not confess?"

"To what?"

"Meeting this woman. Killing her."

She shook her head. "Sir, I did not kill anyone."

"I see," he said at last, then strode toward her to look up at her. "Madam. Do you love your husband?"

This? Now? She turned to find Kendryck's dear face in the crowd. This was not the way she wanted to say this. Not the time or place. But she did not look away as her mind raced to find the right words for this most precious declaration.

"Lady Strade. Do answer the question!"

She took a breath and opened her heart to the man she'd come to cherish. "I do love him. Very much indeed. I have never known a man so honorable or selfless. A man so intent on sharing what he knows so that others may live more freely, more happily. I love my husband quite madly. He is upright and moral. He sees people as they are, and yet better, as they can become and as they should be. He works for that. A man of principle who believes in the eternal goodness of human kind. Yes, I love my husband. Those of you who knew him when he was a child were fortunate. I know him as he has become the finest of men, and I am glad he is mine. To have and to hold. For decades to come."

A pin could have dropped in the room, and all would have stirred.

As it was, even Grant had to clear his throat before he could go on. "Stand down, madam."

She returned to her husband's side, and he took her hand in his strong one.

"We will now ask the jury to decide if the deceased was murdered. Whether by accident, misadventure, or with willful intent to kill. You will take your time and consider all the evidence from all the witnesses. When you have your verdict, send your foreman to me with news of it. We will announce it here in this place minutes after you decide."

He glanced about. "Does anyone else wish to testify? No? Well then, we are adjourned."

Chapter Twenty-Three

SHAKING WHEN KENDRYCK and she were blessedly alone in the family carriage, Tynley let her tears fall. He took her in his arms and let her weep. "It's over now. You foiled him."

The two of them had briefly met Gerard at the rear of the public room of the inn. The young man had ordered his hired coach from Cardiff to wait for him outside, and Barbara and his mother had taken the opportunity to join him in his conveyance for the ride back to the Rambles.

Tynley rejoiced at their solitude and hugged her husband close.

"All of that was hateful. What a horrid man that Silas Grant is. Can we not write to the King's Bench and complain about him? I want him gone!"

"He had his pound of flesh, but I doubt we could remove him. He is well known in Cardiff, though not for good reasons."

He lifted her chin. "Forget Grant for a moment. Listen to me, my darling. I want you to know how your declaration thrilled me."

"Did it?" Oh, she was trying to be nonchalant about it. Failure was not an option, and yet...

"You honor me. Your eloquence. Your sentiments."

"Oh, no." She wanted to curl into a little ball. If he did not love her, she did not wish to be alone out here in a sea of desire only to know that she rode the waves alone. "I…I told the truth."

"I know you did. I heard it in your tone. I saw it in the look in your eyes, your stance." He put his big, warm hand to her cheek. "I know the look and sound of love. To have it from you was a precious gift in so raw a place as that."

She blushed, and novel as that reaction was for a woman of her age and experience, she tried to pull away.

"Don't think I don't appreciate what you said."

"No?" Appreciation was far from what she really sought from him. Oh, she'd been wrong to go so far. If he thought she did it to make him say something he did not feel… "I said what was true. What he and everyone needed to hear, and I said it as best I could. I—"

"I love you, Tynley."

She could not believe her ears.

"This is not the time or place I wanted for this, Tynley. I have thought of how I loved you for days and days. Weeks, I do believe!" His blue eyes danced with merriment. But he swept her closer to him and stole her breath. "I love you, my darling wife. How could I not? You have given me so much. A new perspective on my past, a hope for my future. A helper to make the road easier. I love you, Tynley. And I am so glad you answered my advertisement, darling. I do not know what I'd do without you. But I will work never to be without you, your approval, and your love."

Then she did weep in his arms, and he offered his handkerchief to dry her cheeks. And to her astonishment, as she stopped crying, she noted that he also had tears in his eyes.

"I did not want to love anyone again," he said, and smiled at her as she dabbed at his long, dark eyelashes. "But you are so easy to love. How was I to deny how wonderful you made me feel? Or how I wanted to kiss you and hold you against me forever? I want us to have the full measure of a life, my darling. Birthdays and Christmases, anniversaries and celebrations."

She kissed him full on the mouth. "Babies!"

He drew back and chuckled. "Those too."

"A dozen!"

He tucked her beneath him to the squabs, and as the coach climbed up the bumpy hill to home, she jostled and almost fell to the floor. He caught her.

"That would be wonderful," he whispered. "But if it is not so, I will not count the lack. I want you, Mrs. Hollens. All that you are."

"We will publish your articles."

"And get your plays produced."

She rolled her eyes—and hid her fear that she would once more lay down her arms because of circumstance or need or pregnancy…or cowardice. Her fear that all his political aims would outweigh her goal to be a star in the theatrical world must not be a knife that cut them in two. "A tall order to win recognition in the theater, sir. I am still a woman."

"A very fine woman. And mine." He waggled his brows like a lecherous bloke.

She cuffed him. "My goal is a harder one to achieve than yours. We can concentrate on yours."

"No. We cannot. We each must get what we want. You make me strong. I make you strong. We will achieve our separate desires together."

"I don't know how that works, Kendryck." Her statement was so candid, he stared at her.

"I do," he said, and brushed away a new tear from her cheek. "I do. We love each other well every day, our talents and our ambitions. We nurture them in ourselves and each other until there is no you or me, but us. Only us. Happy and loving, fulfilled in what we are and what we do. Always."

She clasped him in her arms then and cried in her complete happiness.

"And now, you must sit up, Mrs. Hollens. We are about to pull into the yard, and we must face our current challenges. All that we are is good, my darling. Come now. No more tears. A smile for me and all the years ahead."

CARTER MET THEM at the door, anxiety lining his face.

"Mr. Gerard has a coach and is bringing his mother and sister home from the village, Carter," Kendryck told him. "He stopped there on his journey. I assumed as he passed through that he saw or heard that the inquest was today."

"May I ask, my lord, how it went?" The servants knew all about the missing lady, how she'd been found, and the need for an inquest. Seren had been very upset about a death so nearby. Nishan, Kendryck's young valet, was very superstitious about it all and took to praying to his gods about deliverance from evil.

"Not well, Carter. The coroner thinks someone murdered the poor lady, but he has no viable suspects."

Tynley handed over her coat and gloves and removed her hat. "Carter, please tell Cook I think we should have an early supper. Nothing fancy or taxing for her. Something simple. It has been a long day for us all. And that snowstorm looks not far off."

"A fine idea, my dear. We will go up, Carter, to refresh ourselves and come down, say, in two hours?"

"That will be agreeable, sir."

"Please tell the others when they arrive about supper."

"Very good, sir."

IN THEIR ROOMS, Tynley and he had in Nishan and Seren to help them undress. Tynley could not wait to get out of her corset and don her heavy, quilted robe. Underneath she always wore her delicate white muslin nightgowns that Kendryck had had made for her. Today, so early yet, she wore one because she was tired and hated being trussed up in whalebone after such trying scenes.

Sending off their servants, they sat in their sitting room, she in her robe and gown and he in his pajamas and midnight-blue banyan.

"I do not want to go rushing downstairs to deal with the three of them. Can we just sit here for a few minutes and talk and have a tipple or two?"

He raised a glass to her in silent agreement, and the two of them took chairs next to each other before a blazing fire.

"I cannot believe Grant tried to make us the murderers," she told him.

"He has no one as a viable suspect. He thought if he could badger you or me into some slip of the tongue, he could hold us up as culpable." Kendryck regarded her with awe. "You did not give him an inch."

She hated to say the next horrid words. "But to cite a woman with red hair as the last one to see Miss Roundbridge alive means more than I am a suspect."

"Grant needs more than a statement that a lady with red hair and a green dress talked with the woman to make a case that she, whoever she was, should be convicted of murder. Grant was grasping. Foolish. And he knows it. He'll get from that jury a verdict of death by some foul means, but he cannot pin the crime on anyone. Not even anyone who is left-handed."

"I thought that a prudent point. So why not someone who is left-handed?"

Kendryck sighed. "There are a hundred ways to hurt some-one when you are intent or enraged. Grant has no witness to an attack. He has only a body, which has been very badly abused by exposure to the elements over weeks in the open air."

"Still all this business about red hair and green gowns leads me say that I want to have tea with your grandmother and tell her what has happened."

"I doubt she'll understand."

"She might." Tynley wanted to take another look out the lady's window and get her to talk about those who walked in the woods. The baroness was addled, but not confused all the time.

"Please don't put too much store in that."

"I won't. I promise."

"We have much to deal with now that Gerard is home." Kendryck took to viewing the flames behind the grate. "I don't know what to expect. Will he be better now that he's been off and has come home? And if so, how and why? I tell you, darling, I have not any patience left for him. These past few weeks have brought us trouble. I wish to return to the peace of the few days you and I shared on our few days alone. I'm wondering what you might think of you and I moving to London and leaving the three of them here?"

Tynley knew he had thought long and hard about this. He'd mentioned often his deliberation of being able to afford a separation of the family. "Instead of sending them away, you'd like us to go to London? Just the two of us?"

"What do you think?"

She could list a few reasons not to go. The villagers might talk. They might think she and Kendryck were running away. And what of Barbara, who wanted the very best for herself with a London debut? But for once, Tynley prioritized her husband and herself. "I would love it!"

"Good. Then we will do it. After the New Year. As soon as weather permits." He crooked his finger. "Come here."

She went to him and crawled into his lap. Her arms around him, she put her head to his shoulder.

He kissed her, his lips exciting, assuring, his tongue reaching inside of her to bind her to him. "We will do well together anywhere we live. Let me show you."

And in the peace of their bedroom, he aroused her once more to worlds far above the cares that could bind them to the terrors of the earth.

Chapter Twenty-Four

BATHED AND DRESSED, each of them had a plan for the afternoon.

"I will go talk with Grandmama," she said as she tied Kendryck's cravat. "I want to see if she is coherent enough today to hear news of the inquest."

"She tangles much. Do not be disturbed if she muddles it all."

"I won't."

"I must speak with Gerard," Kendryck told her. "I will press him for a decision about his future. I imagine that interview will be short. Shall I meet you in the dining room for our early supper?" He took her in his arms, his lips to her temple. "I'd frankly prefer to not leave this room for the day."

She kissed his cheek. "Supper will be brief, and then we can return here…" She widened her eyes and laughed.

"Then I can remove all these layers of clothing. Your skin next to mine is all I want these days." He cupped her cheeks. "I love you. For a man who did not want to love anyone ever again, I find I cannot breathe without you near me."

Her heart turned over. She rose on her toes to kiss him with all the passion words could never say. "I am yours always, and you are mine. I am so fortunate." She tipped her head. "And you are too!"

He chuckled and grabbed her before she whirled away. Her breasts against his chest, her body flush to his, she sank her fingers into his hair and relished his ravishing kisses down her throat and across her décolleté. "I don't want to go anywhere," she breathed against his lips.

"Come back to me. Not the dining room. We'll have our supper here in bed." He ran a finger over the swell of her breasts. "I shall savor all the delights of your skin."

She shivered. "And afterward?"

He lifted her chin. His eyes were dark blue seas of enchantment. "I will once more taste every inch of you."

"Every inch of me throbs to have you now." But she put a hand flat to his chest and, with a sigh, said, "But we're leaving. Now."

When she turned around at their door, he was standing there, hands on his hips, admiring her. "If you wait another second, my love, I will never let you go."

"GRANDMAMA," TYNLEY GREETED the older lady, and kissed her on the cheek. "You look lovely today."

"I like the pink, don't you?" The baroness spread out the fabric of her dark pink skirts. "I feel young again. I am too old, you know. A lady must be ready for the ballroom. Not the dustbin!" She laughed at her words. "Come sit down with me, Charlotte."

Dear me. She once more thinks I am someone else. Well, I will try to make some sense here.

Tynley gave a look to Lucy, who shook her head and sighed, then went off to the lady's bedroom.

They sat on the settee before the flaming fire.

"It will snow soon." The lady's gaze drifted to her bedroom.

"I agree. The air has the stillness, and the clouds are heavy with it."

"Will you write to Kendryck today?"

The baroness thought he was still in Calcutta.

"Yes. Shall I tell him what you have been doing lately? Have you read a good book?"

"That anonymous writer who does little salon stories."

That brought Tynley up short. "You have read a book lately?"

"Of course! Every day!" The baroness sat up and blinked, insulted. "What else can I do when they won't let me out of here? Ba! And I do like the whisky and brandy at dinner. My husband, God curse his soul, didn't like me to drink. Hell, what did he know, eh, girl? He drank like a fish. Would he had done it more and not gotten all those women with child."

My, my. The baroness trusted Tynley more each time with secrets. Or her own imaginations. *I must remember that.*

"Have you seen any redheads go along the forest path lately?"

The woman stared at her. Thinking, she was. Then she nodded. "This morning."

"Today?" That was news. *Or is it?* "When?"

"This morning. She has to go down there, doesn't she?"

"Where?"

"Oh, Charlotte, do not be thick, will you? You know perfectly well she goes down there a lot the past few days. I told you that yesterday."

Tynley sighed. "Of course."

"You don't believe me! Why do I bother with you, child, if you are not trusting me?"

"But I do, Grandmama. Show me again where she goes. Please. I know I have forgotten. And I am such a numbskull." Tynley stood and made for the lady's bedroom and the window where she purportedly saw her vision of a red haired lady in a green gown.

"Very well." The baroness got to her feet and, unsteady as she usually was, walked like a queen around Tynley, brushed off her assistance, and said, "Come with me."

At the window that looked out over the rolling hillside down through the dense forest, black now as sun set and the first flakes began to fall, the baroness pointed to a footpath into the woods.

"There. There! You see it."

"I do." For the first time, Tynley saw a cleared path that led down in a southerly direction. A path she and Kendryck had never taken. One she'd not known about. One no one mentioned. "Why do you think the red-haired lady goes there?"

"To meet a lover."

"Oh. Right."

"Or to keep her secret." The woman inched near Tynley and pointed a palsied finger toward the path. "To see if she left anything."

"Like what? What would she leave?"

The old woman rolled a shoulder. "A gun."

"A...a gun?" That was absurd. Or was it? Tynley balked. She'd not seen any gun in the house. Not a pistol or a rifle. None.

"She likes to carry it with her."

Tynley would go along with the rambling now. She would get nothing useful today. She might as well surrender and simply humor the lady. "Who does?"

"There." The baroness pointed outside. A dark figure of a woman, her back toward the house, drifted into the woods. "See? She's gone again!"

⇶✂⇷

TYNLEY RAN DOWN the hall to her rooms to fetch her coat.

She had to know if that path was indeed the one near where Miss Roundbridge had trodden—and disappeared.

Because that path, said the baroness, was the one that led to the village. "Come out of cover of trees at the inn, you do."

The path where Miss Roundbridge had met her so-called friend. A lady in green. A lady with red hair.

Tynley darted into their sitting room and to her closet to dig out her heavy winter coat. She yanked it on—and froze.

What she did, where she went, was dangerous.

Kendryck had gone down to his meeting with Gerard. She ran to her escritoire and picked up a pencil. Grabbing paper, she scribbled. Her hand shook and she picked up another piece of paper. *Walking path to the inn. Come! T.*

She screwed up her courage. Now or never.

Now today, for a reason only she knew, Madeline was taking that path down through the woods.

Tynley had to know why.

OUTSIDE, THE CRISP leaves in the trees began to rustle in the onslaught of a rush of wind. Tynley huddled into her coat and lifted the collar. Snowflakes big as her fingertips began to fall in flurries.

She hurried along, glad she'd worn her good half boots. The ground was so slippery and treacherous on the steep incline of the hillside. She wished she'd had presence of mind to get Jericho and Dick to come along. They had the run of the property. Why had the two dogs not discovered Miss Roundbridge's body? Perhaps they had and failed to rouse anyone to investigate. It was not the dogs' fault they had not summoned someone to the poor lady. Not to her rescue, and not to her death scene, either.

But Tynley had never noticed this path on this south side of the house. She and Kendryck had always taken the same path, a more even one than this, less challenging with its highs and lows. This one definitely had its challenges. She stopped at the ridge of one. A four-foot drop to the next level had her shaking her head.

That required her to carefully take hold of an outstretched tree branch and lower herself down to the next level. That too was very slippery, and she skidded along. But she righted herself, thankful her gloves protected her hands.

A few indentations in the ground were footprints in the slick snow. Madeline was not far ahead of her. Madeline in her apple-green winter coat.

Around another clump of trees, Tynley came to a clearing and another drop. She paused at the edge.

Madeline was there walking, it seemed, in circles. Was she looking for something she'd dropped? It certainly appeared that way.

Chapter Twenty-Five

TYNLEY TOOK A step toward her. The crunch of a footfall in the snowy forest brush had Madeline looking up.

"What are you doing here?" Tynley called down to Madeline.

"I could ask you the same thing." The woman turned away as if she had no time for Tynley's inquiries. No concern, either.

But then, Madeline was confident enough and selfish enough not to care about anything except herself.

"Going for a walk, are you?" Tynley would not let her get away without rattling her.

"None of your business." Her head cocked high, Madeline picked up her skirts and walked toward Tynley as if she had not a care in the world. She slipped a little on a snowy path and attempted to climb up to the next level. But she had trouble on the uneven, slippery terrain. So much for holding one's head high.

But Madeline had poor footing, and with the bad time of it, Tynley extended her hand down to her. "Let me help you."

"I don't need your help."

Ignoring Tynley, she scrambled up on all fours to climb the steep rise like a crab.

Madeline righted herself, brushed her muck-covered gloves together to no end, and straightened herself to walk away.

Tynley had had enough of her intransigence. "Why didn't

you say to the coroner that you knew about this path down to the inn?"

"A lot of people do."

"Not me."

"Well, what a lack." Madeline tsked. "You poor girl."

"Did you see anyone here?"

The answer Tynley got was a cold-hearted stare.

"Did you meet anyone here?"

"Only the birds and the bees."

She walked on, but Tynley scrambled after, thankful for the sure footing of her boots. She had all the speed she needed to come abreast of Madeline.

"Why would you come down here?"

"None of your business."

"What are you looking for, Madeline?" Tynley sidled nearer. "Did you leave something here?"

The woman rounded on her, her teeth bared. "Leave me alone."

"Oh, I will. It's what you've wanted from the beginning. Me, gone. That would suit you well, wouldn't it?"

"So what? You'll not get you gone! I cut your gown. I put rotting plants in your bed. And still you would not go! But you are a fool, stubborn, and crafty. A curse on this house!"

Tynley balked at Madeline's confession of what she had done to frighten her. Anger mixed with remorse drove her on. "I'd say you are the problem, Madeline. Your superior attitude. Your haughtiness. Your wielding of influence over your daughter to the point that she becomes your agent, your shadow. Poor girl, she—"

Madeline whipped around. "Quiet! You leech. You ne'er-do-well. An actress come to take my title, my honors, my home. You'll not succeed, I tell you!"

"You have made your own disaster, Madeline. By your attitude, you have poisoned so many against you. Even those in town—"

"Shut up!" Madeline took the path toward her and slipped on the snow. She windmilled but caught herself. "You are nothing but filth. But the whole family is like that."

"Mama!" Barbara appeared at the upper ledge.

"Go home, girl! This bitch and I have things to settle!"

But now there was a witness to anything Madeline might do. Tynley grew emboldened. "You have ruined your chances of a good life."

"Me?" Madeline gave a hysterical laugh. "Your Indian lover. He has ruined me. My plans, too. But I have fooled him. I've gotten some of what's due me."

"Madeline, whatever you think Kendryck has done—"

"Mama," Barbara cried from above. "I'm coming to get you. Don't hurt her."

"Hurt her?" Madeline snarled at her daughter, but whirled on Tynley. "It's you, little Miss Pudding in the Mouth. You need to go back to London. Stop trying to take from me."

"I have never—"

"Shut up. You're like them all. Taking from me. You cannot ruin me. I won't let you. You won't be ruined by your husband. Not like my sweet man. Hell's spawn, he was." Madeline tried to choke back a sob. "My life was ruined by him, who threw up every skirt he could get near. Gave me the clap three times, the bugger. No worse than his father, who ruined me and made me marry his son!"

Tynley's mouth dropped open.

But Madeline raved on. "'You'll come to belong to us both,' he said. 'You'll spread your legs or we'll have trouble here paying for your new gowns. Your husband may take you every other night of the week, girl, but you're mine each Friday at ten.' Oh, yes. Don't look surprised. You knew!"

Tynley's heart broke for the woman. Such evil no one could survive. "No, Madeline, how could—"

"Gerard is the heir here. Not your precious Indian outcast. Gerard's father was the old man. Surprised? Yes, he was a fiend.

His wife, that delirious old woman, even she knew it. She fought to keep Kendryck here when we knew, even then, that Owen would die of the pox. Yes, we knew he would. A roué. Just like father, like son, like grandson. Owen was a rotter of the highest sordid order.

"Then came this woman to tell all in the village that she'd marry the new lord. By God, no, she would not. I found her. I told her she would not. I saw she was big with child. Not Kendryck's, I knew. It could not be. And she laughed and said he'd never learn. She'd make certain he wanted her more than any truth about her baby's father. Another bitch, she was, come to take what's mine. And my son's and my daughter's. No! I would not let her have him."

"And you met her and—?"

"And she was going to hit me. Picked up a rock, she did. Little idiot. Well, I got a bigger one, didn't I? And I hit her. Quick. Easy. Funny, really, how she just…went limp…and dropped to her knees…"

"Oh, Madeline." Hysteria had Tynley gasping and throwing up her arms. "You must tell them."

"What? Who? Who should I tell? No, by God. So you can have everything?" She laughed and took a step toward Tynley.

"You…you must! Tell them how your husband and your father-in-law treated you." It would make no difference. Not really. "That you killed that woman is—"

"Murder? A crime? A sin!" Madeline choked on wild laughter. "Oh yes! You're an idiot. And *you* want to tell *me* what *I* can do? How I can live? *No! No, by God!* You tell me *nothing!*"

She ran toward Tynley, her hands out. Tynley hit the ground with a thud. But Madeline had sailed onward, past her, and sailed over the precipice.

She screamed, and the force of her body as she hit one limb made Tynley gasp and hold her stomach. The thunk of Madeline as her body hit one thing and another made Tynley shut her eyes with each succeeding thud.

"Mama! Mama!" Barbara, her red hair flying behind her, navigated the hill.

"No. Barbara. Go back!" Tynley sat up and ran her forearm over her eyes. Sitting, legs straight out before her in the snow, she checked her own condition. She could move her fingers, arms, her toes, her legs. She glanced up at Barbara. "It's terrible. Slippery. I will go down."

She scrambled to her feet, but her head spun. She stood, her body weaving for a second. She braced herself, her legs apart, and got her balance.

Then she blinked hard and sought Madeline. In the silence of dusk, no sound rent the air.

Madeline had sailed beyond her view, through the white-covered pine needles and leaves, through the cloak of snow flurries that now grew so thick it formed a veil.

Tynley trudged downward, carefully picking her way along.

Minutes later, Tynley spied the crumpled body of Madeline in her green woolen coat.

"Oh, Madeline." She crawled over to her under a branch of a pine tree.

She put a hand to Madeline's neck, then to her wrist. Her mouth was open. Her breath gone. Madeline was dead. Without all her cares and words now. Without all her resentments and angers. Without a need to trudge in snow or rain or sunshine.

She was gone beyond all the travesties of justice and the cruelties of her husband and her father-in-law, beyond the cares of worrying about her children.

She was gone, and Tynley prayed she found peace she had not found on earth.

KENDRYCK HAD CALLED Gerard to him in the library.

His half-brother came in, looking a bit thin and the worse for his misadventure. He was pale, too. If that was due to his broken arm or another reason, Kendryck had no idea. "You do not look well, Gerard. Do have a chair, and we can talk."

"I'll have a brandy if you don't mind, sir."

"Of course." He went to pour for the boy. "I'm glad you have come home. I was worried about you when we did not hear."

"Thank you, sir." When Kendryck held out the glass to him, he said, "May I have a bit more, sire, please? I am staying away from opium. Kills the pain of the arm, you know. Brandy helps. Although I assure you, I've had my terrors from it and cannot drink to excess, either. It is hell to recover."

Kendryck said, "Take it. You may have what you need."

Gerard took the glass eagerly and thanked him. "Before you start, sir, with a list of my transgressions, I wish to talk."

Kendryck took a seat and nodded. "Go on."

"I went away early at my mother's request. She thought it wise that I go to Kent, or appear to, while you were in Cardiff. You see, sir, she likes me here…and was afraid you were going to send me away again."

Kendryck considered the boy's admission with a pity he had not ever felt for Gerard. "You told her of my ultimatum?"

"I did, sir. But truth is, I hate it here. It is an awful, ugly house. No offense, sir, but—"

"You are right, Gerard."

"I am?"

"Hideous from curtain wall to refuse dump. Has been from the dawn of time. Made worse by those who scavenged from shipwrecks on the shore to those who ravaged the villagers. I don't blame you for not wanting to be here."

"I thought you'd hate my saying that."

"No. Gerard. I welcome the truth. Can I have more of it from you?"

"Yes, sir. When I said I did not like school, I meant it. When I said I like my friends, I do. Not all of them are idiots who attack others. I know what is to be beaten…" He hung his head and took a long swallow.

"I know you do, Gerard. I would like to see you rise above that. It was your childhood. This is you as an adult. You can treat others better than you were."

Gerard took another drink and sat forward, his elbows to his knees. "I have one friend. Harold Fisk. Lord Fisk's son. A good man. A fine friend is Harry. I stayed with him and his family in Richmond. The have a full stable, sir, of very fine horses. They breed, sir. Racers and trotters."

Kendryck sighed. If this boy was about to tell him he wanted to raise horses, too, he would give Gerard no money for that.

"I like horses. I always have. We have only one here to ride, and he is old. Plus we have the carriage horses, of course. But while I was with the Fisks, I went riding until I did this." Gerard indicated his arm in the sling. "I want to be a blacksmith, sir. Or a farrier."

Kendryck's jaw dropped.

"I know. You are shocked. Well, so am I. I am not the best person. I know I have been terrible to you, sir, and to your wife. I am not like that when I am not here. I've had some very bad friends, whom I followed. That was my trying to fit in. But I swear I am better than you've known me to be!"

"I am surprised, Gerard. Tell me more. How would you learn the trade?"

The boy licked his lips. "The Fisks have a farrier on their estate. He's good man. I asked if he trained others, and he does. Lord Fisk learned of my inquiry from the man, and his lordship said if I wanted to learn from his farrier, he'd gladly put me up as a guest in their small house off near the stables. I told him I would love to do it. That is…" He looked appealingly at Kendryck. "If you will give me a small allowance to afford it."

"I see. How small?"

Gerard shrugged. "Lord Fisk says he will charge me no rent. Just me getting on by myself, cooking and cleaning and learning. Thirty pounds a month? How is that?"

"Thirty pounds a month." Kendryck could not believe the sum. "That is sufficient."

Gerard held out his glass. "May I, sir?"

Kendryck rose to get the flask and returned to offer him more.

"An inch, sir. Yes, that's good. Thank you."

Kendryck regained his seat. "Thirty sounds like a deal, Gerard. I would be honored to sponsor you in that. And to do it well, you must recover use of that arm." He smiled at his brother.

"Yes, sir." He beamed at Kendryck in return. "Thank you, sir. I must move on, do something that makes me feel better and not so in turmoil all the time. Horses, I don't know why, calm me, sir. They…they understand me. How that is, I do not know."

"Best not to question how you feel, as long as you do feel the difference," Kendryck said. "If a creature makes you happy, like Jericho here…" The dog came trotting in, tongue out, circling Kendryck's chair. "Sit down, boy. Sit."

But the dog gave a yip.

Kendryck would have none of the animal's sass. "Sit!" Then he responded to Gerard. "If someone makes you happy, then it is wise to welcome the joy of their regard." *Like loving a woman whose very smile makes you happy to be alive.*

"Yes, sir. Yes, sir. You will not regret you gave me this chance, sir. I can pay you back, if you want. I know you try to be prudent with expenses."

"No need to pay me back, Gerard. Make a good go of your shop, and that will be all I ask of you."

Gerard gulped down the rest of his brandy. He sat back in his chair again, relaxed from the tension and from the liquor, Kendryck thought.

From his waistcoat pocket, Gerard took out a small pouch. "This, sir, is yours."

The bag was of ordinary chintz. A roughly made, small thing, it could hold little.

"What is it?"

"Three items that belong to you, sir." Gerard's brown eyes grew bleak at his words. "They were given to me to sell."

That last word had Kendryck's ears pricking. "What are they?"

"Diamonds."

Kendryck licked his lips. "Why did you not sell them?"

"If I did, I would never be welcomed by you, sir. I did not care for who I was, as it were, so why would I do that, sir?" He became hoarse with tears and ran a hand over his sniffling nose. "I did not want to, sir."

Kendryck dug out his handkerchief and gave it to the boy. In truth, he could say he almost did not want to know why or how or when Gerard had acquired the three. But in knowing who had given them to him, he would then be required to cast that person out of the house forevermore. "Who gave them to you?"

"My mother."

Kendryck rose and paced the floor. Jericho came with him and barked.

"Sir! Sir!" Carter raced into the room. "Come, sir. Come! My lady! Sir! They've fallen down the hill, and Mrs. Hollens, sir, is gone!"

KENDRYCK RAN OUT in the snowy dusk, Gerard behind him. Conway and Peters, too.

At the top of the path down, Carter stood and beckoned them onward. "Down there, sir."

Kendryck squinted in the faint hollow that the path carved between trees.

Barbara sat on a rock, her coat covered in a thin layer of snow. She shook with her fear and pointed. "Mama is down there. She fell. She's not talking to Tynley. They argued and then Mama went for her and fell. She's hurt."

Kendryck peered down the side of the hill. Was Tynley hurt? And Madeline? Was she alive...?

The flurries were so thick that he could see only vague shapes darker than the trees. "Get blankets and sheets. They need to be brought up. If they're injured...we've got to be careful."

Peters ran off to the house. Seren and Lucy dashed forward. Nishan came after them with Kendryck's greatcoat, a blanket, and a pillow. Kendryck wanted to laugh and cry out loud. Ever in Calcutta, for any occasion good or bad, one always needed the comfort of a pillow!

⇶⫷

KENDRYCK MANAGED THE hill, but he knew not how. He was swift, but stumbled. He saw Tynley, but swore if he ever got to her and she was safe, she'd never be out of his sight again.

The snow was relentless. He'd move back to India, where snow never cut the heat of day or night.

He'd die if she were no longer with him. He loved her, and he'd told her so little of his regard. He'd never stop telling her.

Was that her calling him? Faint but true. He...he heard her. He did!

She was no ghost.

No remnant of his past or illusive beauty of his future torment.

Dear God. He stopped. Only a moment, it was his wife calling his name.

She was alive.

He ran down to her, skidding, sliding, to get to her quickly. She sat in the snow, crumpled like a doll made of old cloth. Beside her was the body of Madeline.

Sprawled, her mouth open, her eyes too, his stepmother looked oddly surprised in death.

He knelt beside his wife and fingered her arms, her neck. "Do not move. Are you hurt? Bones? Broken?"

"Nothing. Nothing," she murmured, and grabbed the froth of his cravat. "She's dead, Kendryck. Dead. She...she lunged for me. I...I could not escape her. She...she killed Roundbridge. She admitted it." And then she burst into tears and flung her arms around him.

He scooped up his wife and just sat there, rocking her back and forth as Conway and Peters came to bundle up the body of Madeline. And Carter, frail old fellow, came as far as he could in the slippery snow, and mumbled his sorrow that Madeline was gone.

"Poor lady," the old butler mourned. "Sorry, sir. Not...not good to speak ill of the dead."

⇻⟫⟫⟩⟨⟨⟨⟸

It took them more than an hour to bring up the body of Madeline. Conway and Peters took her to the ice house to the west of the main house and laid her out on a slab.

Kendryck had then told Conway to go down to the village to find Silas Grant. "If he has gone back to Cardiff, notify the innkeeper to fetch him. We need the man to return."

"Why? Why do we need him?" Barbara sat opposite Kendryck in a chair in his sitting room in his chambers.

Gerard sat in another chair, silent and brooding. His cheeks bore the tracks of his tears for the passing of his mother.

Tynley was tucked up with a cup of tea and a glass of brandy beside her in the settee next to him. She had on her robe and a wool knit blanket around her shoulders. Since he'd brought her upstairs, she'd said little. At Barbara's questions, she stared at the girl blankly.

"We need Grant because, Barbara," he told her, "your mother died by accident, and anyone who dies without explanation must have a coroner's decision of the cause of death."

"She'll be written up in the newspaper. She'll be notorious. She hates that."

Tynley burst out in a sob.

Kendryck took her into his embrace. "It's fine, my darling."

After a minute, Tynley regained her composure. "No one," she said to the girl, Gerard, and him, "ever...*ever* wants to be notorious. She was misused, and abused. Poor lady." She swiped tears from her cheeks.

"Why do you defend her?" Barbara said with resentment. "She hated you."

"Not really, Barbara." Tynley shook her loose curls back from over her shoulder. "I don't believe she did. She saw me as the one who would take from her the only dignity she had been allowed to retain."

"Oh, fiddle-faddle," Barbara said, her dislike of Tynley mellowing.

Kendryck realized few had ever defended Madeline. His father and grandfather, even Owen, had been critical of her.

"Your mother had much against her." Tynley was adamant in her statements. "Her father, her husband, the law. She wished to be free of oppression. And so should you."

"I...I want my mother back! She wanted the best for me. And I promised I would help her."

Kendryck stilled. Even as he brought his wife closer into his embrace, he stared at his sister. "Whatever you promised her now goes with her to heaven. She knew you loved her."

"She did. We were going to go away and live in London on our own. Far from you. Both of you."

Kendryck found that an extraordinary statement. "How was your mother going to do that, Barbara?"

Barbara bit her lip, frowning at him. "She had found means. Good means."

He grew angry. "You mean money?"

She curled away from him. "Yes."

"Did she tell you where she had found it?"

"No."

"Did she tell you how she was going to fund your new life in London?"

"No. Only that…"

"Only how?" he asked her with pointed look. "Tell me."

"She was going to sell things that she…that she possessed."

"I see," he said. "Her family jewels?"

"No. No, I wanted those for my come-out."

"Yes, you did. So what would your mother sell?"

"Gerard was helping her." Barbara glanced at her brother and, wide-eyed, encouraged him to support her statements.

"How," Kendryck demanded, "was Gerard helping her?"

She rolled a shoulder. "I cannot say. You tell him, Gerard. Did you do it? Tell him, for God's sake!"

The young man sagged. "I was to sell diamonds for Mama. Diamonds that were yours, Kendryck. Diamonds that would become the means for her to live as she wished. With you and me, Barbara. Alone."

Tynley shook her head, bewildered at the revelations.

Kendryck curled his wife close and focused on the two siblings.

Barbara grew red in the face as she questioned her brother. "And did you? Sell them?"

"No."

"What?" Barbara was aghast. "Why not? You betrayed her. Your own mother."

Kendryck could not bear the ugliness between people who were meant by blood and felicity to regard each other with love. "What did you do, Barbara, for your mother's dream?"

"Not…" She sat back, petulant. "Not much. I hired a carriage for her and me to go to Cardiff the day after you and Tynley married."

"Ah." This was the incident he'd forgotten. This was the item he'd failed to investigate. "And what did she do there?"

"She…she sold a treasure. A treasure that brought her a goodly sum. She and I could go away. Gerard too, if he wanted. We would go away to London."

"What did she sell in Cardiff, Barbara?" Kendryck would not let this go.

"She took diamonds. Yours, she said. You hoarded them! So she took them. Worth a fortune, she said. Why not? You'd not miss them. You had so much. She took them to a dealer in Cardiff. She knew you would go on your honeymoon and leave us the carriage. But she did not want our coachman to know where she'd gone. Surely he would tell you and she would not be stopped, she said, from going to London. She wanted to take me there for my debut."

Kendryck could not believe the duplicity of his stepmother. "Why did she go out along the path in a snowstorm?"

Barbara looked sheepish. "She went out to look for a bracelet she'd lost in the dirt. I could not understand why or how she had, but she had to go look for it. Mama went out straight away after we arrived home from the inquest."

Kendryck shifted. Tynley looked up at him, her mouth open in surprise at all these revelations. He stroked her cheek and tucked her head beneath his chin. His wife. His treasure. His finest treasure.

"But then," Barbara said, as the tears that she'd swallowed came now and tore her speech to shreds, "she…she and Tynley argued, and Tynley wanted to know if Mama had killed that dead woman. They argued. Mama and that Miss Roundbridge."

Kendryck waited, his heart swollen with sorrow for this young girl who had been so misused and misdirected by her own mother. "You were there? You saw your mother with the lady?"

"Yes! Yes! I was there. I saw. Mama did not know I was. But I saw, and…and Mama got angry at her. That lady wanted to marry you. And Mama said there would be no other lady of the house but her. She slapped her, and the lady picked up a rock. But Mama got to her first with a rock she had picked up. The woman fell, and when she did, Mama said she should make certain she was dead, and she hit her again and dragged her under a tree."

Tynley turned with a groan into his embrace.

Kendryck swallowed bile. "Did you tell your mother you saw her with Miss Roundbridge?"

"Oh, no. Never. She'd hate me. Hate that I… So, no. I didn't meant to be so mean, but I was ashamed of Mama…and me." Barbara's face crumpled in shame at the facts she had hidden from her mother and everyone else. She had borne the fact of her mother's guilt and kept it to herself because she feared her mother would turn against her. Or worse.

"Barbara," he said, "I am so sorry to hear all this."

"You have suffered so badly," Tynley said, leaning forward to take Barbara's hands.

But the girl snatched them away. Then her tears came in loud, racking sobs.

Gerard rose and took his sister in his arms. "This is not your fault or your burden to carry. Not anymore. Come here now. Do cry, sweet girl. We will both cry for our mother who has gone."

Gerard gazed at Kendryck. "I will escort her up to her chambers. She must rest."

Kendryck nodded.

They sat, Kendryck and Tynley, for long hours. In silence, with tears and kisses, they consoled each other. Long past midnight, he lifted his wife in his embrace and took her to their bed.

There they slept in dreamless slumber until the first light of dawn, when Tynley rose to walk the floor.

Chapter Twenty-Six

KENDRYCK CAME THROUGH the door to their bedroom and wrapped his arms around her. He kissed her beneath her ear and cuddled her close to him. "I will build a fire for us."

"I didn't want to awaken you." She turned in his arms and pulled up the collar of his banyan. "I apologize."

"If you cannot sleep, neither can I. You fret about all of this, and what is best about a marriage if two people cannot share their concerns?"

She nestled against his broad shoulders and sighed.

He led her to the settee and, settling her there, kissed her lips, then went to the fireplace to put logs behind the grate. When he had a goodly fire going, he returned to her and settled her against him, her legs out along his. His lips rested against her crown.

She would share with him her biggest concern, that their marriage would limit her in ways that every woman was limited in the eyes of Society and the laws in Britain. She loved her husband dearly, but she knew what the two of them faced, first now with this deaths of his stepmother and of Miss Roundbridge, but also Kendryck's own ambitions to right the wrongs of many in India.

She fingered the embroidery on the label of his banyan. "Madeline's death has shown me much. Things that I knew already, true. But now facts that we both know may prohibit us from gaining what we each so desperately want."

He lifted her chin with the gentle touch of two fingers. "Tell me all of it. Much I know, but it is best to say it, give it to the universe so that we may feel the importance and the necessity to address it."

"Madeline was a victim of men's laws, but also their greed. She had fallen prey not because she was weak, but because circumstances prohibited her from living the life she could as a one of integrity.

"I've been concerned, Kendryck, that my ambitions would fall to second place behind a man's. They did first, because of my pregnancy. But then also with my husband, not because he wanted power or supremacy over me, but because he came to believe he and I would be better off, more financially secure, if I were employed as a manager of the theater. I gave up my ambition to be a playwright because it was easier than arguing. And earning money made everyday life easier than having less.

"But I failed myself, too. Every actress gains a reputation that she does not necessarily earn. Perhaps over time, if she takes a lover, she becomes less than she envisioned in the eyes of others and of herself. But in truth, every actress is assumed to be a libertine. And I left acting partly because I no longer wanted to be notorious.

"Add to that the fact that people have always thought less of me than I am or wished to become." She caressed his cheek. "I know you don't. But one reason I left London, one reason I told myself I could live a new life with a new husband far away from the city, was because I could gain a new reputation. A fine one that was the epitome of prestige and honor."

His dark brows drew together. "And now, after all this death and chaos, how to you think you will deal with returning to London? I am not without myths said of me. Rumors are ugly whispers no one can ever control."

"When we return to London, I know I will want my professional life again. I will want to write. That will be so different from what you write and speak about. If I write, my reputation may diminish yours! And that, my darling, I could not bear. I told you I love you. At the inquest, I told the world I do, and I will not take it back. But I cannot hurt you. Cannot destroy what you need to do for your own satisfaction. You will change the world, my love. What I write can only change one person's evening."

"Tynley Hollens! That is not so!"

"Oh, it is," she groaned. "It is!"

"I would say there are playwrights who have changed more than an evening. Shakespeare, for one."

She scoffed.

"Marlowe, another."

She shook her head with a rueful smile.

"Sheridan!"

She gripped his banyan. "I may never be their equal."

"No. You may be their superior!"

"Now," she said, chuckling, "you are dreaming."

"You dream of writing great plays that bring people joy. I dream of you smiling at the result."

"Oh, Kendryck." She shook her head. "You are so good, my darling. Can you bear it? If people consider me a woman of ill repute?"

"Can you bear it? If people consider me a man demented?"

"Oh, but you are not. You are noble and generous, wanting to give others the rights and respect they justly deserve."

He paused, and his bright blue eyes bored into hers. "How noble and generous could I be, my love, if I advocate giving others the rights and respect they justly deserve, but I deprive my wife of the very same things that make her life sublime?"

Her mouth fell open. "Oh," she said.

"Exactly."

She nestled against him. "You are a very wise man."

"Mmm. I have a very wise wife."

"Do you?" She raised her head and grinned at him.

"There she is. The woman I adore." He kissed the tip of her

nose. "I love you. More than I've said. I will change that and tell you every day."

"Oh, I like that promise," she said, and put her lips to his.

"When I saw you at the bottom of that ravine and I feared you were gone, I swore I would die, too. But you are alive. That is the most vital thing. We have decades before us, and we will march on together, hand in hand, to do as we wish. Become the people we wish. No stopping us because people or time or circumstance is against us. Not even, God save her, because Madeline committed a crime.

"I will speak to Grant," he told her. "We will resolve this in a manner that is polite and respectful of all of us. I wish to see Barbara recover from her mother's influence. I want to help her do it, too. She must have her come-out. I doubt she would be recovered from her grief this year."

Tynley agreed with him.

He curled her close. "But we all need to come to terms with what has happened here. Barbara especially. Gerard, too. He tells me he wishes to become a blacksmith and farrier. He has always liked horses, and I told him I would sponsor his apprenticeship. And as for us, we must think beyond this. We will go to London, as we planned. What do you say to the first of the year?"

"I like it. We will do our mourning there."

"Quietly, away from here. What do you think of closing this house entirely?"

She beamed at him. "We could take any servants with us who wish to come."

He hugged her. "I love you, my darling."

She squeezed him close. "We should go back to bed and rest. We have a lot of work to do to make a future, a good one, for all of us."

Epilogue

**December 1818
Hanover Square,
London**

LADY PEREGRINE LOOKED through her pince-nez and smiled at the sight of Barbara conversing easily with a young viscount the lady had invited to her dinner party this evening. She and Tynley sat together after dinner. The twenty-two guests enjoyed their own conversations while Lady Peregrine and Tynley were ensconced in one corner. "The girl does well, Tynley. I am very pleased with how she has come around. I am certain you and your husband are, too."

"We are, Aunt." Tynley fluttered her fan at her throat. It was December and frigid outside, but very warm in the house—and Tynley suffered. "We've had quite a few dust-ups, but she understands what she must improve."

Barbara and Gerard had grieved for their mother with all due the poor woman. Gerard, who had been eager to get on with his apprenticeship, had left home in February after his mother's death.

Silas Grant had come the next morning after Madeline's demise and, with Barbara and Tynley's statements, had declared Madeline's death an accident. Notice of her demise had appeared in Cardiff newspapers, but, to Tynley and Kendryck's knowledge, not much was made of her passing. Grant had asked about the reason for the argument with Tynley, and Barbara had told him she witnessed her mother kill Miss Roundbridge. Grant had been furious that Barbara had not come forward to tell him, but he could not fault her. He said he sympathized that Barbara wished to protect her mother, wrong as her deception was. After that, Barbara had dissolved in tears and would not speak for weeks.

By the end of January, Barbara had agreed to go to London with Kendryck and Tynley. Kendryck's grandmother had died in early January of a terrible chest congestion. They had buried her in the family plot near the old curtain wall.

Kendryck continued his plans to leave for London, and offered the staff to go with them if they wished. To the two maids and Cook, who decided not to leave, Kendryck awarded pensions. At the end of February, after Gerard's departure, Kendryck closed the Rambles permanently. He had locked the old, massive wooden door behind him, vowing to return only once a year to take whatever seemed valuable to London.

His goods from India were among those. He had them transported with the household, and they were stored under lock and key in the cool basement of the family London townhouse in Grosvenor Square. Soon, he would begin to look for suitable space to rent to put it all on display. He'd charge a fee, he told Tynley, for the exhibition, and that sum would fund a new building to be a permanent exhibit of goods from the Subcontinent.

Meanwhile, he had become known as a shrewd investor. Discarding all those markers for business he considered unethical or immoral, he had redirected his wealth into agricultural machines and cotton and silk mills in the north. Others came to him for advice, and he happily gave it.

Their lives in Grosvenor Square were serene. Their friends were of like minds. Gerard, when he came to visit twice a year, learned from that. So did Barbara.

The transformation of the girl's thinking had been slow. Being introduced deliberately to London Society had been a prudent means to show the girl that the *ton* did not appreciate irrational and selfish behavior. Or, to be honest, those who Kendryck and Tynley favored did not find such characteristics endearing.

Aunt Juno liked the looks of the girl. "I will be happy to sponsor a ball in June in her honor, Tynley, if you think she is ready."

"That is an honor, Aunt. Thank you. I would like to think on it for a few weeks, if you do not mind."

Tynley would discuss it with Kendryck. He was very attuned to people's opinions of them all and careful to avoid anyone who might be so rash as to criticize them in word or deed. Kendryck, protective as a tiger, countenanced no bullies in his midst.

"Of course," said her aunt with a smug smile. "I understand she has done so well as to have attracted the son of Lord Haverford."

"She likes him." That friend of Kendryck's, still a bachelor, had called on the household of the Baron and Baroness Strade of Rhoose and Gary weeks ago. Tynley had been indisposed that morning, and Barbara had done the honors to receive him. Though he had called unannounced that day to renew his acquaintance foremost with Kendryck, Leonard Haverford had returned three times for tea. Each afternoon, it had become increasingly clear, he prized his conversations with Barbara most. "Kendryck and I wait for her to tell us if it is more important to have her debut or to settle her future before June."

"I'm certain the young 'American' has little interest in the past. Americans believe in fresh starts."

Tynley nodded. "And causes."

"Of which you and your husband are so successful."

Tynley regarded her husband, who stood near the window discussing politics with a friend of his, another member of the Lords. Kendryck had written more than two dozen articles that appeared over the past two years. His words had raised consciousness about the East India Company's treatment of native Indians. Two bills in consideration now in Parliament would reform the Company's navy. It was a beginning, Kendryck was happy to point out.

He had taken his seat in the Lords, and in his inaugural speech had launched his attack upon the Company. His work in Parliament and his articles were having great effect. He had started a novel many times, but the plotting was difficult for him. He had decided writing articles was his most effective means of fostering change. But he laid the popularity of his series on the woman who was his erstwhile editor, his wife.

Tynley claimed no glories for polishing his words. She had her own to work over.

While Kendryck wrote in their study each morning, so did Tynley. Last year she'd finished a play that the manager of her old theater in Covent Garden, The Crown, was set to produce in the spring. At the moment, no negative words had yet been published about Baroness Strade's occupation.

"They'd better keep it that way, too," Kendryck had warned when he saw the newspaper announcement two weeks ago of Tynley's sale to the theater.

Her father would not be alive to know of it. He had died last spring. Afterward, her mother had come around to ask if Tynley might speak with her again. She apologized for her treatment of her daughter, and the two of them fell into each other's arms. They took tea every Tuesday at four in the parlor.

Tynley was happy to visit with her mother once more. She had missed her. She also knew that another reason her mother came to visit was to bounce on her knee Tynley and Kendryck's firstborn, a boy they had named David.

Tynley put a hand to her belly and took pride in the fact that soon another baby would delight his grandmother, as well as his aunt, his mother, and his doting father.

Kendryck approached. "I hate to be the one to end this fine tête-à-tête, but you must forgive me, Lady Peregrine. My wife promised me I could spirit her away if I thought she looked frazzled."

"You take good care of her, Kendryck. Do take her home to rest."

He took Tynley's hand to help her up. "Barbara tells me her friend Mary Summers brings her home. Lady Peregrine, I hope you will not mind that we are the first to leave?" he asked.

"Not at all. I need my sleep as well. Too many hang on for too long. Go home, sir, and in so doing, you encourage the others to depart. And I thank you."

⋙⋘

IN THEIR CARRIAGE—THE old one they had brought from Wales—Tynley snuggled up to her husband and kissed his cheek. "I am tired. I'm so glad you suggested this."

"Well, my darling, the clock strikes nearly eleven. We must get home before Carter falls asleep on the tile and Jericho must answer the door!"

She had a good chuckle at that. "And what of Dick?"

"Ah, that fellow. All he does anymore is belch."

She gave her husband a pained look. "He is rather loud."

"Bah! You are too polite. You mean he is gassy."

Her laughter caught him like the unfurling of a rainbow. Outside, it was night. But anywhere with her all of the colors of earth and heaven danced in his vision. Dazzled by the hues and the shades of life's joys and tragedies, he took her to him and touched her lips to his.

"Each time I look at you," he told her, "I marvel at the quality of my life now. You are the red of passion and greens of prosperity, the blues of night when I hold you in my arms, and the golds of my rejoicing.

"I lived in the shadows of grays and in the depths of black when you came to me. I had only the intentions to find the brightness of joy again. But you have brought me from the darkness of my despair and taken my hand to go with you from the abyss of my pain."

He cupped her cheek. "I love you, Tynley Hollens. You are my light, my morning, and my tender night. I love you. Laugh with me through the years. Cry with me at the endings. Know I will always love you, the color of my life."

Fleet-of-Heart Chronicle
Serving London and environs

NUMBER 13 Volume VII July 6, 1818 Price—Sixpence Halfpenny
Published Mondays and Fridays

WANTED: Matrimony!

Frustrated in your search for domestic tranquility?

Search no more!

Place your advert with the *Fleet-of-Heart Chronicle*!

News sheet now totally devoted to marital bliss.

Find happiness in a thrice!

Affordable!

Exclusive. Confidential.

The strictest honour observed!

A Lady seeks the bliss of wedlock!

A Lady of fine repute seeks a husband who will value her. She has money, status, and renown. She has charm, manners and good looks. She seeks a man who will honor her and she in turn will serve him well.

Replies to G. Hammond, Publisher, 140 Fleet Street, London by August 1, 1818. Lady desires to quit London quickly.

A Blacksmith seeks a wife who does not complain!

A man of good means from his shop has need of a wife to assist him in his work. A knowledge of shoeing horses to assume the job of farrier is essential. The gentleman has a home, his own pump for water, two horses, and a dog. He does not have any children. Two have passed on. And he requires a lady of youth who can provide him with more children to work the shop.

Replies to G. Hammond, Publisher, 140 Fleet Street, London quickly as customers need their horses shod.

ABOUT THE AUTHOR

Cerise DeLand loves to write about dashing heroes and the sassy women they adore. Whether she's penning historical romances or contemporaries, she has received praise for her poetic elegance and accuracy of detail.

An award-winning author of more than 50 novels, she's been published since 1991 by Pocket Books, St. Martin's Press, Kensington and independent presses. Her books have been monthly selections of the Doubleday Book Club and the Mystery Guild. Plus she's won nominations and awards for Best Historical of the Year, Best Regency and scores of rave reviews from *Romantic Times, Affair de Coeur, Publisher's Weekly* and more.

To research, she's dived into the oldest texts and dustiest library shelves. She's also traveled abroad, trusty notebook and pen in hand, to visit the chateaux and country homes she loves to people with her own imaginary characters.

And at home every day? She loves to cook, hates to dust, goes swimming at least once a week and tries (desperately) to grow vegetables in her arid backyard in south Texas!